Zebra Books by Madeline Hunter

A Duke's Heiress Romance series

Heiress for Hire

Heiress in Red Silk

The Heiress Bride

Decadent Dukes Society series

The Most Dangerous Duke in London

A Devil of a Duke

Never Deny a Duke

Novellas

"A Christmas Abduction" in *Seduction on a Snowy Night*

"The Unexpected Gift" in *A Yuletide Kiss*

Published by Kensington Publishing Corp.

The
Heiress
Bride

MADELINE
HUNTER

ZEBRA BOOKS
KENSINGTON PUBLISHING CORP.
www.kensingtonbooks.com

For my grandchildren

Chapter One

Some men are born to duty. Others have duty thrust upon them. Nicholas Radnor, the Duke of Hollinburgh, counted himself among the latter group. The uncle who preceded him in the title had been young enough when he died to have assumed a second marriage still a possibility, along with an heir who was his son. That Uncle Frederick had neglected to take care of his succession in a timely manner was, in Nicholas's opinion, a dereliction of the highest order.

A year ago he would have never viewed it so harshly, but becoming a duke entails new perspectives. His own had changed considerably in recent months. He no longer mourned those carefree days so recently in his past. His ambivalence about the title had been put to rest as well. His path forward, obscure mere months ago, now blazed in front of him, marked by awaiting milestones.

He considered one of those milestones while reading his mail on a fine morning in late April. He had saved the letters now in front of him until after breakfast because their contents would not be conducive to good digestion. Two letters, two graceful hands, two female relatives. The letters contained private advice regarding young women these relatives considered appropriate brides.

He had never announced he was looking for a wife, but any duke his age would be. It was high on the list of ducal duties, and, after a long, nostalgic review of his years spent gaming and seducing, he had placed it on his agenda for the imminent Season. He scanned one of the letters that proposed a young lady described as measured and demure. Not so long ago both words would have had Nicholas running away, but duty called. Both qualities were admirable in a future duchess even if her husband was sure to be bored senseless. He wondered if demure meant demure in public and in dress, or demure in bed.

"Your Grace, I have those accounts ready."

He looked up to where Mr. Withers, his steward, gestured with a thick stack of papers near the door. Those papers disheartened Nicholas even more than the notion of a wife who was demure in bed.

Duty, duty. "Come back in an hour and we can assess the disaster."

Withers tried an encouraging smile. "It isn't nearly as bad as we thought. However, the report from the textile mill is still incomplete."

Not nearly as bad but still bad, and that damned mill had become a significant nuisance. "An hour, Withers."

Withers closed the door after backing out of the chamber. Nicholas had just begun treating himself to an hour of daydreaming when the door reopened and his cousin Chase barged in.

"You summoned me?" Chase's blue eyes appeared steely, the way they did when Chase was annoyed.

"I asked you to call when you had the time."

"Barons ask one to call. Dukes summon."

"What nonsense."

"Fine. Since it is not an immediate need, I'll return at my convenience." Chase turned to go.

"Well, since you decided to call—"

"I am responding to a summons."

"Call it what you want. The point is you came, and I do have something to discuss."

"Your future bride?"

"Oh, for the love of—"

"It is all the aunts can talk about. They sit in their theater box—"

"*My* theater box."

"They sit there and all through the performance they are examining the girls, sharing gossip on them, making lists of possibilities. I told them to stop, but they said you have asked for their advice."

"I did not."

"Then you must have ceased scolding them for interfering, and they assume that means compliance."

That was damned close to how it had happened. "They hear things you and I never would."

Chase sighed. "Please do not ask me to investigate some girl. I have my standards."

Chase was Nicholas's closest cousin, and the one to whom he would turn for advice on some girl when the day came. As for investigating—Chase had created a profession for himself in doing discreet enquiries.

"No, although when the time comes, that is not a bad idea. I want to talk about uncle's death. I think it is time to address that again."

Chase's expression turned sober. "Are you sure you want to? Think hard. If it was as we suspect, the culprit is probably among us. Not Kevin, but another."

"I have thought hard for too long. Your investigation after he died was well along when we stopped it. I think you should dust off those notes and lists of yours. If there is a killer among us, I want to know."

"Once you know, then what?"

Nicholas sat taller. "I'll decide then."

"It won't do to have a member of a duke's family hang, cousin."

That had been part of the problem from the start. Justice should be blind to pedigree, but it wasn't. Possibly, a judge would avoid a hanging if a jury found one of his other cousins guilty of murder. Which was not likely to happen, what with juries also bowing to ducal prerogatives.

"Aside from the matter of trials and punishments, I need to know," Nicholas said. "Don't you?"

Chase hesitated before answering. "Of course. Perhaps it will be an obscure business associate, if it was anyone at all."

Chase leaving the cause of death an open question was a nice touch, but they both believed uncle had neither fallen by accident from that roof walk fourteen months ago, the way the official report read, nor thrown himself to his own death, the way some whispers claimed. He was pushed.

Chase sidled close to the desk and paused. His gaze lit on the letters and he sent Nicholas a mischievous smile. Then he lifted the newspaper from the desk.

"Educating yourself on the radicals' demands?"

"I read many papers. Uncle Frederick subscribed to that one. I let it continue."

"And you read it."

"I need to know what is claimed and thought, even by those elements I may not agree with. It is how it is done, if a member of Parliament is responsible."

Chase smiled sympathetically. "No one expects you to be him."

"I hope not. I'm not nearly eccentric enough."

"I was not talking about Uncle Frederick."

No, he was talking about Nicholas's father. The true heir.

The one who should now have the title. The one who had prepared for it while Nicholas enjoyed life as a man-about-town. An image came to him, of the last time he saw his father. He hated that the image his memory summoned was always the last one.

He pretended Chase had not broached that subject. "You mentioned business associates. I also want you to look into several of the partnerships uncle burdened me with. I think my partners in two of them are—" Nicholas was about to express his suspicions when the study door opened once more. Powell, the butler, entered, bearing a silver salver with a card upon it. From the butler's expression of excitement, Nicholas wondered if it was the king who had called.

"I thought you would want to see your caller, Your Grace." Powell thrust out the tray.

Nicholas lifted the card and read it. The arrival of the king would not have surprised him more. He looked at Chase. "She is here. Right here. In this house. Now."

"Stop babbling. Who is here?"

Nicholas handed over the card. Chase's expression fell into one of shock. "Iris Barrington. I'll be damned."

"We have been looking for her for over a year, and now she just knocks on the door?"

"She must have heard about the will and her inheritance. Where else would she knock?"

"After a year? We had to ferret out the other two women who inherited from uncle. For this one to just arrive on the breeze is suspicious."

"Too easy, you mean."

"Hell, yes, too easy." Nicholas felt his cravat and checked his waistcoat.

"You appear most ducal," Chase said. "Hell, that collar is so starched you could probably cut iron with it. You must let me know what she says." He walked to the door. "Wait a few minutes before going down to bring her here," he said over his shoulder to the butler. "I want to sneak a long look at her."

Powell stood there, salver in hand, while Chase disappeared. After a minute he looked to Nicholas, seeking permission to depart as well. After another minute, Nicholas nodded.

Iris didn't really expect the duke to see her, but it was worth a try. Should she fail today, she had several other plans for gaining an audience with him. Those would require a lot of time and a good deal of subterfuge, so it was worthwhile to start with the direct approach.

Having made it to the drawing room gave her heart. With luck, the duke would at least be intrigued. If he was a bibliophile like his grandfather, her calling card might nudge him. She had commissioned cards that included little images of books below her name, so recipients would see at once what she was about.

One could say she had come here about books, too, if one wanted to stretch matters. Not to sell them, although she wouldn't mind making a few sales to the duke, or anyone else. It was what she did, after all. How she fed herself and financed her travels and everything else. Her visit to this massive townhome today was not about trade, however. It was much more important than that.

The question was, would she find this duke almost human like the last one or a lying scoundrel like his grandfather? The strong possibility of the latter had her straightening her spine and gathering her courage.

The door opened and she turned, expecting to see the butler had returned to her. Instead a dark-haired man—a quite handsome one—stuck his head in. His remarkably blue eyes swept the chamber, then came to rest on her. She could not ignore how his gaze sharpened, and how he took her in most thoroughly.

Not the duke, she was sure. A duke did not greet visitors like this. Someone else, then, who had some interest in His Grace's visitors. A secretary, perhaps, although he did not look like one.

He apologized for intruding. His head disappeared. The door closed.

How odd.

A few minutes later, the butler did return. He bid her follow him. When they did not go down the stairs, she realized she would have her audience after all. Excitement built with each footfall.

The butler escorted her to an expansive study. It had been decorated in extreme Chinoiserie, with big urns and heavily carved furniture. Only the desk appeared normal for a duke. Broad and deep, it could hold numerous papers and books on its surface, which at the moment it did not. Very few items rested there. An inkwell, a pen, a newspaper, two letters, and an odd little woven box. The desk gave the impression of either someone having not yet moved into the space, or of someone so neat that nothing personal was allowed to sully the clear surface.

The man standing next to the desk was far more interesting. She realized that the other man, the one who intruded on the drawing room, was a relative. The two looked enough alike, and both bore some resemblance to the last duke. Dark haired and this one had dark eyes as well. The current duke was a very handsome man, with regular features and the kind of countenance that women can't ignore. Dressed as impeccably as one would expect, with a blinding cravat and collar and a dark suite of garments, he presented a tower of correctness and, she feared, dullness. He stood taller than most, at least a head taller than herself, and his manner upon greeting her bore all of the formality that one expected of an important person who had agreed to accept the call of a total stranger.

She figured she had at most three minutes to garner his attention before he politely had her thrown out. She made a curtsy, then stood upright and looked him right in the eyes.

"My name is Iris Barrington, and I have come to request—no, to demand—that you fulfill a promise that your uncle made to me."

At first she received no reaction at all. Just a long consideration. For a moment he reminded her of Count D'Ilio, a friend whose reserve could be either intriguing and mysterious or annoying and boring. It all depended on her mood. She tended to attract men like that. They enjoyed her lack of reserve and lived a vicariously vivacious life through her.

This particular man did not truly fit that mold. For one thing, she doubted he was all that reserved in a normal situation. The duke in him might be, but the man in him probably wasn't. Her reason for thinking that was the sparks in his eyes. The duke was taking her measure, but the man liked what he saw.

How interesting. Perhaps a different tactic was in order.

She flashed her brightest smile and stepped a few paces closer so the expensive scent she wore would waft toward him. "Forgive me. I did not intend to be rude and just blurt that out. However, I am at a disadvantage. I am grateful that you received me at all. It was very kind of you to do so."

"You could have written first."

"I assumed my letter would never make it past the desk of your secretary. I have no references. No family here. I am not an ordinary petitioner."

A half smile formed. He gestured to a settee and chair

against the far wall. "Perhaps you will sit and explain about this promise you claim my uncle made."

She sat, leaving enough space for the duke to sit beside her. Which he did not do. So much for a few feminine wiles gaining her all that she sought.

"You say 'claim.' You probably have had a long line of people approach you and say the late duke promised them this and such," she said.

"A fair number."

"Were they all liars?"

He smiled. Goodness, what a nice smile it was too. The kind that could warm a woman all the way down to—

"A fair number were," he said.

"I am not lying. I met with your uncle not long before his passing. He promised to help me find something that I believed he owned. A manuscript. A very fine one from the early 1400s. A Psalter, full of superb illuminations. I had heard that it was bought by his father—your grandfather—and wanted to know if it was still in the ducal library."

Curiosity joined male appreciation in his eyes. "Why would you care if it were in the library?"

"I have a buyer for it. It is worth a small fortune. I trade in rare books and manuscripts, you see. In such a sale I would act as a go-between." Lies, most of it. It would not do to explain the real reason she wanted to find that manuscript. He would never help her then.

"Did he tell you that his father's library was divided upon his death? Each son received a portion of it."

"He did tell me, and he promised to look into which son had received the Psalter. When word reached me that he had died—I had not heard from him in so long, but I never guessed that was why. I thought perhaps he had not found it, or changed his mind, or that his letters had not found me

yet. I realized then that perhaps he had not even had the
time to look into this for me."

More curiosity. Too much.

"When did you have this visit with him, when you asked
about the Psalter?"

"In February, or early March. I can't remember the exact
day."

"Was it here in London?"

"He wrote and told me to come to his estate in Sussex.
Melton Park."

The duke seemed to ponder that. He stood and walked to
one of the windows and gazed out. Then he looked back
over his shoulder and examined her from hat to shoes. "Is
this the only reason you have called today, Miss Barrington? Is there anything else that you want to address with
me?"

Her mind, which had begun dallying on inappropriate
musings while she observed his tall, lean form and perfect
profile at that window, scrambled to right itself and guess
what else she was supposed to want from him.

"There is nothing else," she finally said, stupidly.

He looked out the window again. "This house has an extensive garden. The day is fair. Would you like to take a turn
with me? As it happens, I have something other than old
books I want to talk about."

She could hardly refuse, since he had bothered to see her
at all. However, while he escorted her out and down to the
garden, it crossed her mind that this could be a very deci-
sive man, and that she was about to hear a proposition that
indeed had nothing to do with old books.

"Where do you live?" Nicholas asked the question after
they had strolled about fifteen feet down a garden path. He

tried to make it sound barely curious but suspected it came out more like an interrogation. The sharpness, he admitted, had a lot to do with forcing himself to train his mind on the conversation to come rather than the erotic speculations to which it had wanted to veer since this woman walked into his study. To desire a woman so immediately, so thoroughly, so specifically—it had been a long time since he experienced that kind of attraction, and it was all he could do not to turn into the worst lecher in London.

"I spend most of my time on the Continent. I was raised there, and of course the best libraries can be found among the aristocracy of those countries. As for a home, I do have a family home in Florence. I am often traveling, however."

"Do you come to England often?"

"Not often. Perhaps once a year. My travels take me to other capitals."

"Looking for old books?"

"It is my trade."

Their stroll had taken them far into the garden, near the wall that surrounded it. Few of the houses in London had grounds like this. The northern section was wilderness, even more rare. Situated as it was at the upper end of Park Lane and across from the park, it formed a little bit of country in a teeming town. Of all of the properties that Nicholas had inherited, he preferred this one.

Beside him, Miss Barrington trod resolutely. Her expression remained passive, but her dark eyes glinted. Those eyes could be mesmerizing if he allowed himself to look into them for long. The glints became stars in the night sky then. That, and her dark hair and very fair skin gave her a distinctive appearance that was somewhat foreign. A taste for flamboyant details in her dress, in this case a long Venetian shawl of ochres and grays, such as most women wore to the theater, not for a morning call, drew further attention to her person. And her manner—not many women would make demands of a duke upon first meeting him.

She was fascinating. A gloss of sensuality covered her much like a veil might cause hazy features. It came off of her like an air or a scent. Her actual scent only increased the effect.

He knew that he wanted her as soon as he saw her, which made the meeting all the harder. It was difficult to remain aloof when in reality you wanted to devour your guest.

"Miss Barrington, there is something I must tell you. It will make little sense, I suspect. If that is your reaction, you will not be alone. I would agree, totally."

He sensed her tense beside him. She stopped walking and faced him. Her expression indicated she was not going to be all that surprised after all. She raised one eyebrow, waiting.

"My uncle's will had some unusual provisions," Nicholas continued. "A large portion of his personal wealth was left to people who are not family, friends, or retainers. Three women unknown to the family received most of it. Iris Barrington is one of those women.."

She blinked, hard. She frowned. Then she burst out laughing. "You are joking, surely. This is a peculiar amusement of yours."

"Not at all. We have been looking for you for months. Here in England, and for some time now on the Continent. Perhaps all that traveling interfered with our finding you there."

She smiled broadly with a luscious mouth. "And this is what you wanted to tell me? This is the reason for this stroll in the garden?"

"Yes." He reached into his waistcoat pocket and withdrew a card. "This is the name of the family solicitor. He is also the will's executor. I recommend that you see him at once."

She took the card and stared at it. Then she laughed again. "Well, I'll be damned." She looked up into his eyes. Those starry glints began beckoning him to join her in the night sky. "I just assumed you brought me here to proposition me."

He laughed, too, as if such an idea was ridiculous.

They headed back to the house. Of course, he had to know.

"Does that happen often? Being propositioned?" he asked ever so casually.

She kept looking at the card. "All the time. A woman on her own—well, you can imagine. But I have never been, and never will be, some man's mistress. I make my own way. Being supported like that carries obligations that I refuse to accept."

"That is understandable."

She aimed for the front garden portal, indicating she intended to leave that way. At the gate she stopped and faced him again. Her smile was sly, but her expression matter-of-fact. "Then again, I am not opposed to taking lovers if they appeal to me. That is different."

Very different. He reacted as if it had been an invitation of sorts, but he also knew it might only be a taunt.

That sensual air seemed to blanket him. In a few moments he would be completely aroused if she did not leave at once.

"I need to ask you something," she said. "Do a duke's promises die with him?"

"Not the important ones."

"I would very much like to find that Psalter."

Hell, he'd give her his eye teeth if she wanted them right

now. "I will see what I can learn. I'll start with the library here. How will I recognize it?"

"If you open a book only to find it is a manuscript full of colorful paintings on vellum depicting the Psalms, that is probably it."

And then she was gone, out the gate, the shawl swaying to her step.

Chapter Two

"Walter will have apoplexy," Kevin said while he swirled the port in his glass. "He has already spent the money he expected to inherit when the third mystery heiress wasn't found. He and Felicity went to Paris, and she bought her whole wardrobe for the Season there. Rosamund says the hats alone cost a fortune."

Nicholas sat with his cousins Kevin and Chase in the library of Whiteford House. They had come to discuss the unexpected discovery of Iris Barrington.

"None of them will be pleased, since her significant legacy would have been split among us all. Bar the door, Nicholas. Word should spread by morning, and they will all show up here, complaining and begging," Chase said.

The provisions of their uncle's will had not sat well on their two aunts and their many cousins. Precious little had been given to any of them, including Nicholas, who, as the new duke, received a lot of land and houses but almost nothing to support their maintenance. The difference, he kept reminding himself, was that he expected nothing while Walter and the others had expected quite a lot and had lived accordingly. When two of the three mystery heiresses had been found, hopes had diminished but not ended. The sad truth was that a lot of people were counting on Iris Barrington being dead.

Not Chase or Kevin. Each had the good sense to fall in love with one of the heiresses. Marriages had followed, which made them above it all in this most recent situation.

"Sanders is making enquiries to ensure she is who she claims," Chase added.

"She seemed unaware of the inheritance," Nicholas said.

"Did you believe that?"

Did he? Once away from the influence of her eyes and smiles, he had to admit that the whole visit had been peculiar. For her to turn up on his doorstep after all these months—it begged for an explanation besides her desire to sell one of his grandfather's purported library holdings.

"If she wanted to claim the inheritance, she did not need to come to me," he said, thinking aloud. "She could have just gone to Sanders. As executor, he is the one she needs to satisfy with her identity."

"I'm sure our aunts will be doing their best to make the case that she is not who is named in the will," Kevin said. "After all, to have another one of the heiresses be in trade— they will think uncle's entire goal was to humiliate them in society."

"Since you mentioned it, I think that Miss Barrington will like Rosamund's hats. Her own had a similar flavor. Just a bit dramatic. It fit with her ensemble nicely, and I could see her patronizing Rosamund's shop."

Both of his cousins just looked at him.

"I'm only saying that—"

"That you were noticing her hat and ensemble," Kevin said. "Under the circumstances, perhaps noticing her character would have been preferable."

"I doubt Nicholas missed much about Miss Barrington," Chase said. "I only saw a glimpse but there was much to occupy one's attention. Wasn't there, Nicholas?"

"It was my duty to pay attention. She is the possible heiress to a large fortune that otherwise would stay in the family."

"True. True. And yet—" Chase raised his eyebrows.

Kevin glanced from Chase to Nicholas. "What? I'm not being told something."

"There is nothing more to tell," Nicholas said. "I have described the meeting."

"You left out some important details," Chase said. "For example, you have not described *her*." He turned to Kevin. "She is very distinctive looking. Dark eyes, dark hair. A bit foreign in appearance. I would call her—vivid."

"An odd word," Kevin said.

"When you meet her, you will know what I mean. She is lovely. Don't you agree, Nicholas?"

"I suppose she is lovely in a way."

"*I suppose she is lovely in a way*," Chase mimicked his sonorously ducal tone.

"When I met Rosamund, it was as if I had been hit by a bolt of lightning," Kevin said. "I trust nothing like that happened with you. We don't even know for certain who she is."

"There was no bolt. No anything. We had a civil conversation. That is all."

"Thank goodness. Otherwise, the aunts will be plotting if she is at all acceptable."

"Our aunts will not find her the slightest bit acceptable." The very notion had him grinning at the reaction of those aunts if they ever met the woman claiming to be Iris Barrington. "She is far too dramatic in appearance—forgive me, make that vivid—and she is clearly a woman of the world."

He caught Kevin and Chase exchanging meaningful glances. He challenged them with a stare. Both went back to sipping their port. He did as well. As the conversation shifted to other things, half of his mind contemplated the vivid woman in question.

He should probably find out when she had met with Uncle Frederick. There were reports of a meeting in the garden with a woman on the day he died. If that had been Iris Barrington, he really needed to know. And despite the way he warmed when he thought of her, he needed to keep in mind that they had only her word that she was ignorant of the inheritance. Hell, for all he knew, she had been aware of it ever since the will was written.

Iris walked out of Mr. Sanders's chambers in a daze. The last half hour had been astonishing. For some reason, the last duke had not only left her a legacy, but a big one. Huge. She had entered that solicitor's office a woman who made ends meet by brokering and selling rare books. She had exited a wealthy woman.

Surely a mistake had been made. She dared not believe this was real because then the disappointment would be all the greater if it disappeared. As it was, she wondered if someone would nudge her and she would awaken from a dream.

It appeared she would have to remain in London for some time, while the nice Mr. Sanders checked to make sure she indeed was Iris Barrington. To that end, she had provided him with the lawyer in Florence who had served as executor of her father's and her grandfather's estates, and the address of the family home where she had lived with all of them along with her mother until, one by one, they passed and left her alone. She had also explained the peculiar decision of her father to use his mother's maiden name, Borelli, instead of his legal name, Barrington.

She told the cab driver to take her to the British Museum, where she alighted. She paused to examine the front façade of Montagu House, which housed the museum. At one end some new construction appeared underway. The museum was being enlarged.

Bookstores tended to congregate in museums' shadows. She began to walk, looking for chambers to let for a short while.

Her stroll took her to Gilbert Street, where she found exactly what she wanted. A small bookstore had a sign in the window indicating an apartment above to let. Its appearance appealed to her, deeply. It reminded her of her home in Florence, with its small panes of glass showing some books, and a story above where the owner would live.

Her mind filled with memories while nostalgia squeezed her heart. She imagined walking in the door and finding an old man there, white haired but handsome still, sitting in a comfortable armchair with a stack of books nearby and one open on his lap. She saw a young girl on a wooden chair beside him, leaning over his chair's cushioned arm and laying her head on his shoulder while he read to her. His scent, so distinctive, a mixture of leather and wine and mint, became real again. She closed her eyes and savored the memories, then opened them and walked to the door.

She entered the shop and breathed in the familiar smells of old books and paper, of dust and a touch of mold.

A woman emerged from among the shelves. Red haired and very pale, she had a soft, full face and a heavy-bosomed form. She seemed of indeterminate age, a woman who had left youth behind but not yet turned matronly. The woman greeted her in a voice laced with the lilts of Scotland. Thirty, Iris calculated. A few years older than Iris herself.

"You be wanting a practical book or a fun one?"

"Always fun," Iris said. "You have a fine establishment here." She eyed a stack of books near the door bearing a motley assortment of bindings. A quick scan told her this store specialized in old books. Very few recent publications could be seen, although they were given prominence of place on a nice little display case.

"Not for long," the woman said. "Was my uncle's shop, and I thought to continue, but I've realized I'd do better selling out and living in the country. This town is not for the likes of me."

"That is unfortunate. I was hoping to see the chambers to let, but if you will be selling that might not be wise. The new owners may prefer to use the space in other ways."

"What ways would that be? It is a little home up there. Only a fool would turn out someone who pays on time. Come with me, and I'll show it to you. It is in the back and overlooks a little garden. They are the best chambers up above."

Since the woman was already halfway up the stairs, Iris followed.

"I live here." The woman gestured to a door right at the landing. "This here is the apartment that is available." She swung open a door and stood aside.

Iris entered and paced through a sitting room. Sparingly furnished, it had tall ceilings and appeared well maintained. One wall held two good-sized windows that looked over the garden. A door took her to a bedchamber with similar windows and views.

"Mattress is new," the woman said. "There's a good shop on the next street if you want to add some furniture. It could use a table and some chairs."

Iris placed herself in the center of the sitting room, imagining herself here on a winter evening. "Does the fireplace draw well? I can't abide a smokey fireplace."

"Never a problem with it. I keep it clean."

Iris pictured the table she would bring in, and the comfortable upholstered chair for reading. "What is your name?"

"Bridget MacCallum. My uncle was Liam MacCallum.

He passed on two years ago now, but everyone on these streets knew him."

"What is the price to let these chambers?"

"Ten shillings a month. Thirteen if you take board."

"Since there is no kitchen up here, it would be awkward not to take board."

"You are welcome to use the kitchen in back if you prefer to cook for yourself."

Iris slipped past Bridget and descended the stairs. "Where do you buy these books?" she asked while they walked back to the front of the shop.

"Auctions mostly. I prefer the ones held at the houses. The prices are better than at Christie's and such."

"So you are a frequent visitor to the auctions? You are known to the other booksellers who attend?"

"We all know each other."

In the light from the front window, Iris faced Bridget. "I also trade in books. Rare ones. Here is what I propose. I will pay you eight shillings a month for the chambers, and two more for board. And I will help you pay less for the books at auction, and you will help me pay less as well if there is something I want to buy. Perhaps if we are both sly, you will not have to sell this shop."

Bridget peered at her suspiciously. "Nothing illegal to this, is there? The helping each other part, I mean."

"Nothing illegal. Also, nothing others are not doing, right under your nose." She eyed the stack of books near the door. She reached down and pulled out one with a very fine binding in good condition. "You should make bindings like this more visible. There are those who care not for the contents, but only the leather. Trust me, this one, if left here on top, will sell within a day or so. Now, what say you to my offer?" She placed the book in Bridget's hands.

Bridget ran her cuff over the leather book, giving it a dusting. "Seems to me we can give it a try if you are willing to take your meals when I do. I've the shop to mind, and that comes first."

"I will even cook on occasion, if you like."

"Well, now, that will be a treat. When will you be coming here to live?"

"Tonight, if that suits you." She pried open her reticule and plucked out ten shillings. "Here is the first month's rent. I expect that I will be here several months at least. Perhaps you will not sell before I am gone."

The sun glinted off Bridget's red hair while she nodded. The light turned her white skin translucent and revealed a few lines that aged her beyond what Iris had calculated. Perhaps thirty-five, she decided.

"Could be. I've a mind to stay if I can, and with those chambers let to you, I may be able to for a bit longer."

Iris opened the door and was almost out after taking her leave when she paused. "My book trade is private. I make use of my chambers to meet with buyers and sellers. I promise that you will not be disturbed when they visit."

Bridget gave her another good look. "There's no reason to ask you your business. Especially if you are paying ten shillings a month and cooking at times."

"Then we are agreed. I will return this evening. I look forward to living above your shop. It will feel like home, I am sure."

Three days later, Iris followed Bridget into a house on Dover Street. They did not look at each other, nor did they speak. Anyone watching would assume they had never met each other.

Once inside, Iris aimed left, and Bridget turned right. They approached the tables with books from opposite directions, examining tomes for sale. With a glance, Iris concluded that the day's outing would prove far more profitable to her landlady than to herself. The library for sale contained very predictable titles, the sort any respectable townhome in London would contain. The bindings that gave them consistency of appearance were also respectable, but not valuable in and of themselves like some bindings could be.

It was such a proper and appropriate library that she wondered why one of the big booksellers had not simply bought the entire thing outright, with an eye to selling it as a whole to a new house owner looking to populate library shelves. Most likely, the heirs who had inherited this house and its contents hoped to get more if they sold piecemeal.

She doubted they would. By the end of the auction the leftovers would probably be sold in large lots and at low prices. She would remind Bridget of that. Bridget bought inventory of a wide variety, and mixed lots like this auction would probably offer might appeal to her.

She left the large tables and strolled around the edges of the chamber. More tables rested here, with a vast variety of books. These were not the sort to be bound in identical leather, but what Bridget called the practical kind. Cooking guides, comportment advice, even husbandry instruction rested on one table.

"Are you seeking advice from older women of experience?" a voice at her shoulder asked. A strong hand reached around and lifted a small blue book. "This one here, perhaps. *Proper Etiquette for Young Ladies*. My cousin's wife knows the author. I have always suspected it is my aunt Agnes."

She glanced askance at the man now by her side. Her gaze fell on the best superfine frock coat, then up to a perfectly tied cravat, then further yet to an exceedingly handsome profile. The duke stood out in this crowd to say the least. He towered above the other heads, and his entire presence announced his status and pedigree.

"Your aunt enjoys writing?"

"Not at all, but she adores giving unwanted advice. It would be like her to decide duty obligated her to impart her views on the behavior of young ladies."

"I always assumed such books were written by women determined to ensure that young ladies have as little fun as they did when they were that age."

She allowed him to hover while she inhaled his scent. Leather and wool, such as one expected, but beneath that a subtle spicy note. It gave the commonplace masculine smell a bit of mystery. She wondered if the duke had a hidden exotic side to him.

She moved on, perusing the side tables. He fell into step with her. Across the room she could see Bridget noticing the man now attached to her side.

"You did not reveal your interest in books when we met," she said. "You might have told me we have something in common."

"Isn't everyone interested in books? It did not seem to be remarkable."

"Men of your sort are interested in reading books. That is not the same thing as attending auctions of libraries."

"I became aware of it, and thought to stop in. One must do something of an afternoon."

"I see. How conceited of me. I thought you were here looking for me."

"Why would I do that?"

She stopped walking and looked up at him. "We both know why, but if you want to pretend we don't, I don't mind."

In the far corner, she found much more interesting books. There, in the dark, assembled as if the auctioneer knew no one would want them, some very old texts in foreign languages had been heaped. She shoved her reticule's cords up her arm and began to move heavy books around, flipping quickly to frontispieces that showed year and city of publication, scanning contents and images. All the while she tried to appear barely interested.

One person was not fooled. "Ah, you have discovered the hidden treasures."

"Hardly treasures, but of some interest. Stop touching them. I would rather the entire assembly did not notice what I am doing."

"Should I stand aside?"

"Just don't draw attention to us by trying to help me. Look bored."

"I can do that." He stepped away and folded his arms over his chest. He all but sighed with annoyance. How much better if he had walked away completely. Not that she really wanted him to. The attendance of a handsome man, especially a powerful one, was always pleasant.

At the bottom of one stack, she found buried gold. She knew as soon as she saw the cover that this one book was worth her while. Published in the early sixteenth century, in Latin, it was a treatise on perspective. There were collectors who wanted any early book on that subject. As it happened, Iris had just such a collector among her friends in Lyon.

She checked the condition as best she could while remaining surreptitious. Other than a few pages with foxing, it appeared in fine shape.

"That one is quite impressive." Her interest had garnered the duke's and he now hovered at her shoulder again, his proximity and breath making her skin tingle. "The images are engravings, aren't they? They are very sharp and appear to have dark lines, not gray ones such as is common."

"That means they were printed from plates not used much yet. An early printing."

"Is it worth something?"

"Something." At least forty pounds. Not a fortune, but a goodly sum for such a book. She could travel for half a year on forty pounds if she had to.

She returned it to the bottom of its stack and stepped away. She found the title in the auction guide she had obtained at the door and made a little mark beside it.

"Do you normally buy books in England?" the duke asked while they continued their stroll.

"No. I normally sell books here when I visit. However, it appears I will remain in London for a while now, so Mr. Sanders can verify my identity. Since it involves letters to Florence and who knows what else, it could be some months before I receive that legacy. You might have warned me that it was a very large inheritance and not the few pounds I assumed. I nearly swooned when Mr. Sanders explained it all."

"It is large, isn't it? There were three heiresses who, together, got the overwhelming majority of his financial holdings. The other two did very well, but your legacy is twice as big." He paced on a bit before adding, "I expect my family will want to meet you."

"Whatever for?"

"To see to whom my uncle gave all that money. Aunt Agnes will probably invite you to dinner so everyone can gawk and be rude."

"Perhaps I will decline."

"That might be wise."

"This has been a very pleasant chat, Your Grace, but I think I will remain for the auction itself. First, I must go and refresh myself. These things can run long and are very boring, so I understand if you want to leave."

"I'll stay too. I'm curious how it all works. I'll find seats while I wait for you."

Cursing under her breath, she made her way to the ladies withdrawing room. There she perched herself on a bench to rest. A little later, Bridget availed herself of the other end of the bench and fanned herself with the auction guide while other women came and went and chatted nearby.

"Warm in there. They should open some windows with so many bodies about," Bridget said.

"I expect it will thin quickly enough. Well before they form mixed lots of the remains. Those are often very reasonable to get. Most of the buyers are men, so the practical books will probably end up in those late boxes."

"Is that what you have come for? Practical mixed lots?" Bridget asked.

"Mostly. Do you think I should buy a few if I can? What would be a good price, do you think?"

"No more than a pound a box and that's assuming at least ten books."

"Thank you for that advice. I'm not familiar with London auctions like this."

The fan flicked again. "Did you see nothing of particular interest? I found it quite ordinary myself."

"Oh, there are a few items that appealed to me." She opened her guide and turned to the page with the perspective study.

Bridget collected her reticule and guide. Only it was Iris's guide that she clutched. "Best be getting back so I get a good seat. It has been pleasant talking with you."

"And I with you. *Bon chance.*"

Iris waited a few minutes after Bridget had left, then followed, carrying Bridget's guide that bore its own markings. She saw the duke had taken a seat in the third row from the front. She caught his eye and headed to the rear. By the time she found a seat toward the back of the rows of chairs he had joined her. She could see Bridget down in front. That was a mistake. Bridget needed to be able to see who else was bidding, and other important things. She never could if it was all happening behind her.

"Why did you want to move?" the duke asked as he settled in. Heads turned to where he sat. Goodness, the man was a liability to her plans. She wondered how one told a duke to go away.

"Because from here I can see what is what," she whispered. "I have already spotted one ring of three bookmen." She indicated who the three were, and the duke's gaze darted from one to the other. "Watch. None of them will bid when one of the others does. They have agreed who will win which lot already. Only an outsider will be able to take one of those lots away, and for good money at that."

"That sounds unsporting. Even illegal."

"As far as I know there is no law against not bidding on a book."

She raised her hand when Bridget's choices went on the block and was able to purchase four of them. Then the miscellanea began to arrive. Some people left then. Most of the ring did. One person did not. The man sitting beside her.

"Look. That is the book you were interested in," he said too loudly.

"So it is."

"Aren't you going to bid?"

"I think not."

"It was very handsome. It would be a shame to let it go for mere shillings."

"I had second thoughts on it."

"That red-haired woman down there is going to get it for next to nothing. I rather liked it myself. I'm going to bid and—*ow*!"

"Keep your hand down," she hissed while she removed her elbow from his side.

"But that woman—"

"*Yes.*"

He looked at the red hair. He looked at Iris. "*Ohhhh.*"

"Yes."

The auctioneer knocked down the perspective study for a mere seventeen shillings. Iris chose to leave then. The duke trailed her through the house toward the entrance. He waited while she made payment and arranged for delivery of the books, then escorted her to the entrance.

"You can be quite devious," he said. "I will have to remember that."

"It was not really about that particular book. I could have bought it for the same price by bidding myself," she explained. "I do not want the booksellers to come to know me sooner than necessary. If they do, and word spreads on my trade, they will follow me at every auction, bidding on what I want and making most items unaffordable. It is in my interest to avoid the kind of attention that would do that."

"Of course, although in several months you can purchase any book you want at any price."

That comment made her stop in her tracks. "I can, can't I? I had not even thought about that. It is one thing to have a change in fortune, and another to learn to live with it, I suppose. Perhaps I will write one of those practical books and title it *Growing Accustomed to Being Nouveau Riche*."

He laughed along with her while they passed through the front entry. She liked how the sides of his eyes crinkled when he laughed. She was occupied with admiring that while they descended to the street. She wondered if in pleasure his countenance hardened or softened, and whether those naughty lights deepened.

Suddenly a vise gripped her waist. She flew, her body making a long circle while her feet left the pavement. When the blur ended and she stood on firm ground again, she was in the duke's arms, being held to that superfine frock coat while shouts filled the air.

She looked in the direction that others did and saw a carriage careening down the street.

"Are you all right?" His voice, deep and quiet, sounded in her ear. She looked up into the duke's concerned expression.

"You almost walked right into the path of that carriage. The horse must have broken loose. There was no coachman or passengers."

He still held her closely, with their faces a mere inch apart. She did not want to pull away because an inner terror began to make her shake, as she realized the close call she had just had. If the duke had not been beside her—

"It was fortunate you decided to pass the time at a book auction today," she murmured.

"That was not the only reason I came," he said. "Unless you want to pretend it was."

Down the street several men had managed to stop the runaway horse. The coachman ran past to retrieve his equipage, his face red with worry and exertion. Just then Bridget emerged from the house, carrying a large flat package. She paused and gazed at Iris.

Iris extricated herself. "Thank you. Truly. However, with the horse caught we risk being the most interesting occurrence on this lane."

He let her go. "I must allow you to finish the day's activity with your partner, and I must attend to other, less fascinating business."

He walked away while Bridget trod down the steps, hugging her package. "Who was that?"

"The Duke of Hollinburgh."

Bridget laughed. "Go on!"

"That is who he is."

Bridget gave her a curious look. "Go on," she murmured. "You've beaus who are dukes? What you doing sleeping above my shop?"

"That, my new friend, is a long story."

Chapter Three

"I have drawn up a list of people to look into," Chase said. "Regrettably, half of them are relatives."

Nicholas had been expecting a list. It was his cousin's way. Chase had a unique profession—the family insisted on calling it a trade in order to feel superior—of conducting investigations. His methodical approach had been developed in the army where he learned these skills. His wife, Minerva, also participated, but operated in a more fluid, imaginative way. Together they rarely failed in their efforts.

"It still has to be done," Nicholas said. "We should not ignore our instincts on the matter. Even if the official report said accident—a conclusion you encouraged for reasons we both understand and accept—you and I should know the truth if possible."

"And you think it is time to do that?"

"I do." One should not ignore the murder of a relative, no matter how convenient that would be. And if there were a viper in the nest, he wanted to know. As to what he would do about it . . .

"It would help if it had been Philip," Chase said. "You have already cut him off and disowned him. Unfortunately, he has a tight story regarding his whereabouts that day and night."

"People lie to cover for friends. It could still be him."

"In this case it was not a friend, but Felicity, who doesn't even like him. She was returning from a friend's home when she saw him staggering out of a gaming hell. She gave him a ride home."

"Was Walter with her?"

"He was sharing wine and conversation with a member of his club."

"We need to make sure all the rest also have such good explanations."

"If so, you will have to be the one to find out. In fact, you will have to do some of the other work on this. Minerva's condition means I don't want to venture far from home."

Nicholas knew he should have started all of this months ago, before Chase's wife got with child. Now she was in the middle of a pregnancy that was proving more difficult than dangerous, to hear Chase tell it. Still, Chase obviously wanted to stay nearby.

"Give me the list. I'll mark the ones I think I can handle without being too obvious." Nicholas held out his hand.

Chase placed the list in it. Nicholas perused the fifteen names. "You have included Miss Barrington."

"Of course. She inherited a very large fortune as a result of his death. We have no idea where she was at the time, and you said she met with him soon before. I would say that right now Miss Barrington deserves to be at the top of the list."

Which was exactly where Chase had put her.

"I could deal with her," Chase offered. "She is here in London, and it would be no trouble."

"I'll do it. She won't suspect that I am investigating, while she would wonder why you are sniffing around."

"True. On the other hand, she would never accuse me of betrayal if she learned what I was doing."

"We do not have a friendship, let alone the kind that uses words like 'betrayal.'"

"If you say so."

He hated it when Chase retreated like that, in a way that managed to insert one more phrase that implied he, Chase, knew better than what had just been claimed. Nicholas let the subject drop, however. For one thing, he did not have a friendship with their third heiress that could be betrayed. For another, if Iris Barrington ever murdered someone, she would never consider it a betrayal if she were found out.

Iris stood across the street from the bookshop, examining its façade. Some paint was in order along the eaves, and the windows needed a good wash. She marched toward the door, as if she were a patron who had just arrived. She glanced in the window where a new tome rested. An old one, opened to show the engraved depiction of the optical effects of proper perspective when used in a painting. Behind the book stood a discreet sign reading RARE BOOKS BOUGHT AND SOLD. INQUIRE WITHIN.

Inside the shop, she found Bridget sitting in the upholstered chair that Iris had bought yesterday.

"That is for patrons, to encourage them to sit and peruse a few volumes," Iris said.

"When a patron enters, I'll stand up. Till then, I can sit here."

"Ideally not. And let's try to keep the cat off the cushion."

"King Arthur has a mind of his own."

The cat in question, a huge blond tabby, snuck his nose around the corner of some shelves and eyed the new chair possessively.

"If he fills that cushion with cat hair, I'll be making cat stew."

"Don't you listen to her, Arthur. No one makes stew here unless I know what is going in it."

Iris examined the other changes she had made in the shop. After pulling twenty books from the many piles and cases, she had assembled them on a special shelf. Like many shop owners, Bridget didn't really know what she had in her inventory, especially since most of it had been inherited. It turned out her uncle had purchased a few items that with a little imagination could be considered rare, and they now held pride of place near the front of the shop.

"What am I to charge if someone wants that fancy book we bought at auction?" Bridget asked. "You may not be here for me to check."

"Forty pounds."

"Go on!"

"That is what it is worth and what I will charge to my collector in Lyon if we don't sell it in a month or so."

"I'll say forty-five, then go down to forty if he haggles."

Iris thought that a splendid tactic, and one she often used herself. Bridget had a talent for bookselling, and she had not objected or even commented much when Iris began making a few changes to the shop. It appeared more inviting now, and more organized.

"You going to tell me about that duke?" Bridget asked while she petted King Arthur, who had decided that the cushion might be out of bounds, but Bridget's lap never was. "I've been bursting with curiosity."

"I met him recently. His family has a very fine library, and I hope to purchase some items from him."

"So he agreed to meet you at that auction? You'd think a duke had better things to do."

Iris decided it was a good time to do some dusting. She poked her feather duster among the books on a nearby shelf. "That was an accidental meeting. Neither of us knew the other would be there."

"Where else would you be, since you are a bookseller?" Bridget's voice carried from the new chair.

"I doubt he thought about it much. Just as well he was there. I might have been run down by that horse and carriage otherwise."

"Yesss. The runaway horse and carriage. Lucky you that a duke was there to save you. I could see how shocked and breathless you were when I came out."

"Quite shocked."

"Took you a long while to recover. Good thing he was there to hold you up or you'd have ended up a heap on the pavement."

Iris worked her duster harder while she scolded herself for enjoying being breathless with the duke. She had to remember that she had a mission here that needed her primary attention and could not allow a handsome man to distract her. A mission and a duty. She was determined to see it through for her family's sake. It was time to purge history of its lies.

Nor did she really know if this duke could be a friend, even if that history had never existed. The story was that his grandfather had been charming and affable too. Even kind and generous. A man can hide much with a few smiles if he is a duke.

She looked around the bookshelves to see Bridget petting the monstrous cat. "Tell me, does that cat ever catch mice? I found two making merry in the storage room this morning."

"King Arthur prefers to hunt in the garden. He isn't partial to the storage room. I think it scares him."

Iris doubted anything scared that cat. He probably weighed thirty pounds. And that wasn't all from catching rodents in the garden. She had also caught the cat eating some leftovers that had not been wrapped and put in the larder fast enough.

She eyed King Arthur. He gazed back placidly. She could imagine his thoughts. *She will pick me over you, so don't even think about it, woman.*

Suddenly the cat was jumping off Bridget, and she was rising. "Mail's come."

The door opened, and the woman who brought Bridget the mail from the office for a small fee handed in several items. Bridget passed out some coins and flipped through the letters. She held one large one up to the light.

"Fancy paper. Fancier hand. Heavy. Postpaid, no less. It's for you, of course. I never get mail that looks like this. Must have cost a lot to send it."

Iris took the thick letter. It had come from Mr. Sanders. Surely he had not heard back from Florence so soon. She had also provided a few references of collectors here in England with whom she'd had dealings, though. Perhaps he was reporting on those.

She tore open the letter only to find another sealed one inside. Even fancier paper, and the seal looked very important. Bridget sidled over to look on. "Seems a shame to ruin that seal by opening it."

Yet open it she must, although she guessed whose seal it was. Sure enough, the letter had come from the duke.

    Imagine my surprise to realize I had no way of contacting you. Nor would Sanders provide your address, which you have told him you want kept private. Thus, I am forced to request he forward this.

    I would appreciate it if you would call on me this Thursday at one o'clock in the afternoon. I have a proposition for you, but, per your stated preference, it is strictly a business arrangement.

Bridget's eyes widened after reading the letter over Iris's shoulder. "A bit flirtatious, isn't he?"

"It is just his way."

"I suppose if a man is a duke, handsome and young, he is at liberty to flirt if it amuses him. Warned him off, did you? Was that before or after the embrace outside the auction?"

Iris felt her face burn. What silliness. She never blushed, least alone at an insinuation like that. She tucked the letter inside her bodice and lifted the feather duster again. Out of the corner of her eye she saw the huge blond tabby stretch out on the new chair's cushion.

"She is here."

Nicholas looked up from the damned accounts. Powell stood near the door, a column of calm competence. Considering that Uncle Frederick had pensioned off all the experienced staff, Powell had been a godsend when he took up his position. After guiding Nicholas on the next few hires, Nicholas had handed the entire project into Powell's capable hands. As a result, he now had a London home and a county seat that hummed with excellent service.

Nicholas began moving books and papers so he could rise. Powell gestured to the stacks that surrounded the reading chair in the dressing room's corner.

"I could have all of that moved to your study, Your Grace."

"So you have said. I prefer to suffer here. Did you put Miss Barrington in the library?"

"Of course, sir. It was what you instructed."

He let Powell leave, then prepared to go down himself. He donned the frockcoat discarded during the torture of examining the accounts and checked his ridiculously stiff cravat. Johnson, his valet, ensured he looked his role rather too well, in his opinion. Someday, after establishing his seriousness regarding the title, he intended to enter the House of Lords with a casually tied black cravat. Perhaps he would even call on the king that way. After all, he was Hollinburgh.

On the way down he reminded himself of the day's intentions. If Chase said Miss Barrington was a likely suspect, he needed to accumulate information that either indicated she required serious investigation regarding Uncle Frederick, or that cleared her of suspicion. The best way to do that was to have her nearby where subtle questions could be asked to ferret out the details of her story. He had found the perfect way to do that.

He found her in the library, perusing the shelves. It seemed the books interested her far more than his arrival did. She merely glanced in his direction before continuing her examination.

She had dressed mostly in white today. Current fashion had rather stiff skirts and more fitted tops than he remembered from his younger days. Women tended to make little noises when they walked as the skirt crinkled and rubbed the fabric beneath it. Miss Barrington, however, had chosen a softer top skirt, one that still managed to flow while remaining current. He was no expert on such matters, but he suspected that the lace festooning the dress would be considered overdone by his aunts.

It was the hat that truly declared her independence of such judgments. Wide brimmed and set low on her crown, it sported three bright plumes. Two russet-hued ones pierced the air to the left, but one jutted to the right. Deep sapphire in color, it angled in such a way as to frame the side of her face, its fluffy ends caressing her alabaster cheek.

Her dress at the auction had been plainer. Almost colorless. But then she did not want to draw attention to herself there. Normally she did, apparently. That lace and those plumes were flags that announced to the world that she was free and a little wild and she made her own rules. With her dress and manner, she told Aunt Agnes and others like her that she did not give a fig for their opinion.

Or his, most likely. She had already let him know that she knew he wanted her. It was disconcerting to have a woman so directly identify desire, and all but name it. He much preferred to lead in the dance. Instead, this woman still considered whether she would even put his name on her card.

He knew how to handle that. He was not green in the least. He needed to put the notion of pleasure aside, however, and learn more about her, and her dealings with his uncle.

Duty, duty.

When he approached, she finally gave him all of her attention. Her full red lips smiled. Her dark eyes, emphasized by that plume and low brim, glinted.

"Why are you keeping your place of residence a secret?" he asked after they exchanged greetings. "Sanders would not reveal it even after I commanded him to do so."

"I thought it best not to have that information out and about. Word of this inheritance is sure to spread, and I would rather not have a line at my door petitioning for loans and donations."

"I am hardly going to do that."

"I was not thinking about you when I gave Mr. Sanders the directions."

"Then you will let me at least know your whereabouts?"

She cocked her head. "I don't think so."

So much for ducal power. He gestured to the French doors that gave way to a terrace. "I have told them to bring you some refreshments. Please join me for some coffee or tea, and I will explain myself and my plan."

He escorted her onto the terrace. A table had been set there, with silver urns and china plates. Coffee or tea waited to be served by the attending footman. A plate of cakes waited too.

She exclaimed and clapped her hands when she saw them. "Viennese. I intended to decline any food, but with these I must indulge."

He could not remember the cook ever baking such a thing before. They did look delicious. Almost decadent. "I sent down word that you had traveled throughout the Continent," he lied. Most likely Powell had sent down that word, but her delight in the cakes made him decide to take credit.

She accepted coffee and two of the cakes. After one sip she bit into her treasure. Tiny grains of sugar adhered to her red lips. Very red. He wondered if she painted them. Not that it mattered. He imagined flicking his tongue to capture each and every grain of sugar on her mouth.

"Your cook is excellent. These are among the best I have had. Please thank him for me." She bit again.

How like her to assume that someone would indeed inform the cook of her approval. How peculiar to believe it might be a duke. He would try to remember to have Powell convey his guest's appreciation.

"You really must try one," she said after swallowing the last of the first cake.

"I doubt my own pleasure will match that of watching yours."

Teeth submerged in the next cake, she paused and gave him a worldly look. Only then did he appreciate the double entendre of his statement. Her lips smiled around the cake, as if she enjoyed the flirtatious moment. He smiled back, as if it had all been planned.

"You wrote that you have a business arrangement to propose." She raised the subject after dabbing at her lips. The two cakes had been consumed in mere minutes. Not a delicate consumption either. One more thing on the list that made Iris Barrington extremely inappropriate to anyone who cared about such things. Being a duke now, he supposed he did, at least more than in the past. Which did not mean he didn't appreciate the stimulation of a woman like her.

"You also assured me it was not that kind of proposition," she added. "Not assured, actually. Implied. It was a little confusing."

"Miss Barrington, if I ever make that kind of proposition regarding an arrangement, there will be no confusion on your part, I promise."

"What other sort of arrangement could a man like you want with me?"

He thought that a cynical thing to say. Perhaps that was the other side of the coin in being a worldly woman. She knew men rather too well.

"I wanted to tell you that I have begun to search the library for the Psalter. However, in doing so, I realized that the contents were not properly appraised upon my uncle's death."

"Estate appraisals are rarely accurate. There is an interest in keeping the values low."

"Even the inventory itself is an unsatisfactory updating of the one done when his father passed on. No Psalter of any kind is in either, however."

"It might not have been included in the inventories. If it was not in the library, for example. Or hidden. It is that rare, and that valuable. It is not the kind of thing one puts on a shelf, binding out, among the Bibles."

"Then a thorough search will be necessary, of this house and the others. However, in realizing the appraisal had been unsatisfactory, I decided to rectify that and have one done. Not only of my uncle's library but of the portion my father inherited. I moved all of that here last year. Is this the kind of thing that you do?"

She appeared to weigh the question. He did not doubt she saw the implications.

"It is not commonplace for me to do it," she said.

"Perhaps you can recommend someone—"

"I said not commonplace. I did not say I do not ever do it. I would consider this under two conditions. The first is that you indeed undertake a thorough search for the Psalter. The second is that, should you choose to sell any of the valuable books, I be given due consideration as the person who will broker the sales. For those books, I will give you two numbers. One would be the amount you might realize at an auction. The other would be the amount I would seek in a private sale."

"That sounds fair enough. Now, regarding your fees—"

"I will not take money for this. I will hope that I find books worth representing. My commission on such dealings is ten percent. That will be my fee."

"It is too generous of you to undertake such a chore for no payment guaranteed. I'm not sure I should agree."

"Your grandfather's library was famous. I'm sure there are many books that are worth my while, and that will bring high amounts. I am willing to risk it."

High amounts? How high? That perspective study was worth forty pounds, according to her, and it was not even all that special. He glanced at the French doors, to the library within. If even five or ten books were really valuable, it might solve the financial straits of the estate for a few years.

He gestured to the footman to pour Miss Barrington more coffee. "We are agreed then. You can start tomorrow."

"Please alert the staff that I will be coming in the mornings at nine o'clock and staying three hours. I will require paper, pencils, and a measure."

"Perfect. Please, have another cake."

He watched her savor it and indulged in a few fantasies about licking sugar crystals off scandalous parts of her body.

Chapter Four

Iris presented herself at Whiteford House at exactly nine o'clock. She carried a little satchel that contained her own measure (having decided she could not trust theirs), an apron, several pairs of cloth gloves, and a little booklet into which she intended to list the really good books that might be worth her interest. She anticipated a very productive project in this library and was already planning which collectors should be approached with each kind of book.

The butler left her in the reception hall while he excused himself. She spent the time waiting by examining the motley collection of objects that decorated the large space. On her first visit, her excitement had only permitted a blur of textures and colors to penetrate her awareness, but she noticed now that each item appeared to be of very high quality. Weapons, armor, porcelain, textiles, statuettes— someone in the family had displayed very eclectic taste here. She did not think it was the Hollinburgh she knew.

To her surprise, the duke accompanied the butler when the servant returned.

"Come," he said. "Let me make sure you are settled correctly."

"I'm surprised you are even awake." They traversed the building toward the library. "Shouldn't you be sleeping off some decadent party or a night of gaming? Pursuing a wife or taking pleasure with a mistress?"

"Despite the commonly held views of us, we do not only live for pleasure."

"Forgive me. Shouldn't you be consulting with the king, or plotting the finances of the realm?"

"You have a taste for sarcasm as well as Viennese cakes, I see."

"My time amidst aristocrats has colored my views."

"And yet you were not opposed to taking such men as lovers, you said."

"I never said my lovers were aristocrats. Although, in real intimacy, no person is. But we digress. Why am I honored by your rising at this hour to greet me?"

"Perhaps I was curious whether your dark eyes still contained stars in the early morning light."

Lest she wonder if he was flirting, those adorable crinkles formed on either side of his eyes while a slow smile broke.

"Also," he added. "I thought it more important to get you started than to lie abed."

Alone? She almost asked.

Once in the library, she immediately examined the shelves.

"What are you looking for?" the duke asked.

"I am reassuring myself that yesterday I correctly ascertained the organization. Each private library is divided differently. Some are by bindings, which is a very stupid way to do it but looks pretty. Others are alphabetical. This one, like most good ones, has been organized by subject matter. It makes for finding the appropriate content easily. However, it makes my work harder, because rare old books are filed in with recent publications."

She spied a northern window. "Could that table be moved to that window? The light will be best for examining anything of note."

He went to the door and called for two footmen, who came and moved the table. Once it was in place, she opened her satchel and set out its contents. The duke himself moved the pencils and paper from the desk where they had been placed.

"I brought these too. I thought you might find them useful." He set down two thick account books. She opened them to see the inventories.

"Those will be very useful. In the least, I will see what the purchaser thought he had bought. Thank you." She donned the apron and a simple white cap, set out one pair of gloves, and approached the section of the shelves that contained scientific books. The same collector in Lyon who might buy the perspective study might also want something that turned up among these tomes.

She plucked four books off the shelf and carried them to the table. The duke still stood beside it.

"I promise not to steal anything," she said. "You can have a servant take the satchel if you fear I will sneak something of value off the premises."

"I am merely curious about . . ." He made a gesture in the air toward her equipment.

This would be a slow morning if he wanted a tour. However, she set down the books and pulled on the gloves. "I use these so I do not do any damage to the pages. Fingerprints and such." She opened the top book. "Now I am checking the frontispiece to see if it is as old as I suspected. If it is, I will page through to consider its condition, if all the leaves are still here, and if the subject matter has appeal to a collector of books of this nature. All these things affect the value."

She finished her explanation and turned expectantly, assuming that now he would leave.

Instead, he hovered. "If a Psalter is found, how will you know it is the right one? Have you ever seen it?"

"I will know it by its description."

"Someone else has seen it and described it to you?"

They were wading into deep water fast now. "It was described to me by someone who in turn knew someone who had seen it. The belief is that it was once owned by Cosimo de' Medici, and that the illuminations are by the artist Fra Angelico. That attribution is far from secure. Enough illuminations were described to give me a fair idea of what it looks like, however." Deciding that more information might avert his attention from the subject completely, she continued. "The first illumination is a full page showing King David with crown on a throne, holding both a book and a lyre in the manner of Christ in Majesty. Most notably there is a city depicted in the background in good perspective. That last part is distinctive, but David is usually shown as a shepherd with the lyre, not as king. I was told that each psalm begins with an elaborate historiated initial. That means the first letter is expanded so a little painting can be included in its spaces. The bulge in a *P*, for example, would include a little scene or figure."

Hoping to move matters forward, she opened one of the books on her table and began examining it. He still didn't leave.

"You are very knowledgeable. Did you tell my uncle about that painting and the perspective city? Did he know how to recognize the Psalter if he found it?"

"I gave him that and more. I believed him when he said he would search for it, just as I am counting on your doing it instead."

She sensed him watching her while she made some notations on the paper. Her private jottings in the booklet would have to wait for when he finally left.

"When did you speak with him? Perhaps he had the time to do the search, but not the time to inform you of his discoveries."

The book she currently examined occupied most of her mind. "Late winter or early spring was when I was in London. March, I think it was. I told you that."

"Did you come here to see him?"

"I journeyed to his country home where he was in residence. He invited me to come after I wrote to him. I was not in Town long, so I went at once." Her current book appeared to be a chemical treatise from 1693. Of interest, it was written in French, not Latin. If written in the vernacular, it was probably intended for less educated men. Tradesmen and such. Its modest size suggested as much too. She set it aside to receive more attention when she had some time to read enough to ensure it contained information of interest. She jotted some notes on her paper.

"Was that your first letter to him?"

The question, asked with forced nonchalance, garnered her attention. She kept her gaze on the books and answered just as casually. "I had written from Paris in the winter. December, I think it was. Why do you ask?"

"No reason in particular. I just find it interesting if he agreed to meet after one letter."

"You agreed after no letter. However, it was not only that letter in March, if that reassures you that he was not reckless with his prerogatives."

She found it hard to ignore him. Not only because of his questions. He was just very much there, intruding on her awareness, beckoning her to forget what she was about and instead contemplate him.

"Did you have a chance to see the library at that house?"

The question came lightly, like the last, as if he merely continued a conversation of passing interest. Yet she heard a note of true curiosity. She looked up from the table to find an intense gaze on her. For reasons she could not fathom, her answer mattered to him.

"I was not in that library, I'm sorry to say. Is it as good as this one?"

"At least."

"Will you be wanting me to assess its holdings too?"

"If not in the library, where did you meet with him?"

He had ignored her question and pushed further with his own. Caution tiptoed up her spine to her scalp. "Why do you ask?"

"I am wondering why he so easily received you. His father collected rare books. He did not."

"I cannot satisfy your curiosity on the matter. All I can say is that I wrote to him upon arriving in England, and received a response inviting me to visit him, with instructions on how to find the estate."

His expression hardened slightly. "Do you maintain a diary?"

"I do."

"I would like you to see what day you visited."

"Why?"

"It matters to me."

"Why?"

"I require it. That is all you need to know."

The duke hath spoken. Well, well.

She would gain nothing from challenging him further. "I will check my diary to see what I noted. Do you *require* anything else?"

Her tone had him half chagrined, but only half. "I suppose I am curious whether, when you met with him, he mentioned the legacy you are receiving."

She wished she could credit him with mere curiosity. "He spoke not one word about his will and least of all about leaving some legacy to me. We didn't even know each other, after all."

He looked at her a long time. His gaze appeared critical of her, but his male interest also showed. She wondered if the calculations occurring were about his uncle or about the undeniable attraction they shared. When he said nothing, she half expected him to stride over and begin a seduction.

She braced herself, and her mind scrambled to decide what to do. Which was stupid of her. Permitting any advanced familiarity would be a terrible mistake.

He did not come to her. Instead, he turned to leave. "Exactly."

She forced her attention back to the books. Exactly what? Exactly that she and the late duke did not know each other? Or exactly that any seduction would be a mistake?

Of all his relatives, Nicholas considered his aunts the most troublesome. The late duke's unmarried sisters, they demanded support from Nicholas that he neither agreed he owed them nor could afford. That did not stop Agnes and Dolores from peppering him with demands, and even having bills sent to him.

Agnes was the more meddlesome, but Dolores could be the most dangerous. Agnes had a forthright nature, so one knew her mind five times over. Dolores often kept her own counsel and could prove sneaky. Each one was a formidable presence and only a fool would neglect to take them seriously. When joined as allies, few men could outflank them.

Nicholas enjoyed only one advantage in any skirmishes. His title gave him authority that his age and brain never could. When he spoke as the duke, the aunts could be cowed. Nothing less would impress them.

Therefore, it surprised him that the two women had outmaneuvered him with a most direct challenge. He learned that they had sent letters to the other cousins and uncles, requesting everyone attend a meeting regarding the possible discovery of Miss Barrington. Normally Nicholas could simply refuse to attend and spare himself an afternoon of misery. That would not be possible this time, because the aunts had the temerity to announce the meeting would be at *his house*.

"Just write to everyone and say the meeting is cancelled," Kevin said. "Or even better, write and say it has been moved to Agnes's house. Let her provide the food and wine."

They lounged at their club, side by side at the vingt-et-un table. Kevin, as always, was winning. Nicholas suspected that Kevin counted the cards and ran annoying calculations in his head regarding odds. Since that would not be sporting, he never accused Kevin of this, but all those wins begged for explanation. Kevin kept his gaze on the cards while they spoke, his deep-set bright eyes peering out from under an errant shock of dark hair, paying close attention.

Normally Kevin did not frequent the club of an evening, but on this one his wife, Rosamund, was visiting Chase's wife, Minerva. His cousins' good fortune in marrying two of the mystery legacies only brought him joy. They had been love matches too. He was almost sure of that.

Certainly, Kevin would have done poorly with anyone other than Rosamund. A milliner prior to her inheritance, she still maintained two shops now managed by others. She kept her hand in designing those hats and bonnets, though. What made her valuable to Kevin was not her money. Her practical nature kept Kevin on an even keel. A dreamer by nature, and an inventor by profession, he could run down a path without noting the steep cliffs that lined it or the deep holes waiting. Rosamund always saw the pitfalls and potential in ways Kevin probably never would.

"I am thinking I will allow the meeting," Nicholas said.

"I will even host it. I am curious about the reactions. I definitely want to know if anyone starts plotting."

"What could they plot? If they do plot, what do you care? The worst that can happen is they unmask a charlatan, if that is what she is. Then you inherit a tidy sum just like they do."

Kevin could be annoyingly logical. He was right, however. Yet Nicholas did not care for the idea of his relatives acting like legacy vigilantes with poor Miss Barrington as their quarry.

No sooner than he thought it, he had to laugh at himself. Poor Miss Barrington? Even penniless she would not be poor, and he doubted all of the relatives banded together could best her. If ever a woman did not need him feeling protective, it was she.

"I suppose all the wives will be there," he said.

"I believe that is being decided tonight by two of them."

"Tell Rosamund her presence is not required. She should feel no obligation to suffer the mayhem."

"I think maybe she believes she does. Having suffered it when she was the victim, she may want to try and spare this third heiress." Kevin called for a card and won the current deal. "There is something I don't think you know. I hesitate to be the one to inform you."

"What is that?"

"Remember that I am a mere messenger. Direct your anger appropriately."

Nicholas experienced mild alarm. "Tell me."

Kevin cleared his throat. "I believe Aunt Agnes invited Philip. Her thinking was—"

"She invited him?"

"Yes. The idea was—"

"To a meeting she arranged at *m*y house?"

"Lower your voice. You may have disowned him, but

uncle did not, and this is about uncle's legacy, not any from you. At least that is how our aunt saw it. Or so I am told."

"I will write to her and demand she rescind the invitation. I will not receive Philip. Nor should you want to be in his presence. As for your wife—"

"If he intends to come, she will not. I have made that clear to her."

"The wastrel will probably say he is not coming but show up all the same. But he will not enter, I promise you."

Kevin called for another round. "Do you want to take on the aunts when you have so much else to manage? No war should be fought on two fronts."

"There will be no fight. The day may come when I go to war with the two of them, but I will pick the battle."

Kevin now had nineteen on the table. Anyone else would hold, but Kevin called for another card. It was a two. Nicholas threw in his own cards and eyed Kevin suspiciously. Then he stood, to cut his losses. "Tell Rosamund not to attend this meeting, or any social event that intends to make Miss Barrington available for inspection. If she and Minerva want to meet their sister heiress, I will arrange it."

Two days later, Iris finished her three hours in the library. She returned the books to their shelf and tucked little slips of paper between them to mark that these had been examined. She arranged her pages, now full of notes and tentative appraisals, and set them on a corner of her table. She removed her apron and left it over the back of her chair, then donned her hat and pinned it. Sliding her shawl around her shoulders to protect her from the overcast, cool day, she left the library.

Activity buzzed in the corridor outside. Servants rushed this way and that, and footmen carried chairs into the drawing room. The butler oversaw it all, but a man dressed as a cook now distracted him with conversation.

She paused to take it all in, then followed the cook down the stairs after he finished his talk with the butler. On her way, she saw the duke striding up. He noticed her and his expression fell. He glanced over his shoulder, then hurried up to her. "Come with me at once. Do not delay."

Taking her hand, he turned and pulled her behind him, down the stairs and around to the servant stairs. No sooner had they left the hall at the entrance than voices could be heard. Feminine voices. One high pitched and the other fairly deep, conversed with each other.

"He forbad me to invite Philip," the higher one complained. "It is my meeting. Who does he think he is?"

"It is his house. I told you not to try such a thing."

"Philip has a right to be here, sister. His interest in this regrettable matter is as great as anyone else's."

"It is Hollinburgh's house, however. You know he has sworn never to receive Philip after what happened."

"Much ado about nothing. So Philip tried to kiss a little milliner. That is hardly a hanging offense."

The voices faded along with footsteps mounting the stairs. Then from the top, the higher voice exclaimed, "These infuriating urns. I told Hollinburgh to move them out of the way. How is a person supposed to enter the drawing room with all these rows of urns tottering wherever one walks?"

Iris had wondered the same thing the day she had first visited. Navigating that forest of Chinese pottery would have been difficult if the butler had not guided her through the most comfortable, if not direct, path.

"Why haven't you moved the pottery?" she whispered to the duke.

He angled so he could peer around the corner at the stairs, then the entrance. "It discourages visitors. My uncle set them out. I thought to move them, but the more often my aunt complained the less inclined I grew."

"They are very valuable. It would be a shame if one fell and broke."

He glanced back at her. "How valuable?"

"Did you not get those properly appraised either? I know a man here in town who can do it for you."

He took her hand. "We will talk about it later. Right now, I need to get you out of here without anyone seeing you. That means the servants' entrance, I'm afraid."

"In a manner of speaking I am a servant at present."

She tripped after him. He handed her down the stairs to the basement. With a nod at a few astonished footmen and a smile from the cook, he ushered her out a door and up into the garden.

"Stay close to the house so you are not seen from the drawing room windows," he instructed, urging her along.

"From whom am I hiding?"

"The family."

"Which members? The infamous aunts?"

"All of them. At least all the ones who will be out money once you get yours."

"No doubt they want to upbraid me."

"More likely they want to kill you."

As soon as he said it, he stopped in his tracks. She stumbled right into him. He turned and looked down at her. "You are very sure no one knows where you are living in town?"

"If you don't know, it is safe to say that other than Mr. Sanders, no one does."

"I thought that a silly precaution on your part, but perhaps it was wise."

She laughed, loud enough that he placed his fingertips on her lips. "You don't really think someone will kill me," she whispered. "Wouldn't my own heir get the money then?"

"If you have not yet received the legacy—I don't know.

I will have to ask Sanders what would happen. Best if your home remains a mystery in any case." He began leading her toward the front garden portal again.

She noticed that he had not released her hand the entire time. The warmth of his hold charmed her, as did his protective attempt to spare her his relatives. As for the talk of danger—

"You don't really think one of those relatives would harm me, do you?" The very notion struck her as too dramatic to be believed.

"Probably not, but better to be careful." He opened the portal gate, checked the path, then handed her outside. "There is a good chance that one of them has killed before, you see."

It was the oddest parting words she had ever heard. She just stared while he closed the garden portal behind her.

"He was distraught," Aunt Agnes intoned. "He was so happy to be brought back into the fold, but I had to write and let him know he would not be received."

She spoke to the air around her, and the ears nearby, but Nicholas knew her words were really for him.

"He is a scoundrel, Aunt Agnes. I have, and will have, nothing to do with him," Nicholas said. "If you wanted Philip to attend, you should have had this meeting at your own house, not mine."

"It is our home too," Aunt Dolores said. "We grew up here. It is the family home in London. We should all be welcomed here."

"No, it is my home, and I welcome whom I choose. That does not include my cousin Philip. Now, Aunt Agnes, you arranged for me to be the host, but you are the director of this theater. Perhaps we can begin, so we can also end in a timely manner."

Agnes inhaled in a peeved way, which made her substantial bosom expand. Dark haired like her sister Dolores, but very large compared to Dolores's slight frame, Agnes used her heft like a weapon to demand attention and deference.

"You are most ungenerous, Hollinburgh," she said. "I think I much preferred the old Nicholas, who was so affable. You have hardened in the last year in ways that are not attractive."

"You mean he no longer gives you whatever you want," Douglas said from where he sat with his wife, Claudine, near the window. It was so rare for Douglas to speak, that when he did everyone noticed. "He is a duke now. Accommodate yourself like everyone else has."

Agnes looked like she had been slapped. She peered dangerously at Douglas. Claudine, who served as her husband's protector and squire, peered back just as darkly. Agnes shrank just enough to indicate she had decided to forego that skirmish at the moment.

"Yes," Chase said. "Why are we here, Aunt Agnes?"

Agnes drew back in shock. "I think that is obvious to everyone. It is this Barrington woman. The situation is most distressing, and highly suspicious. You say she just turned up at your door, Hollinburgh? She materialized out of thin air?"

"She did."

"How? Why? If she had heard about the legacy, it could be explained. What did she want of you if not that?"

All eyes turned on him.

"It was another matter concerning uncle. That is all I intend to say because it involves no one in this chamber."

"I must insist that you enlighten us."

"Insist all you want. I have spoken my last words on the subject."

Agnes huffed.

Dolores toyed with her skirt, her long, thin fingers playing with the embroidery spiraling around the fabric. "Sanders said she is a bookseller." Her brow puckered. "Barrington. Mmmm."

Agnes turned in shock. "He did? He did not inform me of that fact."

"He likes me more than he likes you. And I ask, not demand. She is a bookseller who specializes in rare books. She travels all over the Continent plying her trade. She has English blood, but she is not really English. She has barely lived here."

"Then she will be taking that legacy and living like a queen in Europe," Walter said. "Hell of a thing."

Nicholas usually avoided talking to Walter. Their conversations often ended badly. Walter was the eldest of the cousins and believed he should be the duke. This despite his father not being the eldest brother of his generation, and everyone knew how these things worked. Walter tried to have the last word nonetheless, issuing opinions and directions as if he possessed greater authority anyway.

"I think she is a charlatan. This story is too odd," Agnes said. "Chase, you must investigate her. Do whatever it is you do when you sniff around someone's life. Check into her family and such."

"Sanders is doing that," Chase said. "He has people to contact and will be writing to officials who know this woman. If she is a charlatan, it will be uncovered soon enough."

"You must investigate yourself," Walter said, repeating that which had already been spoken and answered. "Check into her family."

"She might not only be a charlatan," Felicity said. As Walter's pretty, blond wife, Felicity rarely left his side. Rosamund and Minerva may have avoided this meeting, but Felicity had come and wanted to have her say. "She might be a murderer. She is inheriting a lot of money, if she makes good on this claim. She might have—"

"You do like to point fingers about that." Chase spoke lightly but his gaze darted from Felicity to Kevin, then back. "The official report said an accident. It is time to accept that and cease making accusations that have no basis."

"Something else you should look into," Walter muttered. "Felicity is right. She might be the one who did it."

"It remains conjecture that anyone did anything," Nicholas said decisively. "I will brook no more talk of that here today."

His tone subdued them all for a few minutes. Walter and his brother, Douglas, helped themselves to more wine. The wives reached for cakes.

"What are we to do?" Dolores demanded with a voice close to a wail. "Just wait for her to take all that is left? She isn't even really English, and she is a bookseller. Another tradesperson."

"Calm yourself, sister. It is apparent our brother was not in his right mind when he made that will. Unless his goal was to humiliate us all," Agnes said.

"Perhaps there is still time to contest the will on that basis," Walter said. "That he was not in his right mind."

"You will not contest the will," Nicholas said with as much finality as he could muster.

"No, you will not," Chase added.

"I think I smell desperation," Kevin mused. Kevin had a habit of stirring the pot at gatherings like this. He neither pretended to like his relatives nor allowed them any leeway in being stupid when they spoke nonsense.

"Easy for you to say," Felicity all but snarled. She looked less pretty when she did that, even when wearing an obscenely expensive French dress. "You got yours, didn't you? And Chase. Clever of you to marry two of the heiresses."

"Maybe Philip will marry this one," Kevin said. "Then three of us will be set for life."

"And the rest of us can starve."

"Hardly starving," Kevin said. "We all know what the late duke's brothers received upon their father's death. With a little care, the income should be more than enough to live in style. And if it isn't, Felicity, you can always sell that French wardrobe. I think Rosamund would give you a fair price on the hats."

Felicity turned in shock to her husband. Walter glared at Kevin but had nothing to say.

"Actually, the funds our fathers received might not be the whole of it." Nicholas spoke more to divert the conversation, lest there be fisticuffs, than to impart information. "The portion of the library each received is probably quite valuable. I doubt most of us ever paid much attention to those old books. There might be a respectable fortune in them, however. In fact, I am having the library here appraised."

"Books? Books!" Felicity cried. "We are not going to be able to pay our way with old books."

"Then I guess it is the hats," Kevin said with an unkind smile.

That did it. Walter strode over to Kevin and grabbed him by the front of his frockcoat. His fist was halfway to Kevin's face before Chase got to him. Nicholas rushed in to help and they managed to restrain Walter. The ladies all screamed. Felicity urged her husband on. Douglas ate a cake.

Nicholas helped Chase force Walter from the chamber and into the arms of two footmen. Then he returned and stared at his aunt. "I trust that you are satisfied. Now please declare this family meeting over."

Agnes's nose rose into the air. She sat taller so she achieved maximum formidability. "I am not inclined to end the meeting yet, Nicholas. We have not finished by far."

Nicholas narrowed his eyes on her. "That was not a request from your nephew Nicholas, Lady Agnes. It was a command from Hollinburgh."

She looked at him in shock. Dolores patted her arm in warning. Agnes stood. "I suppose the rest can wait for another day." With Dolores in tow, she walked out of the drawing room, grabbing a final cake as she passed.

Chapter Five

"I sold that book," Bridget announced when Iris returned from the library in early afternoon. Forty pounds waved at her as soon as she entered the shop.

"Who bought it?" Iris took the money and handed back four pounds.

"Some man."

"Did you not get his name or card?"

"I got his money. That's the important part."

"Bridget, always get their cards. If you sell a man one book like that, you are likely to sell him others. Only you need to know how to contact him."

Bridget's expression fell. Iris felt bad for correcting her. "However, getting the money is indeed the most important part, and you did splendidly." She gave the pounds a little kiss and tucked them into her reticule. "I will buy us a joint to cook on Sunday, and I'll prepare it in your honor. Lamb or beef?"

"It's been months and months since I've had beef," Bridget said dreamily. "Although King Arthur prefers lamb."

"Beef it will be."

She found the feline in question at the foot of the stairs, sitting like a sphinx protecting the pyramids. He pretended to be asleep, but Iris was not fooled. She bent down and spoke to him. "If I find you anywhere near that joint, you will be very sorry."

King Arthur yawned, exposing his fangs. He began grooming, starting with his extended claws.

Both Chase and Kevin let Nicholas know that their wives wanted to meet Miss Barrington. However, as with Nicholas himself, Sanders would not provide information regarding her abode. Perhaps Nicholas could arrange a meeting, so the three heiresses could gather?

He was not opposed to their meeting. Yet he dallied in attempting to accommodate his cousins' wives. Eventually, on a lovely morning that promised to give way to a glorious day, he reflected on why.

Iris Barrington had much in common with Minerva and Rosamund. She was a commoner, and a woman of business. She made her own way. Her connections to her benefactor had been very tenuous. Mystery surrounded all of their bequests, and he expected the explanation for Miss Barrington's would be as peculiar and capricious as those for the other two.

Yet he experienced some trepidation when he thought about bringing them all together. The fact was that none of them were appropriate in a way that would satisfy the enforcers of propriety in the world. Too independent, too confident, too lovely, too so much else. However, Iris Barrington was more "too" than the others. Minerva and Rosamund had not traveled the world, and alone at that. They did not flirt with men on first meeting them. They lacked Miss Barrington's overt worldliness.

Sensuality did not pour off them like water breaching a dam.

The truth was, he finally admitted, that he did not think Minerva and Rosamund would approve of this third heiress.

Also he worried just a bit that his cousins would, in the end, not thank him for any introduction. They might even blame him for sins yet unknown, if Iris Barrington influenced their wives.

Ridiculous, of course. Minerva and Rosamund weren't young chits who would follow a vivid character into perdition. He was being an ass.

Having faced and resolved his concerns, he ventured to the library, where he found Miss Barrington crouched low before a bookcase. This particular one had a cabinet at its bottom, the doors of which were now open, and the contents of which Miss Barrington was examining. Her pose caused her skirt to stretch around her rump, giving him a pleasant view. Enough so that he paused to appreciate it and imagine that pose with no clothing at all.

She must have heard him because she glanced over her shoulder. She did not, however, move. It was as if she knew exactly where his mind had roamed, and now teased him with his own thoughts.

"I wondered if there were any rarities in the cabinets. Often the valuable ones get secreted away." She reached in, lifted something, and peered. Then she stood, closed the cabinet, and dusted off her gloved hands. "Nothing in that one. At least not that which I seek. Just some old papers."

"Pity. How convenient if you opened such a cabinet and your Psalter lay within."

"It may still happen. There are a lot of cabinets left to search." Not today, it seemed, because she lifted several books from a shelf and carried them to her table near the window.

"It seems too lovely a day to spend in a dusty library," he said. "What do you normally do on an afternoon?"

"I preview auctions. I ingratiate myself with collectors. Late in the afternoon I have been known to cook."

He barely heard her, because the way the northern light

on this fair day suffused her skin made it appear even more like alabaster. He found her looking at him and realized she had ceased speaking some moments before.

"Don't you ever enjoy yourself?" he asked.

"Yes. I enjoy previewing auctions and meeting collectors."

"I mean with entertainments and outings not about books."

"I visit the parks on occasion."

He made a show of looking out her window, which meant he had to stand quite close to her. "I was thinking today would be perfect for a turn in the park. Why don't you join me after you are finished here."

She laughed. "I think the English all think as one unit. Nice day means visit the park. Of course, you have so few of them. Nice days, that is. It is a wonder you haven't all moved to warmer, sunnier climates."

"Then you will indulge me?"

She opened a book, suddenly all business. "I regret I must decline. You see, I have already agreed to meet a friend in Hyde Park later today. But thank you."

A friend? What kind of friend? How could she even have friends in London? She never lived here and rarely visited. It entered his mind that the vivid Miss Barrington was already accumulating men in her wake.

"Oh, dear. I have insulted you. It was not my intention, but I truly have this other appointment. Perhaps another day? Or after this appointment?"

Now she was treating him like a petitioning green swain. He was Hollinburgh, damn it. "I don't know how long I will be there, unfortunately. Should we pass each other, perhaps you would introduce your friend?"

She appeared not the least impressed by that, although any friend would be agog at being introduced to a duke. Men had made fortunes out of less.

"That is very kind. I will look for you."

"How good of you." He didn't even try to keep his annoyance from his tone.

He sent messages to Minerva and Rosamund, saying the introduction would not happen today, but the footman returned to report neither lady was at home. So at four o'clock Nicholas had his horse brought around, and he paced along the Hyde Park fence to its Grosvenor entrance.

No sooner had he entered than he spied a carriage that he recognized. He pretended not to see it, but a footman jumped into his horse's path, then came over to explain that his aunt had asked him to attend on her. At the same time, another footman opened the carriage door and handed down Dolores and a sliver of a young woman dressed all in virginal white.

He tried to remember which appropriate young lady this might be. Dolores had been peppering him with information on one in particular. The oldest daughter of some earl's brother or something like that. The girl now stood in all her demure glory beside a sharp-eyed Dolores who waited for him expectantly. He dismounted, handed his horse to the footman, and walked over.

"Aunt Dolores, I should have known you would be here. It appears all of London has chosen this day to visit the park, and before the fashionable hour at that."

"The afternoon was too good to waste," Dolores said, offering her cheek for a nephew's kiss. "Miss Paget called on me, and I decided our visit would be much enhanced by some fresh air."

Miss Paget. Yes, she was the one Dolores kept chattering on about. Pure and demure and worth twenty thousand a year. According to Dolores, if the girl caught a duke, it would be closer to thirty thousand.

She looked like a child. That was because she was a

child, but it would help enormously if she did not still have that ungelled prettiness to her. He had no trouble picturing her playing with dolls.

Duty. Duty. "Why don't we take a turn," he suggested after introductions. They strolled down the path. The footman followed with his horse. The river of people parted in front of them. Sometimes it was good to be a duke.

He chatted with Dolores. Miss Paget said nothing and kept her gaze down. Dolores asked her a few questions and received answers. He offered a few pleasantries and received the same in return. After fifteen minutes of such nonsense, he had learned nothing about the girl, nor she about him.

The goal was an heir, and he assessed her potential there. Thin as a reed. He wondered if that mattered. She hardly looked hearty enough to bear children. Dolores was thinner yet, but Dolores had never needed to produce heirs, preferring to remain unmarried like Agnes. The rumor was that since neither was going to marry a duke, any husband would be below their unmarried status and a step down. Therefore, both decided to remain single and enjoy their current place.

They also assumed that whoever was duke would enhance their incomes and pay some of their bills. Uncle Frederick, their brother, had done just that, as had their father before him. Now they wanted Nicholas to be the source of the largesse. Only he could not afford it, even if he wanted to be so generous, which he did not.

Thinking of money had him viewing Miss Paget in that regard. Thirty thousand would reestablish the estate quite nicely. An heir and a massive fortune all in one stroke. He'd be a fool not to propose on the spot.

Except he didn't want to.

There were rules about the marriage dance, and Dolores knew them better than most. When their stroll had lasted exactly the allowed amount of time to avoid implications that would be awkward to endure, she extricated herself and Miss Paget from his company. He took his horse from the footman, mounted, and paced along the edge of the path, acknowledging the greetings of those he knew and suffering the stares of those he did not.

The park was jammed with carriages, strollers, and horses. From atop his mount he surveyed the faces, looking for Minerva or Rosamund. He spotted them standing in the grass to the side of the path. Minerva was fanning herself, as if being amidst the crowd had been too much for her. The slight bulge beneath her garments indicated she was pregnant, but he doubted most men would notice. The women, however, would spot it immediately. Those like Aunt Dolores could probably name the week of conception with one glance.

He dismounted and walked over to them.

"So where is she?" Minerva demanded. Her sharp, dark eyes glanced behind him. "We keep trying to guess which one she is, but of course, that is impossible." She scrutinized him. She could size up a person in five seconds, and she did so now. "She isn't coming."

"No?" Rosamund pouted just enough to make her beautiful face adorable. Kevin spoke of being hit by a lightning bolt on first seeing Rosamund, and any man would understand why. Not only beautiful, but voluptuous, there was nothing slight about her.

"I apologize. Miss Barrington had another appointment. I sent word around to your homes, but you had left already."

"How disappointing," Rosamund said. "I so wanted to meet her. We are three peas in a pod, aren't we? And I wanted to warn her about the aunts."

"I have already issued the warnings."

"It is smart of her to keep her residence a secret," Minerva said. "Inconvenient for us, but also for the other relatives, none of whom will be friendly." She speared him with those eyes. "You wouldn't happen to know—"

"I must go through Sanders like everyone else. If you send her a letter in his care, he will get it to her."

"We must do that," Rosamund said. "We will invite her to come to us, where it will be safe. You must tell Sanders to refuse any letters from the others, however."

"Mr. Sanders is wise enough to make his own judgments. Nor are his fees paid by the aunts, or anyone else."

"I hear we missed a colorful meeting at your house," Minerva said with a crooked smile. "Fisticuffs no less."

"Not quite, but almost. It was good that you chose not to attend. The other wives were there, however. Felicity in her Parisian wardrobe. It was Kevin's sarcasm on that which invited the trouble."

"He has a way of doing that," Rosamund said without apology. She and Kevin knew what they had in each other.

"Chase said you have told him to reopen the investigation into your uncle's death," Minerva said. "I wish I could help more than Chase will allow. He is very protective." The last came out a bit resentfully.

"He is adorable, how he takes care of you," Rosamund said.

"Yes, adorable. Also a little annoying. I am not ill as such. The morning malady is very common, and hardly grounds for imprisoning me. Anyway, Chase is already busy ferreting out information on those business associates. He said that you would be aiding him, Hollinburgh, so my services might not be missed."

"Of course, they will be missed," he said. "However, he and I will—"

"Hollinburgh!"

The shout pierced the air from behind them. They looked to see a curricle sweeping by, its horse going full tilt and its wheels making ruts in the grass. A man with wild blue eyes and an abundance of blond curls sat in it, holding a lady's hat onto her head while he laughed. At the reins was none other than Iris Barrington.

She waved her whip in the air while she barreled away, drawing the attention of everyone on the path.

"Goodness. Who is that?" Rosamund asked.

"He is the son of the Baron Doubry," Nicholas said, his gaze following the curricle. "He is called 'The Blond Adonis.'" Nicholas personally found the young man's appearance almost feminine, but word had it those curls and eyes had gained the lad entry into some of the most exclusive ladies' bedchambers by the time he was twenty.

"Not the young man," Minerva said. "Who is that woman?"

"Oh, her. That is Iris Barrington."

Rosamund's eyes widened. "Oh, my."

Minerva gazed at the equipage. "How delicious."

Nicholas glared at the curricle now being turned while its occupants laughed and laughed, all but falling over each other. "One is not supposed to take carriages onto the lawns."

"Pfft." Minerva made the indelicate noise of derision while the curricle bore down on them again, this time at a slow speed. "You sound like one of your aunts. You get more ducal by the day, and it does not become you."

He turned his glare on Minerva, not that she would care. The curricle rolled to a stop right beside them. Miss Barrington hopped down and handed the whip to her Adonis, who saluted and guided the horse and carriage away.

Iris strode over. "Would you by chance be the other two heiresses?"

"We are indeed," Minerva said. "Hollinburgh, please introduce us."

He made the introductions, noticing how the women all ate each other up with their eyes. Rosamund appeared in awe. Minerva looked fascinated. Iris wore all the signs of a woman who thought it would be great fun to go looking for trouble arm in arm with two new friends.

Chase and Kevin would have his head for this.

Minerva and Rosamund gave her their cards while they all walked to the park entrance.

"Next Tuesday," Rosamund repeated. "At two. Kevin is in his study then, so he won't interfere."

"You are too kind."

"We are all going to be great friends," Minerva said. "We need to stick together too."

The duke trailed behind them, leading his horse. He appeared a little sour.

He put the ladies in Chase's carriage that waited outside the entrance. "And you, Miss Barrington. How did you arrive for your appointment? Did that young man call for you at your home, or did you make your own way here?"

"I came in a hansom cab."

Without one word of explanation, he walked his horse over to Chase's carriage and spoke to the coachman. The horse was tethered to the rear.

"He will return it to my stables so I can see you home," he said upon returning.

"If I came alone in a hansom cab, I can return that way as well."

She might as well have turned voiceless. He slipped some coin to someone else's coachman, who stepped into the street to fetch a vehicle. It arrived soon and the duke handed her into it. Then he entered himself. From his expression, she did not anticipate lively conversation.

They were well into Mayfair before he spoke. "You need to give the driver your directions."

"If I do, you will know them."

"Miss Barrington, I am the last person to be a threat to you. Not only is it safe for me to know where you live, it is necessary. I may need to inform you of something important. I am not going to send every note and missive through Sanders. That adds at least a day to communication when, for all I know, I could walk the distance in twenty minutes."

"Actually, I live on the other side of town." Deciding it could not hurt too much for this one person to know her circumstances, she gave the hansom driver her directions.

"How did you come to know your escort? He normally frequents the most fashionable parties. Have you been doing so as well?"

"I met him at a Bonham's auction preview. There were not many books there, and he happened to be looking at one I wanted to examine. He politely allowed me to do so, and one thing led to another, and—"

"And soon you were making a spectacle in the park with half of London watching."

"He is a nice man who enjoys himself."

"He is a boy."

"A nice boy."

"A sly seducer of a boy. For a woman who doesn't want to draw attention to herself, you did a fine job of it today."

He sounded like an old bean. On impulse she reached over, grabbed his cravat, and made it wrinkle and fall askew. Then she ruffled his hair with her palm. She sank back into the cushion. "There. Much better."

He patted his head and glared down at the ruined linen at his neck. "Why in hell would you do that?"

"To make you less . . . less . . . starched. I refuse to believe you were always like this, all fussy and old sounding. Is it because you are a duke now? Goodness, I would think that a duke could do anything he damned wanted in any way he damned wanted. Why would you choose this?"

As if to show he had not chosen this, he left the cravat a

mess. "You are not to cause trouble with Minerva and Rosamund."

"I have no intention of causing trouble. I doubt I am capable of it. Both of them looked to be women of some intelligence, not young girls who can be led astray by the evil Iris Barrington." She fussed with her reticule and added, "Not like that child you were walking with along with that harpy."

"That harpy is my aunt Dolores."

"Oh. My apologies."

"None needed. She is indeed a harpy, with much sharper talons than her appearance implies."

"Was that the girl she thinks you should marry?"

Long pause. "Yes."

"She appeared quite pretty and sweet. Young enough to mold into whatever you want, I suppose. Virginal, most likely."

"Surely."

"There is no surely. These girls don't live in towers. Even if they did, the gaoler might be a strapping young man who—"

"Do you always talk this way? Just blurt out whatever enters your mind?"

"You have no idea what truly enters my mind. If this conversation annoys you, that is just as well. I fear you would be very shocked."

His gaze met hers evenly. "Try me."

The challenge had been made. She debated whether to take it up. "Fine. I think that you are far too nice to marry such a girl. You will not mold her but allow her to mold you. You will avoid her bed, lest she feel too imposed upon. Your heir will be long in coming, and by then she will have grown enough for you to wonder just a bit whether the child is yours. Have no illusions that the girl is a blank slate and you are the chalk. She knows exactly what she is about, young though she may be. She will make your life hell within five years." She turned her gaze to the window. "I see we are on my street. Would you like to see the shop?"

"Shop?"

"I live above a book shop. I have made some improvements that I am quite proud of. I am even thinking of offering to purchase a partnership in it."

The carriage rolled to a stop. He peered out, then shrugged. "Why not?" He paid the hansom driver, hopped out, and handed her down.

"It appears pleasant," he said.

"It is owned by Miss MacCallum," she said. "The red-haired woman from the auction."

Bridget did not greet them, but King Arthur did. The duke made the mistake of reaching down to give the cat's head a scratch, only to have a long hiss warn him off.

"That is a big cat." He turned his attention to the shelves, then to the upholstered chair.

"Do you want some coffee? Ale? There is a kitchen in back."

She expected him to take his leave, especially since they had not had the best afternoon together. Instead, he accepted the coffee. She led him to the kitchen, where they found Bridget cleaning a big fish. She almost dropped her knife upon the duke's entry. Flustered, she wiped one hand on her apron, then tried a curtsy.

"We are honored," she said.

"I am going to make some coffee," Iris said. "If you don't want to see a fish gutted, Your Grace, you might prefer to wait in the shop."

"I don't mind," he said. Then, to Bridget, "Carry on. Pretend I am not here."

He propped one shoulder against the door jamb. Bridget cleaned the fish, trying to hide its innards beneath an old piece of paper. Iris put the coffee on. "We are in the way here. Come with me."

She led him out of the kitchen and up the stairs. "I was fortunate to find a suite of chambers here," she said. "As you will see, it has a room where I can meet with collectors. It makes perfect sense to do so above a book shop, don't you think? I am hoping the location makes me appear more interesting than frugal."

She opened the door to her sitting room. She had made improvements since moving in. A blue upholstered sofa hugged the wall across from the fireplace. A small table stood near the garden windows that now showed dusk falling. A larger table for displaying and examining books had been tucked beneath a window on the other wall beside the hearth. Bridget had provided a tall bookcase that in turn flanked the study table.

He stood in the chamber's center, looking around. "Miss Barrington, I hope that you will be careful about inviting men into this chamber. Many of them will misunderstand. Nice boys surely will."

"Have you misunderstood?"

"Regrettably, no." He peered out the window. "However, others might. Lest I compromise you and know little pleasure in exchange for the scandal, let us take that coffee out in the garden there."

They went below and collected the coffee and cups on a tray, and he carried it outside. Bridget had set a tiny table and two chairs on some stones that gave way to an over-grown garden full of ivy and shrubbery and way in the back, some kind of fruit tree.

She poured. "I am feeling chagrined by your scold."

"That was not my intention."

"No, it was a warning, such as an uncle might give. I don't think I've ever really felt chagrined and wonder if that is what this even is. A bit subdued and a little embarrassed.

Neither emotion is normal to me. It was kind of you to alert me to how I might invite misunderstandings from other men."

His eyes, bright in the twilight, captured her gaze. "I was not being kind, but honorable. It was not of other men that I spoke, but myself. And the warning was not that of an uncle, but the fair warning of a man who was over halfway to deciding to misunderstand you himself."

No longer embarrassed, or even chagrined, but churning with very different emotions, she leaned in toward him. "Is that why you insisted on learning where I live?"

He leaned in as well, until their heads were very close. "Is that why you allowed me to find out, and accompany you here today?"

They remained like that, gazes locked, speaking only with their eyes. An entire conversation took place without words, one that acknowledged the attraction they had shared from the start.

"I have wondered on occasion what it would be like to be kissed by you, Your Grace."

"Nicholas. My name is Nicholas." He stood and raised her up and placed one careful kiss on her lips. "Not like that, normally."

"No? Like what, then?"

Crashing pots rang through the kitchen window. He glanced toward the sound, then took her hand and led her quickly into the garden. He turned her into his arms. "Like this."

A much better kiss claimed her mouth. A wonderful one. Her excitement soared on the quickly rising passion that swept her up. She had anticipated this for so long, not really expecting to experience it, so the reality of it overwhelmed her.

He knew how to kiss very well. A little rough, a little sweet, part demanding, part cajoling. She tasted every moment of building arousal as if she licked at the best Viennese cake. She hooked her arms around his neck so they were closer and she could feel his warmth against her body. Feel all of him that was possible when fully clothed in a garden. She imagined more—gazing up at the shoulders under her arms, only they were naked and those naughty lights in his eyes had turned dangerous and compelling.

No. You mustn't. The inner voice of reason tried to divert her attention. She silenced it by kissing him back, hard, erotically. It was all the encouragement he needed. He held her close with one arm while the other hand began caressing her. She mentally urged that hand on, and almost cheered when it ventured to her torso, then higher. She ached for his touch on her breast and prayed he would not be a gentleman. They would go up to her apartment and throw off their clothes and share pleasure while the garden breeze cooled their ardor. They would relieve this almost unbearable desire that had plagued them ever since they—

An old stone bench stood nearby amidst the shrubbery. He moved her to it, sat, and pulled her onto his lap. Mouths sealed, tongues engaged, their kisses released higher passion yet. His fingers stroked into her hair so he could hold her head to his erotic assault. His caresses explored all of her, pressing against her garments, finding her breasts and legs and even her vulva. She doubted they would make it to her chamber and did not care. Let it be here, on a bed of ivy in the moonlight. His hand slid to her back, toward the tapes of her dress—

Suddenly he stopped. He stiffened and looked right and left. He pushed her to her feet, then stood and thrust her behind him while the nearby shrubbery rustled and cracked. Two howls broke the evening silence. One was human. The other, far more primitive, sounded like an infant screeching, then crying once in distress. Both sounds obliterated her euphoria and righted her senses.

The shrubbery moved and swayed, and a dark form emerged from it and ran toward the house. Nicholas took two steps as if to go after but stopped and returned to her.

"What was all that?" she asked while she accepted the refuge of his arms.

"Someone was here. An intruder. Perhaps a thief. He probably did not expect anyone to be in the garden this evening."

"But the cries. The rest—"

"Stay here." He ventured into the shrubs and growth where the man had been. When he returned, he carried a limp animal in his arms.

"King Arthur!" she cried. "Oh, is he— He looks dead."

"Not dead, but badly wounded." He shifted his arms so she could see the dagger in his right hand. "This was on the ground by him. He must have attacked the intruder and was stabbed for his efforts."

"Bring him inside, please. At once. Poor Bridget is going to be inconsolable. And to think I have spoken badly of this cat. He may have saved our lives if the intruder carried that dagger."

He bore the cat into the house and Iris pointed him toward the storage chamber. Then she went above to get Bridget.

Chapter Six

"It is a cat."

"Yes."

"You sent for me with a message to come at once, that it was an emergency, and it is a cat."

"A very noble cat, Thompson. A heroic cat. He may well have saved a life tonight."

"Yet, still a cat. Hollinburgh, I am a surgeon in His Majesty's Naval Service. I am called to the sides of admirals when they are wounded and consult with the king's own physicians. I do not treat cats."

"Look here. He was stabbed. We stopped the bleeding such as we could, but I'm sure in a few minutes you could fix him up."

Thompson gazed down at the feline. King Arthur gazed up at him. It seemed to Nicholas that the cat was in pain but being stoical about it. Presumably, cats don't expect human surgeons to rush to their side after such a mishap.

With a dramatic sigh, Thompson began examining the gash on the cat's side. "How did it happen? This is a bad slash. Deep. I'll have to sew it in the least, and we can but hope no vital organs were harmed."

"He was in the garden when I was, and I heard what sounded to be an intruder. Then I think this cat attacked the man, because there were human cries along with feline ones. It was all very fast, and I saw someone running to the portal. Then I found him—the cat—lying on the ground along with this knife."

Thompson held the knife up to the bright lamp that Miss MacCallum had brought in. Miss Barrington now sat with her in the kitchen, since the landlady's emotions would not do well in a surgery.

"It appears clean enough. Hopefully, there will be no infection. I trust you are feeling brave tonight. Someone must hold that monster while I sew, and he is not going to like it."

How bad could it be? After Thompson prepared his needles, Nicholas found out. On his first attempt to hold the cat, he received several gashes on his hand. He reached for his ruined frockcoat and wrapped his hands in it, then tried again. King Arthur began a series of loud, guttural sounds, whether those of pain or indignation it was hard to tell.

Naval surgeons were quick with their work, and Thompson finished in mere minutes. He began cleaning the wound of blood and snipping fur away from his work. "Almost done," he soothed when King Arthur objected again. "There, now. That wasn't so bad."

Nicholas imagined Thompson talking like that to a sailor who had just lost his arm. King Arthur growled in a way that said: *Damnation, yes, it was so bad.*

Thompson stood back. Nicholas released his hold. King Arthur lolled on the table a bit, then carefully stood. Nicholas reached for him and placed him on the ground.

Miss Barrington's head poked into the room. "Will he live? Bridget is beyond distressed."

Thompson wiped his implements. "I suspect it would take more than one knife wound to kill that one. We won't know for a few days, of course. Try to keep him quiet and calm and feed him lightly if at all. If he is hungry, he will find his dinner as he always has."

"The surgeon will come by in a few days to take a look at him," Nicholas said.

Thompson just looked at him, and subtly shook his head.

King Arthur seemed to be deciding what to do and where to go. Bridget's weeping flowed into the chamber from the kitchen. The cat cocked his head, then walked in that direction, favoring his left side.

Nicholas showed Thompson out, then returned to find Iris fussing over his frockcoat. When she saw him, she ran to him and embraced him. "Thank you for finding him and bringing him in, and for the surgeon, and for showing such kindness to a big, ornery cat, of all things. Your coats are utterly ruined too. We will make good on them, I promise."

He enjoyed her honest gratitude, and the feel of her in his arms and pressed against his body. He placed a kiss on her crown. "I am glad if we saved the house cat. I am less glad at evidence there was an intruder in the garden, perhaps trying to enter the house. I don't want to upset you further, but I worry it was not a cat he hoped to stab."

She looked up at him, astonished. "Are you suggesting he was not a thief, but had more dangerous designs? On me? But no one knows I live here."

"We could have been followed from the park. I should have thought about that." Thought clearly, in other words, instead of being distracted by jealousy and desire. There may not be many people who even knew what Iris looked like, but everyone knew what he looked like, and could surmise the rest. "I will check that the back portal is bolted. My concerns may be unfounded but take care just in case."

She still nestled in his arms. She ran her fingertips over a stain on his waistcoat. "I will make sure Bridget is careful too. She has lived alone here. I tremble to think what might have happened if she had been inside when an intruder sought a few pounds."

It was not a garden in the moonlight, but a rough storeroom with one bright lamp. The feel of her, and her lack of artifice tonight moved him back to where they had been before those eerie cries had pierced the night. He placed another kiss on her crown, and when she turned her face up, he pulled her close and kissed her soundly.

Her sensual air had been subdued by the cat's wounds, but now it flowed over him. Into him. A gentle nip on his lip invited more. He moved them away from the doorway and held her face to a long, penetrating kiss of exploration. She responded in kind and his arousal surged, blotting out any other thoughts, caring not at all who might see or whether this might not be wise.

He wanted her. All of her. His hunger possessed a raw edge such as he had not experienced with a woman in some years. Her mouth tasted sweet and he imagined other tastes. His caresses moved, learning what lay beneath the skirt and petticoats and finally the stays. Her full breast rose into his touch, inviting again. He nuzzled her decolletage, inhaling feminine musk, while his hand sought the tapes of her dress.

"Iris, are you still in here? I'm thinking to take King Arthur up to my bed to rest but I fear hurting him." Bridget plodded into the storeroom's center, looking around.

Iris stepped away adroitly. "I am begging the duke to leave his waistcoat along with the other. You and I can try to get the bloodstains out. He is being too noble and refusing. Tell him he must."

Bridget turned and saw them. If she suspected more than conversation had been taking place, she showed no sign of it. "You must at least let us try, Your Grace. Even if you never wear them again, we might fix things so someone else can. Would be a shameful waste to discard such fine garments."

Nicholas had barely regained control of his body, but enough sanity returned for him to play out the game. "If you insist. As for your cat, perhaps you will allow me to carry him up the stairs for you. There is no reason for your dress to suffer the same fate as my coats, and I think I found a way to carry him that does not hurt him too much."

And so he once more lifted the big cat, cradling him in his arms, and mounted the stairs quickly. Bridget skipped ahead of him and opened the door to her chambers. She pointed him to her bed, and he set the cat down. King Arthur sat like the monarch he was and began to groom his paws.

"Thank you," Bridget said with tears in her eyes. "He looks to be better already. Whoever thought a duke would send for a surgeon for a cat. That fish is done cooking, if you would like to share some dinner with us."

"I must decline. As for the rest, it was my pleasure to help, especially after King Arthur's bravery. One expects such devotion of dogs, not cats, but he risked all to protect you."

She petted the striped, blond fur gently. "He did, didn't he? Iris doesn't want him to sit in the new chair, but I'm thinking he can sit wherever he wants now."

He left them together and went down to Iris. He drew her into the shop and held her head with both hands and kissed her deeply again. "I should go," he said, hoping she would beg him to stay.

"Yes, you should," she said quietly, almost sadly. "We quite lost our heads, didn't we?"

"You don't know the half of it."

"Just as well, since what I do know will keep me from sleeping tonight." She slipped out of his hold and walked to the door. He forced himself to cross the threshold into the night.

Chapter Seven

Nicholas galloped his horse deeply into the park. The air still held that dewy moisture of early morning, and few other visitors could be seen, least of all back here.

He often rode in the early hours, to avoid the crowds and to give his mount sound exercise. Today he did so for his own benefit. He was still out of sorts from the events in Iris's garden. The attack on the cat was the least of it, although he pondered the likelihood of that intruder merely being a thief. What affected his mood, and his body, was the incomplete passion they had shared. Every kiss and touch repeated in his mind, on and on, along with imaginings of what should have happened before the drama with King Arthur brought it all to an end.

Often of a morning he rode alone, but today he did not. Chase galloped right behind him. When they had given the horses a good run, they pulled up and walked together.

"You are much distracted," Chase said.

"I have much on my mind."

"Try to ignore whatever it is for a few minutes, so you hear what I have to say. Sanders agrees that something is peculiar about that textile mill, and also the shipping company. Both are delaying and dodging too much. If you are ever to decide whether to hold or sell, you need to find out what is what. To that end, I want to send agents to Manchester to look into the mill. I can handle the shipping company from here."

"We have sent a man to Manchester already. He returned with nothing new."

"I am not sending a numbers man in the front gate. I want to send Jeremy and Elise, to work there. A letter of reference from you will ensure they are taken on."

Nicholas looked out over the park from the slight rise on which their horses stood. Jeremy was a young man of considerable talents, and one of Chase and Minerva's best investigators. He did not, however, work in the typical way, but with subterfuge and, at times, questionable actions. Elise was his young wife. Both had been in Minerva's employ when she met Chase.

"Is this necessary?"

"I think so, unless you want to be arguing with that partner of yours for another two years. Let's find out what is going on, for good or ill." Chase gathered his reins, as if to ride again. "Also, Minerva gave the accounts to Rosamund to peruse, and she is now convinced something is amiss with both businesses."

"Did our milliner find something suspicious?"

"Not outright, but her nose itched." Chase gave a little shrug after he said it.

"Her nose itched?"

"Minerva was watching, and she definitely saw Rosamund's nose do this little twitching motion that happens when she sees figures that are in order, but she still smells something bad."

"You are going to send two people clear across the realm to suffer the labor of a textile mill because of a twitching nose?"

"Don't look at me like that. You know she has a special sensibility with figures. That nose has done well for Kevin, you have to admit. Minerva thinks we should pursue this outside of the usual means, and I agree."

"I much prefer your lists. They are solid if at times dull. A twitching nose—" He looked to the sky in exasperation. "If you want to do this, I will have Withers write the letter. One from me would be odd. A steward might have knowledge of a young couple going to a new town. I will have him say they have been in our employ but are in Manchester because her mother is ill."

"That should work nicely." Chase turned his horse. "I have lured Kevin out of his current project to box later this morning. Join us."

Nicholas moved his horse to a gallop and aimed for the front of the park. Boxing held appeal. Strong exercise might subdue this irritating lust that tormented him.

Iris bent and peered into the cabinet. This one, at the bottom of a bookcase like the others she had searched, appeared empty. Except that she thought she saw something far in the back, in a corner where this cabinet flanked another one, resulting in a space that ran behind its neighbor.

Short of calling for a footman to help her, she would never reach it. Unless . . . She lay on the floor with her arms and head inside the cabinet, then inched forward while she stretched her hand toward the flat object back there. Finally, her fingers closed on it, and from feel alone she knew it was a very old binding. She dragged it toward her and backed out of the cabinet, hitting her head twice before she emerged.

She sat on the floor and set the book down on her lap. As soon as she saw it, her blood began racing. Surely, she was mistaken. She hesitated to open the cover lest she experience enormous disappointment. Gingerly, she slipped her gloved fingers under the cover and lifted it open.

She stared. It was not the Psalter, but almost as good. She couldn't contain her excitement. She jumped up, tucked the book under her arm, and ran from the library in search of the duke to show him her discovery.

A footman explained the duke was entertaining a visitor in his study. She hesitated no more than two blinks before her excitement won over discretion. Marching to the study, she barely contained herself. She barged in past an objecting footman.

The guest that the duke entertained was seated on a chair, smoking a cigar. The window had been opened and puffs of smoke formed currents of haze that wandered out. The gentleman was old enough to be the duke's father, by her guess, and bore some resemblance. His ginger hair stood in contrast with the duke's dark mane, and his florid face suggested that the man enjoyed his drink more than was healthy.

They both looked at her in surprise. Did she only imagine that the duke looked relieved to see her, rather than annoyed by the intrusion?

"Miss Barrington, you are in quite a state," he said. "Is something amiss?"

"Hardly amiss. I've wonderful news. You must see what I unearthed from its hiding place." She strode over and placed the book on his desk and ceremoniously opened the pages to the frontispiece. "It is only the most significant incunabulum printed in Venice, and much sought after. It is justly famous. I've only seen one other copy in my life."

The duke sidled over and looked down. His proximity reminded her of those kisses two nights ago in the garden and the storage room. Mistakes though they had been, the memories had warmed her at night while she debated just how bad an error she had made to allow such familiarity. He was a Radnor, after all, and perhaps as ruthless as his grandfather. She knew better than to believe that acting on every passing desire was a smart path. For women, it could be treacherous.

His gaze fell on the page, and she could see him trying to sound out the pronunciation.

"*Hypnerotomachia Poliphili*," she read for him. "Although as you can see the actual title is much longer than that. It is commonly known as the *Poliphili* to save time. It translates—to the extent that is possible—as the dreams of Poliphilus." She turned the pages. "The layout is magnificent enough to secure the fame of the printer, Aldus Manutius. Even the typeface is superb, being Roman derived. But the illustrations are woodcuts, perfectly placed on their pages for superb design. See?" She opened the book to one such woodcut. Spare and elegant, it depicted a triumphal cart with figures and antique decoration. "Some think the illustrations were created by Botticelli, but that is not universally accepted."

"It is impressive." The guest had joined them and reached down to run his fingers over the image. Iris almost slapped his hand away. "It would be better to wear gloves when viewing it, so the pages are not damaged. I have some extras if you like."

"I've my own gloves." He turned to the duke. "This is what I meant. If your library contains valuable books, mine does too. I want to see what is what with an eye to selling them."

The duke's thin smile showed what he thought of the conversation continuing with a stranger present. He gestured to the man. "Miss Barrington, this is one of my uncles and brother to the last duke, Lord Felix Radnor."

His uncle beamed a blurry-eyed smile at her while his gaze took her in from head to toe. "You've caused quite a stir in the family. No reason we can't be friends, though. I knew nothing was coming to me, as did my brothers. It is my sisters and the cousins who want you dead."

Considering recent events in the garden, they were unfortunate words. Felix chortled as if he found his sisters' and nephews' situation humorous.

"If you are taking a look at this library, Miss Barrington, maybe you can do the same for mine," Felix said. "You can see to it, can't you, Hollinburgh? I'll be in Town for a month or so. As to that other matter, I do hope you will reconsider."

He took his leave then. Once he had left, the duke returned to the *Poliphili*. "You say it is much sought after. Valuable then?"

"Very valuable. I could sell this for four to five hundred pounds. As I said, this will be a prize to any collector of incunabula."

She paged through so he could admire its exquisite design. That it also kept his warmth right on her side was a mere coincidence.

"Your uncle does not seem much like you," she said.

"I hope not. He is a wastrel and shows no conscience in living off expectations he does not have. He normally resides in France but has returned here because his debts have made Paris much too warm for him. He heard that the libraries might hold more than the average value, and he came to ask that I convince you to appraise his with an eye to selling out the ones that will bring him some money."

"Did you refuse? Was that the other matter to be reconsidered?"

He angled his head as though to view one page better. "I have cut off his son, my cousin Philip, for bad behavior. I do not receive him, and everyone knows it, which means many other houses will not either. His father was hoping to put in a few words on his behalf."

"Was he successful?"

"I came close to refusing to receive Uncle Felix too. He

raised a man lacking good character. Like father like son, I'm sorry to say."

"After I am finished here, I would like to look at his library too. If he wants to sell, I'd love to be the first to see what he has."

"He can find another appraiser. I am hardly denying you your daily bread. You don't need the fees—and you would need to require some with him, because you would never see any commissions he owed you on the sale of his rare books."

"It isn't the fees that appeal to me."

"Then what?"

"It is what I do." Although she doubted he would understand, she added, "It is who I am."

Surprisingly, he seemed to indeed understand. He closed the book and handed it to her. "I will arrange for you to see his library. I will go with you, however. You are not to enter that house alone, ever."

It was an emphatic command. She did not doubt he was very serious in issuing it. She carried her treasure back to the library, wondering about this uncle and cousin, and also how she could persuade the duke to let her sell the tome in her arms.

"He assaulted Rosamund." Minerva gave the story bluntly after Iris asked why the cousin named Philip was not received. "It had been a horrible night in all ways imaginable, and that was the worst of it. Fortunately, Kevin thrashed him soundly before the others could stop him."

They drank tea in Rosamund's drawing room. Iris had called at the time Rosamund had instructed in the park and found Minerva waiting for her as well. Rosamund's husband, Kevin Radnor, also greeted her, but after introductions he took his leave of them.

"Philip had already tried the same with Minerva," Rosamund added. "I think learning that from Chase is what finally made Nicholas—Hollinburgh—decree the social death of one cousin. Philip has wormed his way into Aunt Agnes's good graces again, but the duke will not be moved."

"You say his father is in Town?" Minerva asked. "Normally he lives abroad. While he does, Philip makes free with the family home. I hear he has sold some of the nicer objects from the premises."

"At present, the father is looking to do the same with the library, if there is anything worth the effort," Iris explained. "He wants me to do the assessment, and make the offers, too, I think."

"Quiet, private sales are always preferred by men in dun territory," Minerva said. "An auction would announce his dire straits and also that funds are available to creditors."

"I would not mind doing it. I'm not sure the duke wants me to, however."

"Why wouldn't he?" Rosamund asked.

"He said he must accompany me at all times there. Like father like son, he said. Escorting me and waiting while I appraise an entire library would be very inconvenient for him."

"I doubt he will allow himself to be inconvenienced," Minerva said. "If he is willing to do it, perhaps you should accept the offer when it comes."

That made perfect sense. Iris doubted she would have much time on any visit, however. Dukes only wait on others just so long. Still, an hour here, an hour there might be arranged.

Minerva arched the way women do when they are with child in order to stretch their backs. Her movement was most subtle, but Iris could tell that physical discomfort was setting in. She was about to take her leave when Minerva spoke again.

"Did you only meet the late duke one time?"

Iris nodded.

"In March?"

"Yes." She had checked her diary. That little journey to Melton Park in Sussex had been on March 2, which meant she had seen the late duke on the third.

"You must have impressed him a lot," Rosamund said. "Considering the will."

"I can't imagine how or why."

Minerva's gaze turned heavy with thought. "It is quite odd. You see, the last will, the one that names you, was written before March. Late January, I believe. It was not composed after the two of you met, but at a prior date."

"Are you sure?" Rosamund asked, astonished.

"Quite sure. I asked Chase last night. It is a detail that he finds interesting. I do too."

Iris felt her face warming. "I assure you that was our first encounter. Why would he leave a fortune to a woman he had never met?" She peered at the two women sitting with her. "Had he met you both?"

"I had one conversation with him," Rosamund said.

"I had never actually met him, but he knew of me," Minerva said. "He must have known of you, too, obviously." Her expression invited confidences.

Iris had none to impart. "I had written to him, of course. Approached him requesting an audience in order to ask about a book I believed he owned. That was hardly a friendship, or even an acquaintance."

"Perhaps it was all caprice," Rosamund said. "It always had that quality, didn't it, Minerva? An impulse of generosity, for reasons only he would know. I have often wondered if the true goal was not to give the funds to his family."

"That would be understandable," Minerva said. "Be aware, Iris, that I am not prone to think kindly of most of them."

Iris found herself smiling. "What if it were just impulse?

Can you picture it? Him sitting there with Sanders, spinning a big joke without planning, and he plucks our names almost out of the air. Was he the sort of man to be so reckless with a fortune?"

"Not entirely. He was eccentric, to be sure, but the legacies were not completely without purpose," Minerva said. "At least ours weren't. We two have each discovered what we think inspired the late duke to bequeath to us. His thinking became clear in time."

She and Rosamund described what they believed to be the duke's reasons. Iris found the connections thin but reliable.

"I have no similar history that would cause him to favor me," she said.

"Perhaps you do," Rosamund said.

Minerva nodded. "You just don't know what it is yet."

"I don't like it."

Nicholas finished his description of the episode in the bookshop garden with those words. Chase and Kevin had listened to the story without comment.

"And, prior to our meeting today on your behalf, Kevin, I peppered Sanders with a few questions regarding what would happen if Miss Barrington were to perish prior to receiving the inheritance. I didn't like his answers either."

They sat in a tavern not far from Sanders's chambers, near Lincoln's Inn Fields. The meeting that had called them there had been to witness the establishment of a corporation to house one of Kevin's inventions. Shares would be sold soon.

Nicholas had already decided to invest some of his personal funds. Such investments had secured his uncle a fortune, and his grandfather as well. He had studied this new endeavor closely, and concluded it was worth the risk.

The corporation and the business to be built within it had been Rosamund's idea. The little milliner had a business mind as sharp as most financiers. A sensibility with numbers, Chase had called it. Taking her husband's dreams and notions and turning them into paying concerns had come easily to her once she had Sanders explain the options. Nicholas did not doubt that this corporation would be successful. Certainly, it would not lack investors. Buying a piece of Kevin's creations had become quite the thing for men of the ton.

"Presumably, Miss Barrington's heirs would receive the legacy instead," Kevin said.

"Not quite. First, there is the ambiguity over whether, at the moment, she has in fact inherited. The estate has not yet settled on her. This period of investigation is a window that someone could try to exploit."

"Which means that when the investigation concludes, if she is dead, the money—"

"Gets split among the cousins."

Kevin turned thoughtful again. "Her family could fight such an interpretation. It would be in the courts for years."

"Or not," Nicholas said. "As far as I have learned, she has no family to wage war over the bequest. Not even in Italy where her family lived. You can see why I don't like it. The runaway carriage might have been an accident, but the intruder in the garden most definitely was not."

"It might have just been a thief," Chase said.

"Tell that to the cat."

His cousins both smiled at the reference to King Arthur. Nicholas had avoided describing the end of the tale, the surgeon and all the rest, lest he appear too foolish. But they knew the intruder had been foiled not by Nicholas's own bravery, but that of an oversized feline.

"He is recovering, I hope," Chase said with forced seriousness.

"He is, according to Miss Barrington."

"I'm told you are going to take her to Uncle Felix's so she can see if anything of value is to be found. Uncle Felix is telling everyone that he expects a fortune resides on his library shelves, after what she found in your house. He is getting impatient, according to friends to whom he has waxed eloquent," Chase said.

That impatience had shown itself in several letters, each more pointed, from Uncle Felix. "I suppose I should bring her there at least once this week to appease him for a while. She is very busy at Whiteford House, though."

"She is there every day?" Chase asked.

"In the mornings."

"And you see her? Every day?" Kevin asked between two gulps of his ale.

"Most days, I suppose I do."

"That is a lot of time in her company," Kevin said.

"She is very busy. All business, she is. Very single-minded."

Chase leaned in. "Have you developed a new appreciation for rare books as a result of meeting her?"

"I have, actually. Grandfather had excellent taste it turns out. It appears he invested a fortune in his library, if my holdings are any indication."

"So you loiter around while she makes her appraisals, learning at her feet," Kevin said. "I'm impressed that you devote hours every day to furthering your education."

"Perhaps under her tutelage he will become a great collector like grandfather," Chase suggested.

Nicholas heard the notes of sarcasm. Both of them were merrily, if subtly, implying his interest in Miss Barrington had little to do with rare books. They were almost right, although her enthusiasm had rubbed off on him in those moments when he was not calculating rather different things in her presence.

Kevin's smile took on a different aspect. "Have you kissed her yet?"

"What a question." Nicholas tried to look shocked.

"A damned good one, if you ask me. Have you? If not, what is wrong with you?"

"It would not be . . . " He groped for a good "not be" to throw out.

"Appropriate? Since when do you worry about that with your mistresses? He really has turned dull this last year, hasn't he, Chase?"

"I was going to say it would not be gentlemanly to entertain such a question."

"It never was in years past either, yet entertain you did." Kevin blithely turned to Chase again. "He has, it seems. Kissed her. At least."

"It would perhaps be wise to cease this line of enquiry, Kevin. He is still dull enough not to take it well."

Kevin's smile turned sly, but after another glance at Nicholas he retreated.

Was it so obvious that he disliked Kevin's jabs to the point of imagining fisticuffs? Had he really become that dull? They were like brothers. They often discussed matters in private that no gentleman would broach with less intimate friends.

Yet he resented the easy way Kevin had assumed Iris would welcome kisses. At least. And, for inexplicable reasons, he also intensely disliked his reference to her as a potential mistress. Which was ridiculous, since he had himself speculated about that at length. Yet Kevin's saying it had sounded like a high insult, not a casual comment.

He was being an ass. Acknowledging that helped him get his rising temper under control. Of course Kevin and others would make assumptions about her. She was no child, no demure debutant, and she did not present herself as a woman who had retired to the shelf. Her entire persona announced her sophistication and experience.

He stood. "I am going to ride up the river. Come if you want. I don't give a damn either way."

Chapter Eight

"This is where one of the uncles lives?" Iris examined the façade of the town house on Charles Street. It was respectably large and on a good street, but not on a square. She got the impression that at some point it had been bought or let when a different, more impressive residence had grown too large or expensive.

"Felix," Nicholas said as he handed her out of the carriage. "He has been pestering me about having you take a look at his library, so today you will do so, quickly. I have appointments to attend to, and we can't stay long."

"I can continue without you."

"No, you cannot. Every family has weak branches, and this is the residence of one of ours. You are to have nothing to do with Uncle Felix or his son unless I am present. I will brook no argument on this, so do not even try disagreeing with me."

The set of his expression told Iris he meant it, so she bit back her argument for being allowed free access to this library. A man in need of money was a man amendable to very reasonable offers. If given a free hand she might fill her coffers on these shelves alone.

Not that she needed to anymore. She had to keep reminding herself of that. A fortune inherited was not a fortune in hand, however, and she was not one to live on expectations, common though the practice was. She had learned early that the only way to be a free woman was to pay her own way, and she never bought on credit or loans.

The servant ushered them in and brought them immediately to the library. On the way, Iris noticed that there were obvious gaps in the furnishings. Some squares on the walls shone brighter than the walls themselves, indicating paintings had been removed. A table in the entry hall displayed pewter, not silver, candlesticks.

"I can see why he is eager to sell," she murmured to Hollinburgh. "The house has been pillaged."

"It is reported that some of its items were identified in shops. My cousin Philip has made free with the objets d'art to pay his many debts."

She had heard plenty about this cousin whom the duke no longer received. The duke's presence at her side implied the worst of the stories were true.

They waited in the library a few minutes before the duke's uncle Felix joined them. A younger man, ginger haired like Felix, walked by his side. They advanced all smiles and jovial manners.

"I'm delighted you have come, Miss Barrington," Lord Radnor said.

"Good to see you, Nicholas," the younger one added with a beaming grin.

Nicholas fixed his gaze on his uncle, totally ignoring the younger man's address. His expression firmed into one of ducal hauteur such as Iris had never seen. His eyes glowed with anger. "Miss Barrington is here to make a quick assessment only, Uncle. Her time and mine is limited. Shall we begin? In private, please."

The younger man's face flushed a deep red at the complete denial of his presence. He glanced furiously at his father.

Felix flustered for a moment, but then offered another

big smile. "Come now, Nicholas. Your home is one thing, but this is mine. You might bend a little under the circumstances."

Iris hoped that she was never the object of the cold glare that Nicholas now fixed on his uncle. "It appears that importuning people runs in your side of the family. I am unmoved by your concern for your son's situation, and he knows why, so do not test my patience. If you want Miss Barrington to give you her views on the library's value, you will tell him to leave now, and he will never be on the premises whenever she calls again."

"Perhaps you should allow her to decide that," Philip said, as if he were part of the conversation.

Iris gave Philip her attention just long enough to know what she had in him. The way he assessed her said it all. He was the sort of man who lacked any subtlety, and whose thoughts showed in his eyes. Right now, his mind insulted her even if his words and actions did not.

She turned her attention onto his father. "Shall I start?" She paced over to the shelves, aiming for the ones that showed the oldest bindings. She removed her gloves and replaced them with the cotton white ones in her reticule.

"We will send for you when she is finished, Uncle." Nicholas dismissed both men by following her.

She heard the two of them walk to the door, muttering lowly as they went. The door closed. Nicholas visibly calmed.

"My apologies for that." He took a spot near a window. "If you are foolish enough to come here without me, and Philip is here, you are to leave immediately."

She thought it charming that he wanted to protect her. She had known her share of Philips and believed she could manage such as he. All the same, the rule now set down suited her. She did not want to have to watch her back when engrossed in books.

She scanned the shelves and pulled out a few volumes. She discovered a good number of incunabula, and a few codices with illuminations. She wondered if the cases below held treasures like the *Poliphili*.

"How was the library divided up?" she asked while she paged through an early sixteenth century emblem book with fine engravings. "As a holding of known value, surely it was not each son choosing for himself."

He sidled over to peer at the engravings. His shoulder grazed hers and his warmth flowed toward her, distracting her from the pages that she carefully turned. "That is a good question. I will find out if Sanders knows. Perhaps his predecessor as the duke's solicitor at the time kept some papers on the process."

"Each son would want to be sure he received his fair share. You say it was not appraised, but it must have been for the division to have been fair. Were any of them bibliophiles like their father?"

"Not the last duke. As his homes show, he collected other things. Kevin's father does as well. Chase's father left him little, so any books he inherited were sold. I suppose Uncle Quentin might have such an interest. He is the father of Walter and Douglas. He never comes up to Town, and I haven't been to his country home in years. He has some scholarly interests, so perhaps he appreciated grandfather's library sufficiently."

"And the sisters? Your aunts?" *And your father?* She wanted to add that but decided not to. She realized that he never mentioned his own family, and this father who had once been the last duke's heir.

"My grandfather was old-fashioned and saw no reason to include his daughters in the division of the books."

She had to smile, not at his grandfather's notions but at the way his voice alone made her tingle. She glanced askance at him, so close by her side, and pictured him without that starched cravat and shirt and all the rest. A mistake that. She almost ripped one of the pages that she handled.

Impossible, of course. A mistake even to have indulged in those kisses in the garden. Even as she had succumbed, she had known she shouldn't. She had half hoped she would discover the spell broken if she followed her inclinations. Alas, apparently not. Rather the opposite.

She knew intimacy would complicate matters, and it had. If she succeeded in her goal regarding the Psalter, he would not thank her. The last duke had agreed to help her find it, but this duke might be less generous if he learned how it involved his family's history. And if he also helped, what then? The past would stand between them no matter how she fared.

Better to see to business first, where he was concerned. She doubted the delicious attraction they shared would survive that business's conclusion, unfortunately.

She snapped the book closed and returned to her perusal of the shelves, making a mental list of the most valuable tomes. She would have little trouble finding buyers for most of them. She wondered if she could shed the duke when she gave her preliminary report to his uncle.

"I am ready." She pulled off her white cotton gloves and replaced them with her good ones.

The duke sent for his uncle, who almost burst into the library in his eagerness to learn her opinion. Some tea had arrived during her examination, and she sat and helped herself to some since the dust had parched her. The gentlemen joined her, and she poured for them. She made Felix wait until she drank half a cup.

She set the cup down. "As with all household libraries, many of the books are recent and predictable and will fetch commonplace amounts. However—"

Felix leaned forward so far that she feared he would pour out of his chair.

"However, even in this brief study I found ten volumes that I could sell quickly for one hundred twenty pounds. If you waited on selling them at a first-class auction you would receive more. A dealer would offer only about eighty on the spot, though."

"But you can sell them for more?" Felix looked confused.

"I would not pay you for them until they were sold. I would broker them for ten percent. I know collectors both here and on the Continent who would buy them. As I said, it would be quicker than a public sale, especially waiting for one of the premier ones such as will be held this week. It must be a major one that attracts the top collectors. Otherwise, they may go for a song. That is the danger with auctions."

"I will put them in this week's auction, then. This good one you speak of."

"It is too late. The grand preview is tomorrow evening. Mr. Christie closed the listings some time ago, and I doubt he will make an exception for such as these. They are valuable and notable, but not so rare as to upset the cart for them. There will be several more high-quality auctions during the Season, however, if you choose to take that path."

She could see the man calculating the time involved in using an auction and the question of amount received versus the quicker money of going with her. She held her breath waiting. She sipped more tea in order to stop herself from speaking too eagerly.

"And the rest?" Felix asked.

She looked at the two walls of books. "I would need at least several days to do it justice. If you do not choose to have me broker the books, I would expect payment for my time and expertise as would any appraiser."

Felix flushed. She didn't know if it was because he found himself discussing money with a woman, or because he did not have the funds to pay her.

"In advance," the duke murmured casually, answering that question.

"Which can you sell the fastest here in England?"

She named five books, including the emblem book. "I am confident I can find buyers for those within a fortnight."

"Then let us start with those."

"And the rest of the library?"

"Come and do what you do and let me know what can be had out of it."

She stood and the men did as well. "I will arrange for buyers to view the books either here if I am planning to be appraising that day or at the bookshop I use, if I am not."

"I don't fancy the idea of valuable books being in a shop where any fool off the street can steal them."

"Fools off the street will have no idea they are valuable. They will only see old, dusty books on boring subjects."

"She can show them at Whiteford House if you prefer, Uncle," Nicholas said. "I don't mind, and she is still busy there most mornings."

His uncle thought that a splendid solution. She did not.

"You do not seem pleased," the duke said when they exited the house.

"I would be grateful if you were not so generous with my time. The buyers will not accommodate my morning hours in your library, so I will be waiting on them in the afternoon."

"It isn't as if you will be bored while you wait." He opened the carriage door, waving aside the footman.

She stepped in and flopped onto the cushion. She waited for him to join her. "I have other things to do of a day."

"It will not be many afternoons. You are only speaking of five books so far."

How like a man to assume he knew best how others should spend their time. He irritated her enough that she almost didn't care how handsome he looked with the sun falling on the side of his face and the way his eyes appeared in the shadow above that singular beam.

She began planning which collectors she would contact for each book, and how quickly she could procure these sales. Felix would be very glad if she finished it fast. Fifty pounds or so was hardly a fortune, but a man in need of real money could stretch it far if he needed to. Some well-placed pounds with creditors could buy him a lot of time on the balances.

"Are you going to that preview that you mentioned?" the duke asked while the carriage rolled down the streets toward her home.

"Of course. It will be the finest of the Season. All year Christie's holds off many of their best lots for it."

"You received an invitation then. Your presence in London has become known quickly, it seems."

She had not received an invitation and her presence had not become well known. That was by plan for reasons she had no interest in explaining to the duke. Nor did she want to say how she planned to attend without an invitation by merely entering in the wake of a good-sized group.

"Allow me to escort you," he said. "I have never used my invitations in the past, but I find myself more interested in books these days. You can point out the true rarities to me. We can share a late dinner after. The cook has learned of your continental wanderings and is eager to show off for you."

She looked over to find him looking at her *that* way. Unlike his cousin, he could be most subtle, but only a very inexperienced woman would be ignorant of the male interest now arching over the space between them. She suspected that if she agreed to that dinner that there would be more kisses, in the least. She needed to decline his offer, even if entering the preview on a duke's arm ensured she would gain admission in ways nothing else would. Unfortunately, that would also bring more attention to her than she wanted.

Good sense insisted she ignore the fluttering in her stomach and the way her mouth again felt parched. She should turn her gaze to the window and pretend interest in something outside and decline. He wasn't stupid. He would understand.

She didn't turn her gaze away. She looked right into the depths of his eyes and found her voice. "That would be very nice. Thank you."

Chapter Nine

His valet knew. Any servant who has attended his master for years can read that master without words being said, and Johnson adapted accordingly. The evening of the preview, Nicholas found that the routine that said "Master preparing for a dinner party" was replaced by the one that said "Master preparing for a seduction."

The bath water was subtly scented. The meticulous shaving was even more precise than normal, if that were possible. Attention was paid to his nails, and the best linens were laid out. By the time Nicholas went down to the carriage, he did not doubt that word had spread. The footmen would attend at dinner, then retreat. No one would be visible in the hours after that meal. His valet would not wait in the dressing room for him to retire. Two silk robes, not one, would be waiting over a chair.

The arrival of his coach caused significant interest on Gilbert Street. At least a hundred eyes watched the footman bring out Miss Barrington and hand her into the coach. Nicholas noticed Bridget and King Arthur watching from the shop's window.

Iris settled in neatly across from him. She wore ice-blue silk and a lovely ivory Venetian shawl. He wondered how many dresses she had with her. This wasn't a woman who probably traveled with several portmanteaus.

Of course, she could be buying a massive wardrobe now. The inheritance might be delayed but her expectations would get her whatever she wanted. He did not think she was doing that, however. For one thing, no rumors of such had reached his ears. Instead, Chase had informed him that Minerva had told him that Miss Barrington refused to buy on credit under any circumstances.

"I heard from several of the collectors about your uncle's books. I have even convinced two to come see the books at his house in the morning hours. One, however, will have to be scheduled at your house during an afternoon."

He nodded approvingly and congratulated her, but he didn't really care about collectors right now. His attention focused on how the twilight's silvery glow made her appear mysterious. He speculated on what the rest of her would look like right now, or in the moonlight at a later time.

"I also have something to tell you," she said mischievously. "I have decided to buy Bridget's shop. She will stay on and keep a quarter interest, but I will own the rest. I need to make some improvements if I am to use it properly, and it makes no sense to invest like that if I am not an owner."

Mention of the shop jolted him out of his increasingly erotic thoughts. "I trust there have been no more incidents in the garden."

"I would have told you if there had been. King Arthur is much recovered too. He has resumed trying to make me go away."

"Does he come with the shop?"

"I suspect Bridget held on to a portion to ensure his remaining there. That will be no problem. He and I will eventually arrive at a right understanding."

"My money is on the cat sleeping on your bed in a month."

"You have very little faith in me."

"He is a bit wild still. Most cats are. He will not accommodate you if it doesn't suit him."

"Like most men, you mean." She smiled while bending to see the passing houses. "We will see."

No one asked for Miss Barrington's invitation. They entered the exhibition room with its high skylights already showing the gathering night and the sconces and lamps throwing out their gas illumination. The room was bright enough for viewing but eerily so with those lamps.

Society had arrived already, flowing around, pretending to understand the importance of the books in the auction. Other objects that would be sold were also on display. Some Renaissance paintings, a collection of Roman cameos, several bronze statues, and a few large Chinese urns. There would be many auctions here and elsewhere in the weeks ahead, but this one included only the best of the best.

"It is unfortunate that you did not find the *Poliphili* earlier," he said while Iris bent to view a manuscript. She angled her head this way and that while she examined it.

"Why?" she asked absently.

"I could have put it in this auction."

She straightened immediately. "You want to sell it?" She appeared shocked.

"I do."

"It can't be easily replaced. Sell it and it may be gone forever."

I could use the money. He almost said it, but now was not the time to admit to the estate's finances, if he ever did.

She returned to the manuscript. "If you are determined, speak to them. For the *Poliphili* they would alter the listings, I am almost certain. However, I do believe that I have first claim on selling it, if I can trouble you to remember our agreement."

He encouraged her to leave the manuscript behind. "Let us take a turn and view the paintings."

The women had dressed for dinner or the theater, with this preview being a first stop on a long night. Dresses dripping in pearls and embroidery and lace paraded by, with headdresses sporting more embellishments. In comparison, Iris appeared quite simple in her ice-blue silk and lack of jewels. And yet he doubted anyone noticed. Her confidence cloaked her more surely than the silk shawl. He pictured her in Vienna or Paris, wearing the same dress again and again and never caring if anyone noticed because she knew her own worth.

A few of the curious approached him and he introduced her. Some knew she was one of the heiresses, but most did not. In a few instances there were peculiar reactions by elderly ladies on meeting her. Smiles thinned. Eyes gleamed unkindly. Other friends were spotted who required immediate attention. They were not cuts exactly, but damned close.

If Iris noticed, she did not indicate it. She chattered on about the paintings, enjoying herself.

"Goodness, is that Minerva?" she exclaimed when they had made their way to the back of the chamber.

Indeed it was Minerva, holding court from a bench against the wall.

They approached her and she waved them in. "I knew you would be here," she said to Iris. "I came to offer whatever help I could."

Chase hovered over his wife, looking vaguely disapproving. "She insisted," he said to no one in particular, although Nicholas guessed the explanation was for him.

"That was kind of you, but His Grace seems to be providing what help I can hope for," Iris said.

Her words and expression indicated she had, in fact,

noticed the almost cuts. He began a mental list of elderly matrons whom he no longer favored.

Minerva scooted aside. "Sit with me for a spell and rest."

It was a clear signal for the escorts to go away. Nicholas wandered off with Chase. "No Kevin, I assume," he said.

"Of course not. Aunt Agnes is here, however, so beware."

Hell. "Where is she?"

"Let's just say that Minerva is as far away from her as possible."

Nicholas glanced to the other end of the chamber, where he spied his aunt talking to two other women. The topic at hand had her engrossed, so he trusted he might escape any meeting.

"Look. You can buy them and add them to uncle's forest." Chase gestured to two large urns standing sentry beside a large silver and gold figurine.

"I won't buy them, but I will be curious to see what they fetch."

"I'm sure this house would be happy to give you an idea. In fact, here comes one of the auctioneers. You have been seen."

"Perhaps he is coming for you."

"I have little of value, while everyone knows about uncle's collections. It is a wonder you were not waylaid as soon as you arrived, but then they have no introductions. Unfortunately, this one has been introduced to me, so he will expect—"

"Yes, yes. Get it over with."

The man greeted Chase. Chase returned the greeting, then introduced the man, Mr. Nutley, to Nicholas. Nutley feigned a fluster and fluttered his gratitude in meeting His Grace.

Chase drifted away after that, leaving Nicholas to his

fate. The man welcomed him with a flourish of a bow. "Your Grace, we are honored."

"Yes, well . . ." He never did well with unctuous persons, least of all those wanting something from him. This one got right to the point.

"We hope that you will attend the auction itself," he said. "As you can see, much of what is being made available is similar to what the late duke prized."

"I do see that. Very interesting."

"If we can be of any service, of course we would be honored to discuss it with you. The library, for example—"

"I have someone for the library, as it happens. Should I choose to sell anything."

Mr. Nutley appeared surprised. Then pained. He glanced over his shoulder to where Iris and Minerva were laughing. "I can only pray you do not mean Miss Barrington."

"You know her?"

"I do not. However, her grandfather was well known in the trade. Until his fall, that is." The last came out a confidential whisper.

Nicholas decided he did not like Mr. Nutley and that this auction house would not receive any rare items out of Whiteford House. He was too curious to end it there, however.

"His fall?"

"Oh, dear. You were not aware." Mr. Nutley acted torn and worried, but quickly recovered. "It was well before my time, and I don't know the particulars. However, he was proven to be a thief, you see. He had to flee to the Continent as a result."

"You are prepared to disparage a woman's reputation based on something that happened two generations ago, and about which you do not even know the particulars? I was not aware that this auction house traded in rumors as well as collections."

Mr. Nutley could not have looked more stunned if Nicholas had thrown down a gauntlet. Nicholas left him gape mouthed and went looking for Chase.

She knew she should not have come with the duke. If she attended at all she should have slipped in, examined the books, and left as soon as possible. Once more the man was interfering with her plans by luring her into womanish distraction.

Those older women had known who she was. Or rather who her family was. Their expressions and abrupt departures said as much. It had been just shy of rude, but the duke must have noticed. She doubted she could rely on the duke assuming it was harpies disapproving of her lack of high pedigree that caused the oblique cuts.

Now one of the auctioneers was talking to the duke and glancing her way.

She felt sick, but for the wrong reasons. She should be distressed that her intentions in coming to England had just been made more difficult. Instead, she experienced wistfulness that the duke would probably want nothing more to do with her.

It wasn't fair. Even if the stories were true, they were not her stories. She had faced them down all over the Continent. Through tenacity and determination, she had built her own reputation there, one of scrupulous honesty and fair dealing.

England was a different place, however. Not only would her presence here become common knowledge among bookmen by morning, but so would ancient history about the rumors regarding her grandfather.

"Are you unwell?" Minerva leaned close, watching her with concern.

She forced a little laugh. "It is I who should be looking

after you, not the other way around. I am quite well, just distracted by my own thoughts."

"Unhappy ones, from your expression. If I can be of any assistance, I hope you will allow me to offer it."

She almost told Minerva then. It was all on the tip of her tongue. Her new friend appeared so genuinely interested and sympathetic that she wanted to blurt out why the evening had disheartened her. She swallowed the impulse. Minerva was a Radnor, and her loyalties would be to that family. That thought made her sadder. Whatever friendship they had forged would probably not last.

"Oh, dear," Minerva said. "We have been seen, and I fear it is too late to help you escape."

Iris looked up to see a tall, buxom woman dressed in dark-rose silk laden with pearl trim bearing down on them. Dark, hawklike eyes peered unkindly right at her while the woman traversed the gallery.

"That is Aunt Agnes," Minerva said. "I will be hard put not to introduce you." She glanced around the crowd. "Where are husbands when you need them?"

"Do not concern yourself. I think it is time to meet the infamous aunt." The approaching woman was of the same age as the ladies who had been rude. Perhaps she even knew something useful.

Soon that significant presence towered in front of them. "How unexpected to see you here, Minerva. I trust you are not making a night of it, in your condition."

"How good to see you too, Agnes."

"I always attend the first preview of the Season here, in honor of my father." Her attention turned emphatically on Iris. "Won't you introduce me to your friend?"

"Of course." She made the introductions. Agnes's utter lack of surprise on hearing Iris's name showed that she knew exactly whom she had encountered.

"We finally meet, Miss Barrington. I would have expected

it to happen sooner. Hollinburgh understands my interest in you, and he should have arranged this introduction days ago."

"I suppose dukes are far too busy to remember such things," Iris said. She smiled up at Agnes, then stood. "Please allow me to offer my place here so you can sit."

Agnes thought that a splendid idea and lowered her bulk onto the bench. Minerva tried to be subtle when she scooted farther away.

"So you have come to claim your fortune." Agnes's brow furrowed more.

"I knew nothing of it when I came, as it happens."

"A surprise? Of such surprises dreams are made."

"That is a good description of my reaction. It still feels very unreal."

"I suppose Sanders is busy with you now."

"You mean looking into me, so he can confirm my identity? Yes, he is busy."

Agnes seemed a tad shocked that Iris would so bluntly name that which occupied the solicitor. "Do you know how long it will be?"

"Weeks, at least. Perhaps months."

"It appears we can expect you to grace us with your presence throughout the Season."

"Iris has other matters to occupy her besides social ones," Minerva said crisply. "She is here tonight to examine the books in the preview, not merely to see and be seen."

Agnes slowly turned her head and looked down her nose at Minerva. "Seen she was and will be." She made a display of turning her attention back to Iris. "What are these other matters that occupy you?"

"She is a bookseller," Minerva said. "She can spot the value of a book within moments and give a fair appraisal with a short examination. Her expertise is sought all over the Continent."

Iris just stood in front of them both while they discussed her. She assessed what she had in Lady Agnes Radnor, and how much trouble the woman might cause.

Those hawk eyes narrowed on her. "You are an attractive woman. It is a wonder you are not married."

Minerva rolled her eyes.

"I often travel," Iris said. "Such a life does not allow for making a home for a man. And, of course, some women choose not to marry, don't they?"

Agnes did not miss the implication being set out. She must have decided that a discussion of just why some women choose not to marry would not favor her, because she abruptly turned the conversation to aristocrats whom she knew in various European cities, quizzing Iris on which ones she had met.

Iris admitted to several of them. Agnes would probably be writing letters tomorrow, lest Mr. Sanders not do a proper job in vetting her.

"Really, Agnes, do you intend to ask her about every person she has met in the last five years?" Minerva made little attempt to say it lightly. "If you do, I hope she has more patience for the conversation than I do."

Agnes treated Minerva to a dangerous glare, then gathered herself and rose. "We can continue another time, Miss Barrington." She lost no time in leaving.

Iris turned to sit again and saw why Agnes had retreated so quickly. The duke and his cousin Chase walked toward them. One look at the duke's expression and Iris knew that he knew. That auctioneer had indeed shared old gossip. As soon as he drew near, she stood.

"Your Grace, you must excuse me. I think I will leave now, if you will permit it. I find that I am very tired."

"Tired of rude old women, I daresay," he said.

"Some besides Agnes were rude to her?" Minerva glared around the chamber. "Which ones? I'll—"

"Do nothing," Chase said. "If anyone was rude to Miss Barrington, Nicholas will deal with them in due course."

"I will indeed," Nicholas said. "Let us depart as you requested, Miss Barrington, as others are beginning to do."

He escorted her out of the preview. She felt more eyes on her as she left than when she arrived. Near the door she saw that auctioneer speaking confidentially to a colleague. The latter could not resist a glance in her direction.

The duke said not one word about his conversation with the auctioneer. He would eventually, though. Iris began planning what she would say in return.

Chapter Ten

Miss Barrington emerged from her silence when she heard him give directions to the coachman.

"I did say I was tired," she complained while the footman handed her in. "I would prefer to return home, please."

He settled across from her. "You have to eat sometime, and the chef has gone to considerable trouble from the telling of it. If you don't taste his artistry, he will be most disappointed."

"I would dislike that, but I must insist."

"Indulge me. I would like to discuss the preview. And the sale of that book. The *Poliphili*."

He knew that would tempt her like nothing else. She might be an heiress. She might not need her trade any longer. But the woman who had created a life out of her expertise could not resist the idea of selling that treasure.

She toyed with her reticule and glanced around the coach. Miss Barrington nervous? He wished he could believe it was feminine flusters at being alone with him, but he knew it was something else.

"Minerva appears fine and healthy," she said by way of small talk. "Chase does watch her closely."

"It is his way."

"She may not find it charming, but I do. It is rare to see a man treat his wife as his most valuable treasure."

"It was a love match." He didn't know why he said that. It wasn't as if Chase needed an excuse to dote on his wife. "There are those with less kind interpretations."

"That his love of one of the heiresses was convenient? I expect that is the prevailing view. I suppose I will have to be careful once it is known who I am."

The heiress part was the least of it. He would wait to ask her about the story regarding her grandfather, but eventually he would have to. Chase or Minerva could do it for him, but that would be cowardly.

At the moment, with her within reach and the night surrounding them, he wasn't really interested in that gossip. It became something for another time.

The servants were waiting. Miss Barrington was handed down and escorted to the door. He took over inside and they strolled to the dining room. It had been set for a feast for two. Their places faced each other at the closer end, with only low candles between them.

Which reminded him of the low lighting in that storage room corner. She appeared even more beautiful now.

"How au courant your household is." She dipped her spoon into the soup that had been placed in front of them. "Serving course by course is not even commonplace in Europe yet."

"A few families here do it, to show just how fashionable they are. I find it a bit of a nuisance. We do not normally serve this way." He found it a nuisance tonight because the damned footmen were always around. "I suspect it is one more way the cook is trying to impress."

"It is also practical. We could hardly have ten dishes surrounding us at once."

She appeared to like the soup. He had no idea if he did. Cold, not warm, it had cream and lots of herbs in it.

More wine was poured. More food came, each course on its separate plate. The ritual began to annoy him.

"What did you think of the preview?" He'd be damned if all he did was put food in his mouth while he watched her lips do the same. She remained subdued. He would probably have to broach the reason why sooner than he wanted.

"It was full of surprises. I hardly expected to meet your aunt tonight."

"You met Agnes?" What an appalling development.

"Don't look so aghast. Minerva protected me, to the extent it was needed." She described the conversation. "She will probably do her own investigation into my identity now."

It didn't sound too bad, but he still wished he had noticed and put an end to it at once. "I wasn't speaking of the people there, least of all my aunt. I was asking about the offerings in the auction."

"I was a little disappointed."

"Were you now?"

"I expected better paintings, for one thing. With the financial situation in this country, I thought more families would be selling their finest art."

"Perhaps they are, only privately."

"Perhaps."

"If I were of a mind to buy one of those paintings, which would you recommend."

"The Guercino. He is not one of my favorite artists, but that was a very good painting."

"And the books?"

A few of the familiar sparks glinted in her eyes. "The Newton will go for the most. It was published during his lifetime, and everyone knows who he is. It is easy to talk about and word will spread."

"Why do I think you would not buy it?"

"Because it will go for too much."

"So nothing of interest to you then."

The smallest smile formed. "I did not say that." A moment of indecision flashed, then she leaned in. "There was a small, illuminated prayer book. It was not described correctly. Only someone who knows manuscripts well would know that. It is not German and sixteenth century, but French and fifteenth. I suspect it is worth twice what it may fetch."

He enjoyed watching her mind work it out, calculating the value and profit to be had. It animated her and returned something of the woman he knew her to be. "Are you going to bid on it?"

"Not myself. I suspect my presence in London will be well known by the time of the auction."

"Miss MacCallum then."

"I doubt we have the cost between us. Christie's does not sell on a person's expectations."

"How much would it take?" He could ill afford to fund the gamble, but her excitement about the purchase infected him, and he so loved seeing her vibrant again.

"I would not go above sixty." She laughed. "It might as well be six hundred."

"I will—"

"No." She leveled her gaze on him. "You will not, generous though the gesture would be. I could not allow it."

Damnation, the woman could be vexing. Here he was, offering to essentially loan her the funds to buy her prayer book, and she would not accept. "It would not mean anything. It would not break your rule."

"It would mean too much, and you know it. It would indeed break my rule." She had set down her fork and knife. All of her attention now rested on him. He would be delighted if she were not subjecting him to a very strict examination.

"Tell me, Your Grace. Was it your intention to wait until

after you seduced me to ask me why those women risked your displeasure to insult me?"

She astonished him. Hell, she was different. He found her bluntness both refreshing and irritating. "Something like that." He shrugged. "It probably had to do with your station. I was surprised how much it distressed you. It can't have been the first time you suffered such treatment while mixing with the aristocracy on the Continent. I would expect other women to be cowed by slights like that, but not you."

"Have I disappointed you?"

"A little."

"I think you know that it was not that alone which distracted me while I sat with Minerva. The auctioneer spoke to you about me, did he not?"

It appeared they were going to do it now. "He did."

"Not about my lack of station, I think."

"No."

"Nor was that the reason those ladies raised their eyebrows. They are of an age, after all."

"Old rumors die hard."

"Oh, yes."

He reached across the table and took her hand. "You do not need to explain anything to me."

"Before this evening goes much further, I think that I should." Her gaze contained all that the evening might contain, and an assumption that it would never happen after she spoke.

He almost forbad her to go on. The soft squeeze she gave his hand told him not to bother.

"My grandfather was a bookman here in England. London, mostly, but he had dealings with many of the prominent families. He also had contacts on the Continent and was able to find wonderful incunabula and manuscripts for his patrons here. He was well known as among the best rare booksellers in the world."

"So well known those ladies recognized the name? It was long ago."

"Scandal has a way of branding names on people's brains." She inhaled deeply and extricated her hand. "One of his patrons accused him of theft. He had taken a very rare book, with permission, to leave with another patron for consideration. It is a commonplace practice. Except when it came time to either return that book or purchase it, the buyer claimed he had indeed returned it. A lie, but my grandfather was branded a thief by the seller from whom he had borrowed it. He had to flee England it was so bad. He was ruined. Even in Europe, the story became known. The few sales he made after that were through a go-between, and out of his own small collection."

"Did he teach his son his trade, who then taught you?"

She cocked her head as if that were not the question she expected. "His son—my father—refused to trade in books. He worked for a picture seller. Not his own shop. There was no money for that. I loved the books, however, so while my grandfather lived, he indulged me. I never believed the story of the theft."

"Of course."

"You say that like any dutiful granddaughter would not believe it of the man she loved. As if my judgment on the matter has no weight because of what he meant to me."

"I am saying that of course you would not believe such a thing of him." Which was what she was saying, but he trusted he made it sound better. "Did you have cause besides your belief for concluding that?"

"He neither owned nor sold the book in question. Why

steal something of value if not to either profit or possess? I am sure that it was not among the books he owned, nor among those he sold."

"Then perhaps you are correct, and it was all a misunderstanding."

"I think it was deliberate. I just don't know why." She sat back in her chair, then looked to the door. "Now you know about my family. If you choose not to have me continue with the appraisal, I understand. If you send for Mr. Christie tomorrow, he will accept the *Poliphili* into the auction, I am almost certain. It resides in the third cabinet to the left of the entrance in the library."

She began to stand. He stood and stopped her by taking her arm. He eased her back onto her chair.

"I see no reason to find another appraiser. Whatever happened long ago with your grandfather does not reflect on you."

Her gaze fell to where he still held her arm, then up into his eyes. "Like father, like son, you said. Could you truly trust me now?"

Still holding her, he angled around and lowered his head until he spoke in her ear. "Of course." He pressed a kiss to her neck. "It is an old rumor that does not matter."

Nothing else did right now, either, except her scent and her soft skin beneath his lips. She inhaled sharply, then cocked her head to give him better purchase. She did not hide her arousal but melted into it. He could not see her face but knew what she looked like, lips parted and eyes afire. He lifted her to her feet so he could see with more than his mind's eye.

He made to kiss her. To his surprise she angled back and placed both of her hands against his chest. "You are allowing desire to govern you, and I can't allow that. This of all nights is not the one for this."

She appeared a little sad after she said it. His darker side said with one kiss he could change her mind.

She must have seen the indecision in him because she smiled slowly. "You are not a Philip. I would not want you if you were."

No, he was not. His mind accepted defeat, but his body still rebelled, urging reckless behavior. He stepped back. "I will have the carriage brought around."

She asked to wait for the carriage outside in the portico. He stayed with her. It seemed a long time before the horses' hooves sounded on the drive.

"I will be in the library tomorrow," she said. "I want to meet with the two collectors at your uncle's house the next day, however. If you still insist on being there, would you let me know tomorrow if that will be a convenient time for you."

"I will check my diary."

"And if you could let me know if Mr. Sanders discovers anything about whoever helped disburse the books to the uncles when they inherited, I'd appreciate that."

He just looked at her. Here they were, mutual desire thwarted for Zeus knew why, and she was chatting about books and inventories and libraries. For a worldly woman she did not know men well. He was in no mood for small talk on such matters. It was all he could do not to grab her and be more a Philip than he had ever imagined he could be.

The carriage mercifully arrived. A footman jumped off and came to hand her in. Nicholas watched, feeling sour and annoyed. Before the carriage moved, he walked to it and looked at her through the window.

"What was this book that it is said your grandfather stole? I feel as if it has damned me as well as him right now."

She moved her head to the window. She bent out to kiss him. "It was a Psalter with magnificent illuminations."

Then she was gone, the carriage carrying her into the night.

It had been a mistake to tell him. She knew that as soon as the words emerged from her lips. Sentiment had moved her to blurt it. She had not even made a choice. She had looked at him, so handsome and vexed and confused, and it just bubbled up and poured out. Her own disappointment and her own desire and her sad acceptance of what she could not have had defeated her.

She went to bed churning with emotions. She slept little and woke at first light still in chaos. She almost stepped on King Arthur when she slipped down the stairs to get water for washing. Bridget was coming down when she began mounting the stairs with her pail.

"Up early, even for you," Bridget said, pushing back her full mane of flaming curls.

"I thought to walk to Mayfair. The day is fair, and I could use some time in the sun."

"You be careful. A woman dressed like you, walking alone, gets attention from the wrong sorts."

"I will be careful."

"You hear the sounds of a crowd, even in the distance, you stay far away. Those demonstrations are like brush fires, starting without planning or purpose sometimes, just suddenly there."

Iris had become adept at avoiding the political demonstrations that wreaked havoc on London streets. Her preferred method of staying safe was to find a hansom cab when she heard the sounds of one.

She dressed and broke her fast, then headed out. The activity felt good, and she pondered her dilemma while she strode. If she were lucky, she would not even see the duke today. He would avoid her. If she were not lucky, they would have to have a conversation about the last thing she said to him. If she were truly unfortunate, he would demand far more information than she wanted to give him.

What more to reveal and what to keep to herself, that was the question. With one sentence she had created complications for herself that the duke was unlikely to allow her to resolve easily.

Each step convinced her she had been exceedingly stupid. Better to have gone to his bed and enjoyed herself and distracted him from the entire evening's revelations. She cursed herself for having a peculiar honor that would not allow that kind of deception.

She was marching down the Strand when a dark form loomed in the road beside her. She glanced over at a horse drawing a carriage.

"What are you doing?"

She looked over to see the duke at the carriage window.

"I'm walking," she replied.

"You can afford a hansom cab. Hell, you can afford your own carriage."

"Not yet, and I need my current funds to start paying for the bookshop. I would be walking in any case. It is healthy. I would do it more often, but your city is so wet and misty, or dangerous and angry, that it rarely is practical. Today it is."

That seemed to answer him because the carriage either pulled away or stopped moving. A few moments later, boots fell into step with hers. She glanced back and saw that the carriage followed them at a slow pace.

"You are up very early, Your Grace."

"I am often awake early. I watch the sun rise, then go back to sleep. Today I decided not to await your arrival at

Whiteford House. I just called on you at the bookshop and Miss MacCallum said you were on your way already, walking."

"Why did you call?"

He laughed, not altogether pleasantly. "You know why. I almost came last night and roused you from your slumber. You can't just throw out such a thing and think I would accept it as anything other than a provocation."

"Do you think to have this conversation here, with all these people hurrying past?"

"Is that not to your liking? Then get in the carriage."

"I think not." She trod on.

For a moment she thought she had discouraged him, but soon those boots strode beside her again.

"The Psalter you seek was the one your grandfather was accused of stealing." His voice presented the sentence as if he mused through a problem.

"Yes."

"You have some reason to think it is in my family's collection. That it was either purchased by my uncle or owned by my grandfather."

"Your uncle did not purchase it. He did not collect books. I believed him when he said he had no knowledge of this one."

"That would mean my grandfather owned it and was the person who accused your grandfather of theft. If you can find the Psalter in my library, you can prove that he lied. That is your goal, isn't it? To show that indeed your grandfather had returned the manuscript to him. That notion is absurd, Miss Barrington. My grandfather was not perfect, but he would never do such a thing. What reason could he have?"

His tone had turned incredulous. Astonished. Angry. If she indulged his speculations, it would only get worse when he toyed out the various possibilities.

"My only interest is in clearing his name," she said. "He was ruined and known as a thief. He died with his good name stolen from him. In order to earn a living in antiquities, my father had to adopt his mother's maiden name, because his own father's carried a taint. I am sorry if my duty means that your grandfather's own name might be called into question, but my obligation is to my family not yours."

His hand closed on her arm, gently but firmly. He stopped her walking. "Now I must insist that you get in the carriage."

He gestured and the coachman brought the carriage up to them. He more than helped her inside, entered after her, pulled up the steps, and slammed the door.

"Now you know why I thought it might be better if you found another appraiser."

She said it to end the icy way he looked at her.

"Damn the appraisals. Did my uncle know what you were about in seeking that book?"

"I did not think so."

"And now you do?"

She sighed. "I don't know what I think. If he knew what I was about, it would explain why he even saw me. Why he agreed to look for the Psalter. He had no reason to, unless he was aware of what had happened. Really happened. I did not even consider this at the time but looking back—and if he knew what had happened, perhaps that is why he left me the legacy."

"As reparations for ruining a man for no reason?"

She shrugged. "It is the only explanation I have thought of so far."

It was enough to turn him thoughtful. Not that the anger left him completely. She did not think that would happen for some time, if ever. No one likes their relatives' honors besmirched, which was what her mission would do to his.

She understood his dark mood. Her own resentment of her grandfather's loss of honor was why she was here, wasn't it?

She knew enormous relief when the carriage stopped. She saw they were at Whiteford House. She had not expected him to bring her here, not after this conversation. He waited while a footman handed her out, then emerged himself.

"Miss Barrington will visit the library as usual," he told the footman. Then he strode to the door.

Chapter Eleven

"Why have you demanded this ride with me?" Chase asked the question after they had ridden several miles up the Thames.

"I need your services."

"Besides investigating uncle's death, several business partnerships, and possibly a few debutants who might serve as future duchesses?"

"Yes. In fact, put all of that aside for this."

"It sounds important. What has happened?"

Nicholas told him about the revelations regarding Iris's grandfather, and how they might implicate their own. "I want you to find out about him. Barrington. Have Minerva help with the older ladies. Quiz our uncles, search every library—"

"Slow down. Would it not make sense to start with your houses and your libraries? If this manuscript was owned by a late duke, the current duke is the one most likely to have it."

Nicholas gazed at the churning river. "That is why she agreed to appraise the library at Whiteford House, I suppose. So she could search for it on her own. She has been diving into the lower cabinets, which is really not required."

"She sounds clever and methodical. Perhaps we should

be as well. Allow her to make her search. Help her to do it. Then when nothing is found, she will believe nothing is there."

He knew Chase. This was his cousin's way of reining him in, much like one handled a headstrong horse. "Fine. I will give Iris free rein in the estate's libraries. As for the old rumor, let us look at the most likely sources of information first." He pondered that. "I think I know what to do before anything else. As for you, tell Kevin to search his father's books for this manuscript and to quiz his father about this scandal. One never knows how long stories persist in families. After that, we can decide how to tackle the other uncles."

Chase turned his horse, assuming the required ride had ended. As they headed back to Town, he cocked one eyebrow. "Iris?"

"Miss Barrington."

"I know who Iris is. It was the familiarity that caught my attention. Far be it for me to advise you, but perhaps you should wait before you—"

"I know that, damn it." Of course, he did. Miss Barrington had already said that to him.

Iris shoved aside a stack of vellum. Even in the dark, she could see the cloud of dust rise. She sneezed and swept her hand into the back of the cabinet to see what else might be there. Nothing. She began inching the top of her body out.

When her head emerged, she saw that boots stood right beside the open cabinet door. She looked up those boots and the legs above them until she gazed right into the eyes of the duke. He did not appear any friendlier than when they had parted this morning.

"Are you done in there?" He offered his hand to help her stand.

"Most done. I expect that there are generations of papers stored in most of them."

"No more books like the *Poliphili,* you mean."

"You never know." She dusted off her skirt and bodice. The apron needed a good washing.

"Let us be forthright, Miss Barrington. The *Poliphili* was a happy accident. You are crawling into those lower cabinets looking for your Psalter." He gestured around the library. "That is the only reason you are here, isn't it? Why you agreed to do this appraisal."

She strode to her table and lifted a stack of papers. "I am doing the appraisal and making good progress on it. See here, if you don't believe me. I reserve half an hour at the end to see what else might be tucked away."

"Hidden, you mean." He stood back a few steps and gave her a quick look. "A bit dusty, but almost presentable. Come with me. We have somewhere to go."

Somewhere meant east of Mayfair. They rode in silence in his carriage. Mostly the duke gazed out the window, but he sent a few dark looks her way. She hardly expected small talk, let alone flirtatious banter. That was over now that he knew she hoped to impugn his ancestor's name in order to restore her own family's honor.

She noticed the route of the carriage. "Where are you bringing me? St. James's Park?"

"Not quite. Our destination is close."

It turned out they were visiting the Queen's House. They alighted from the carriage in front of it. She spied construction beginning on one side of the handsome building.

"What are they doing there?"

"The king is expanding it, to serve as a palace."

It would make a splendid setting for a palace, situated as

it was at the western end of St. James's Park and the southern tip of Green Park.

"For now, the last king's library resides there," he added.

"I am aware of that. How nice of you to think I would like an outing, Your Grace. However, I don't have time for one today. Nor do I believe it is open to the public."

"It is open to scholars." He strode to the door and grabbed the handle. "And it is open to me."

Indeed it was. Dukes have their privileges, and his included entry to this building whenever he chose, it appeared. As soon as they entered, a man approached them. "Your Grace. We are honored."

"Mr. Barnard, this is Miss Barrington. Mr. Barnard is the royal librarian, Miss Barrington."

She knew who Mr. Barnard was. The man was famous. He had traveled the world for the last king, purchasing rarities and whole libraries. Although aging now, he appeared spry enough to be able to purchase many more.

Mr. Barnard smiled kindly, but she saw the light of recognition in his eyes. He knew the name. Of course, he would. He might never have met her grandfather, but he would have heard that story.

"I have some questions about the king's library that perhaps you can answer. Shall we go there?" The duke walked away, assuming that of course they would indeed go there.

Iris hurried to keep up. She never thought she would gain access to this library of all libraries. The last king had owned a magnificent one, famous around the world.

Mr. Barnard gave a little history while they walked. "It now comprises well over sixty thousand books. The king is giving it to the nation, and it will be moved to the British Museum once the expansion there is completed. Once combined with the museum's own holdings, the total library will contain well over one hundred seventy thousand volumes." He beamed with pride at the number. "It will be the late king's finest legacy, to enrich generations down through time."

They entered an octagonal chamber full of bookshelves. Iris felt a little heady from the sheer number of books.

The duke set down his hat on a table. "My grandfather was a renowned collector of books, as was the late king. I want to know if a particular book once in my grandfather's possession was ever given to the king, as a gift. Is it possible to know that without a lengthy search?"

"The library was inventoried in detail over twenty years ago, and the lists have always been updated. We are in the process of printing the catalogue. What is this book?"

The duke looked at her.

"An illuminated Psalter from the early fifteenth century," she said. "Probably Florentine. Certainly made below the Alps."

"A manuscript. Well, that makes it much easier. There are only four hundred of those." Mr. Barnard went to a shelf of large bound journals, eyed it, and pulled one out. He opened it on the table. "This contains the inventory of manuscripts. Let us see if one of that description is listed."

The duke hovered over Mr. Barnard, who in turn bent over the inventory. Iris turned her attention to the library itself. Case after case, row after row. A king's accumulation. What riches must be here. And the chamber itself, all wood and bright windows—she could be happy living right here.

"Do we know what year this gift might have been made?" Mr. Barnard asked while he ran his finger down a page.

Again, the duke looked at her.

She had worked out the possible chronology long ago. "Between forty and sixty years ago."

The duke peered down at the inventory. "Here is something from my grandfather but not a Psalter. Some treatise or other."

Mr. Barnard smiled indulgently. "As you said, they were two collectors who probably traded items now and then over port."

Iris poked around the closest shelves and even pulled a few volumes. The bindings were superb but not especially ornate. The condition of the books looked to be of highest quality.

"I'm afraid that is it. The evidence is they indeed found common ground in this interest, but there is no Psalter such as you describe in the inventory." Mr. Barnard closed the tome.

"Thank you for looking for us," Iris said. "It has been an honor meeting you."

"Actually, Miss Barrington, we have met before. Many years ago. You were a child at the time." He smiled kindly. "I was in Florence and called on your grandfather. He and I sat in a little garden on a beautiful day, and he served me wine and figs. Fresh figs. I had never had one before. He plucked them off a little tree right there in the garden."

Her eyes misted, not only because she saw that tree in her mind, and her grandfather tending it, but also because this librarian to a king had sought out a disgraced bookseller and spent time with him.

"I believe you have followed in his footsteps," he said. "There is little in the rare book world of which I am un-aware." He gestured to the library. "I believe you qualify as a scholar. Should you want to visit here, write to me and I will arrange it."

She could barely speak her thanks and pulled out her handkerchief as soon as she walked away.

The carriage waited outside. The footman opened the door.

"I will walk," Iris said. "Thank you for thinking it might be here. I had never considered that possibility." She gazed at him, hoping her sincerity would be clear. "Thank you for bringing me here. It was a wonderful outing, and an unexpected gift to meet someone who knew—" She sniffed and dabbed at her eyes.

His gaze warmed and he waited for her to compose herself.

"One possibility checked off the list at least," he said. "There are many to go. Tomorrow, while we are at Felix's house meeting those collectors, I will have the footmen make searches of all my library's cabinets with the command they remove any book found within them, no matter what the subject or type. You can then examine all of them without having to crawl on the floor."

"Another possibility checked then."

"Yes."

"Are you arranging to investigate all the other possibilities too?"

"A few."

"Do you promise me that if it is found you will let me know?"

That he hesitated gave her heart, because it meant he considered the implications and sought an honest response.

"I give you my word as a gentleman, Miss Barrington."

There was no greater promise than that. She began her walk home and he entered the carriage. It rolled past her, and she looked through the window at his profile. The familiar wistfulness drenched her again. Then she trod on, making her own list of possibilities that the duke knew nothing about.

"Is Philip on the premises?" It was the first thing the duke said when they entered Felix's library.

They had arrived separately, he on his horse and she in a

hansom cab. She had gone through some efforts not to come with him because she had meetings after this.

Felix did not respond at once. "He is above stairs in his chambers with instructions not to come down," he finally said.

"Actually, I would like you to send for him. I have a question to put to him."

Felix showed surprise, then delight. He sent a footman for his son.

Iris began arranging the library for the collectors. "The first arrives in less than half an hour," she said. "I should meet them alone, so both of you will have to make yourselves scarce."

"I should be here," Felix said. "They are my books."

"I need to do what I do without you speaking and trying to negotiate before it is time. Please, sir. Allow me to represent you to the fullness of my abilities."

He grudgingly agreed but didn't like it. Iris imagined him with the collectors, extolling virtues he knew nothing about, nudging them to decisions before it was time. The duke's dark presence would hardly be better. She looked at him until he nodded his agreement.

Philip's red hair appeared at the doorway. He beamed a big smile and advanced on the duke. "Greetings, cousin."

The duke's strict posture did not bend. Nor did he return the greeting. "I have a question for you. If I ever learn that you did not answer honestly, I will ensure that even Aunt Agnes will not receive you. Do you understand?"

Philip flushed. An ugly gleam entered his eyes as he realized this would not be the rapprochement he had hoped for. "Ask your damned question."

"Philip," his father admonished quietly.

"You can bow if you want," Philip responded. "You may see Hollinburgh, but I see Cousin Nicholas who only became a duke because of too many accidents. So, Nicholas, ask your question."

The duke looked like he'd rather thrash the bold young man challenging him. "You have sold some of the contents of this house while your father was gone, correct?"

Philip glanced at his father. "A few small things."

"Did you ever sell anything from this library? Any book or manuscript or anything that might be considered one? Ever?"

Philip laughed. "Sell a book? What would I do with old books? To whom would I sell them?"

"It turns out some are valuable," his father said, as if to show he knew more.

"I had nothing to do with any of them. Are we finished now? I find I don't care for the company here much."

The duke merely turned away. Red faced, Philip strode out of the library. Another box checked off.

Felix appeared shocked. He glanced askance at the duke. Then he noticed Iris. "My apologies, Miss Barrington. My son is not feeling well and did not mean you when he referred to company."

The duke meandered to the garden doors, opened them, and stepped out. Felix took his leave. Iris prepared herself to lock horns with a collector from whom she intended to extract a goodly sum, all the while wondering what Philip had meant when he spoke of too many accidents.

Chapter Twelve

"I think that about finishes it." Kevin announced the conclusion of the search at ten o'clock. After an early dinner, Nicholas and Chase had joined him in going through the library at his father's home, seeking the Psalter. The chore was made easier by Kevin using the library extensively and being very familiar with its contents.

He poured out spirits while Chase closed cabinets and stacked books that had not been reshelved. Nicholas accepted the whiskey and sank into a chair. "I will speak with Sanders tomorrow. Perhaps lists were made of who received which books and they are buried in the family documents that he holds."

"It would save a lot of time," Chase said.

It certainly would. It would take a small army to search all of the houses of all of the relatives. Like the army he had set on his own home. Twenty footmen can make quick work of a search, even if they are ignorant of what they seek. He had returned to his house after the morning at Felix's to find the job more than half done and a few books stacked on Miss Barrington's table. No Psalter, however.

Kevin brought a glass to Chase, then settled in himself.

"Where is Rosamund?" Chase asked. "I'm surprised she did not greet us. She is always about."

Kevin took a good while to sip his spirits. "She went out tonight. Some meeting or other."

"Maybe she is becoming a reformer," Nicholas said, his spirits rising as the whiskey went down.

"Perhaps."

It was an odd answer. Kevin had little patience with reformers. Too much talk and not enough action in his view. If Kevin ever involved himself in politics, he would be the worst radical, which was odd considering his increasing involvement with men of finance and business, who were never revolutionaries.

Chase set his glass aside, folded his arms, and studied their host. "Some meeting or other, you say?"

Kevin nodded.

"And you let her go alone? With the trouble that erupts in Town so often at night?"

Sip. "She met up with a friend, I believe. But Rosamund knows how to take care of herself. As does Minerva, of course."

"Minerva? Are you saying they went to this meeting together?" Chase spoke sharply this time.

"I don't know. Unlike you, I don't interrogate people," Kevin snapped.

Nicholas wondered how the mood among them had changed so quickly. "His wife's doings aren't your concern, Chase."

"I wonder." He leaned forward and examined Kevin hard. "You have never been a good liar. Just as well that you don't try it too often."

Kevin did look guilty now that Nicholas noticed.

"No wonder Minerva quizzed me about this evening in such detail," Chase said. "Would I be dining with you. How long I might be gone. They have plotted something, and Minerva is out and about in her condition."

"They wouldn't have to plot if you would stop being an

ass about it all," Kevin said. "The woman can't breathe with you standing so close and keeping a watch."

"There is nothing wrong with showing concern for a pregnant wife," Chase said.

"There is if you turn into a gaoler," Kevin shot back.

"What nonsense." Chase turned to Nicholas. "Tell him that is ridiculous."

Nicholas had hoped this would all pass with him saying nothing at all. Now both cousins waited for his opinion. "You may be overdoing it, Chase."

"See? SEE?" Kevin all but howled in triumph. "Small surprise that the ladies arranged to do something fun while you were here."

"So they are meeting at my house then?" Chase said.

Sip.

"Where did they go, Kevin?"

"I'm not sure, truth be told. I was distracted when she told me, working out a problem in a project."

Nicholas pictured Rosamund waiting for just such a distraction. She was not especially sly, but she knew what she was about.

Kevin appeared to think hard. "A private theater, I think."

"What is that? How can you have a private theater? If it is private, you have no audience," Chase said, too sarcastically.

"Maybe she said a private music hall. It is some place that Miss Barrington heard of."

Oh, hell.

"*She* is with them?" Nicholas asked.

"Oh, yes."

Nicholas stood. "Let's go." Either they found these women before trouble happened, or he would end up blamed for everything. He just knew it.

Chase strode up behind him. Kevin remained seated, watching them, perplexed.

"You too," Nicholas said. "We will need your help."

With much sighing and grumbling, Kevin got out of his seat. "Much ado about nothing. They will be fine. At least two of them are very sensible. I can't speak for Miss Barrington, of course."

That was the problem.

"What fun. Whoever knew places like this existed," Minerva whispered.

Iris just smiled. Rosamund appeared not to have heard. While Minerva had found the description of their destination audacious and novel, Rosamund had not. Iris suspected that Rosamund knew a bit more of the world than Minerva did.

On a long dais in front of them, five handsome young men in notably tight pantaloons sang a song. A rather bawdy one. All around them, women laughed and giggled. Of all ages, but notably not of middling means, the women had arrived at this unassuming house just like the three of them had, in a hansom cab, before hurrying into the private playrooms within.

The dining room hosted gaming. The drawing room held this small theater. Iris had decided not to wonder what might go on above stairs. Their hostess, the third daughter of a baronet, now widowed, had found a way to pay her bills with this creative endeavor.

Iris had learned of it from Bridget, who had learned of it from the wife of a tradesman down the lane, who had learned of it from her sister who had married an army officer. Curious, she had proposed to Rosamund and Minerva that they visit and see what it was about. Neither one had gainsaid her in the least.

Some women nearby hooted with laughter at the song's lyrics. They appeared foxed. Not ratafia here. No, indeed.

Iris sipped at the very good wine that had been placed on the small table the heiresses shared. Rosamund did the same. Minerva had declined, concerned it would make her nauseous.

Not that Minerva needed wine. She was enjoying herself thoroughly. She might have just been released from the workhouse, she reveled in their adventure so much. Nor did Minerva miss that this was a peculiar private house of enjoyment. She had been the first to note that, other than the woman who owned the house, all the other servers and helpers and performers were men. Young men. Flirtatious young men. It was like having a party with the footmen of one's fantasies.

Iris speculated again about what occurred above stairs.

"This was a wonderful discovery," Minerva said. "There should be more such places for women to gather."

"I believe there are," Rosamund said.

"Really? Why did you never tell me about them?"

"I did not think Chase would appreciate it if I did, and I never have come to one myself. But I've heard of them in passing."

Minerva did not exactly scoff at the notion of Chase's disapproval, but at the moment it did not weigh much with her.

"You don't have to worry about a husband's disapproval, of course," she said to Iris.

"No, but then I have no one to disapprove of either. There are two sides to the singular life."

Minerva acknowledged that with a passing moment of seriousness, then returned to her joy.

"You have been seeing a lot of Hollinburgh," Rosamund said. "What with appraising his library. Minerva said he escorted you to the auction preview."

"He did at that. It is where I met his aunt Agnes."

A series of groans from both ladies greeted that. Minerva

treated Rosamund to the story of that meeting. Iris followed up by mentioning that the duke had accompanied her to his uncle Felix's house, and that she had met the infamous Philip again. They began talking over each other in disparaging Philip.

"He said the oddest thing," Iris mentioned. "Philip that is. He said to the duke that he was only Hollinburgh because of accidents."

"He referred to the last duke's death," Minerva said.

"Yes, except it was plural. Accidents."

A slight pause, awkward and silent, dimmed the fun.

"He might have meant how Nicholas's father died," Rosamund said. She looked to Minerva for confirmation.

"When the last duke died, and Nicholas inherited, he was somewhat stunned," Minerva explained. "It should not be me, was what he said. Several times. He has come to accept the role, but he was not born to it and never expected it. It would have gone to his father, if the late duke had not sired a son. Since the late duke was still young enough to do that . . . You can see how his inheriting was somewhat accidental."

"Did his father die in an accident too? That is too tragic."

"Not an accident as such," Rosamund said. "A duel. His father was shot in the shoulder. He should have recovered, but as such things happen sometimes, he did not. I suppose it might be seen as an accident."

"Nicholas was furious when it happened. Inconsolable for months," Minerva said. "At least that is how Chase described him when he told me about all of this. And suddenly he was the heir to the title. He still assumed the duke would make a second marriage and have a son, but then—" She held out her hands.

Another accident.

"What was the duel about? What could be worth taking such a chance?"

Minerva shrugged. "I only know it was a matter of family honor. Now, I think I want to go to the gaming room. I brought some money. Should we try the wheel?"

Nicholas and Chase stood outside the house, waiting. Chase's mood had worsened the last half hour, and this delay had done nothing to improve it.

Finally, they saw Kevin emerge.

"It took you long enough," Chase snarled. "What, did they throw a party to celebrate your return?"

"It was damned awkward, let me tell you," Kevin said.

"Why? Because you are no longer one of their regulars?"

"I'm not a patron at all now, damn it. To arrive and tell the owner that I need information— We could have sent you for that, Chase. It is what you do."

"I don't have a long friendship with the brothel owner in question, like you do. Did she know where they are?"

"Possibly. It seems there are several such places, but she guessed women of their quality would go to this one. The finer types do." He handed over a piece of paper. "Those are the directions."

Chase just looked down at it. "Please tell me this is not another brothel, only with men for sale. If it is, I will strangle Miss Barrington with my bare hands."

"I believe it is a gaming hall," Kevin said, not convincingly. "There may be entertainments as well. Hence Rosamund's reference to a music hall."

"Entertainments?"

Kevin shrugged. "Parlor songs and such."

"As I said earlier, you have never been a good liar, Kevin. Your utter lack of interest in how your words might be taken has caused you never to develop the skill. Tell me exactly what that woman in there told you or it is you I will strangle."

"Try it. Last time we boxed, I bested you easily. As for what we will find when we visit this establishment, your wife would not be there, dragging mine with her, if you had not turned into an insufferable bore who treats his wife like a prisoner just because she is with child."

"Dragging Rosamund with her, indeed. More likely Miss Barrington lured Rosamund who then lured Minerva."

Kevin's eyes narrowed. "I trust you are not implying . . . be careful or you will be the one strangled."

Nicholas decided it was time to insert himself. "If it were a disreputable place, the ladies would leave upon discovering it. Let us go and see if they are there before anyone decides to strangle anyone else."

They all climbed into Nicholas's carriage. Chase dropped onto the cushion with an emphatic thump. He eyed Nicholas dangerously. "This is all your fault. You are responsible for Miss Barrington, and I see her hand in all of it."

Nothing of note had even happened yet, and he was already being blamed. He should have followed his instincts that said the three heiresses together would mean trouble. "I am not the least responsible for Miss Barrington. I'm not responsible for any of them. Unlike you."

Kevin, who often managed to say provocative things at exactly the wrong time, leaned between them. "Well, you did kiss her."

"I—"

"Not well enough, if this is the kind of establishment I suspect it is," Chase snapped.

Nicholas decided it was time to watch the town pass outside the window.

"That was wonderful." Minerva allowed Rosamund to drape her in a warm shawl at the house's threshold. "We must return someday."

Rosamund nodded. She shot a glance at Iris, then another to the staircase at the end of the reception hall. She raised her eyebrows.

Regrettably, at least one lady had been seen mounting those stairs with one of the young men at her side. While it was possible these ladies had only been going up to the music hall, there were some indications in the moods of the couples to suggest otherwise.

Minerva, busy winning at the wheel, had noticed none of it. Iris and Rosamund did, at which point Rosamund had suggested somewhat firmly that they end their adventure and return home.

"Do you think . . . ?" Iris whispered while they followed Minerva to the door.

"I believe it better not to think," Rosamund said. "It might be better not to know."

"But do you do think . . . ?"

"I saw no evidence to indicate this is anything other than a gaming hall with some musical diversions. Did you?"

"No. Of course not. You are correct. We don't know anything."

They emerged into the damp mist of the night. Minerva sent one of the handsome, young, male servants to go fetch a hansom cab. They waited in the small portico.

Rosamund looked out into the night. She squinted her eyes and leaned forward. Then she straightened abruptly. "Oh, dear."

Iris peered as well. Minerva noticed and joined in.

"Oh, for the sake of—" Minerva frowned furiously. "He followed and found me. You said Kevin was engrossed in some project and didn't even hear you when you explained where you were going."

"Apparently he heard enough," Rosamund said.

Three figures emerged out of the mist and lined up at the bottom of the steps to the portico. Three men examined the women waiting to leave. Iris did not miss that they were angry, nor that their anger all seemed aimed at her.

She stepped forward, to be better positioned to fall on her sword. "Gentlemen, how good of you to come and help us. I fear that I may have led my new friends astray. It is a harmless place, but they both would have left immediately if not for my desire to hear the songs and indulge in a bit of gaming."

"Oh, tosh," Minerva said. She marched down the stairs. "It was I who delayed our departure and Rosamund all but dragged me out."

Chase looked down at his wife. "Did you enjoy yourself?"

"Enormously, although I suspect there are entertainments here in which I did not participate."

Chase glared at Iris. She trusted Minerva would have the man in hand quickly. Otherwise, the meeting that she had arranged for tomorrow with Minerva would have to be delayed.

Kevin came up to Rosamund. "I assume she means private entertainments. Shall we go? There is a stand for hansom cabs on the next block. Best to be off. There is trouble afoot in Town tonight."

Rosamund took his arm and they walked away. The hansom cab they had called rolled up, and with one more glare at her, Chase handed Minerva inside. That left the duke standing below and Iris still in the portico.

"My carriage is down the street. I will take you home." He stepped back and gestured. The sound of horse hooves sounded. He made another gesture and the two servants manning the door disappeared.

"I would prefer to ride in a hansom cab, thank you."

"Why?"

"Because your expression and tone are not pleasant."

"That may be because we spent an hour looking for all

of you. And upon arrival, we were refused admittance, so we then got to wait in the damp for your late departure. It appears that no men, other than those employed here, no matter what their claims or station, are allowed in. Perhaps the lady who owns this house fears the magistrate will take exception to her enterprise."

"I wouldn't know why he would. It is all harmless enough."

"My dear Miss Barrington, if Minerva noticed matters untoward, you surely did." He held out his hand, to escort her to the waiting carriage.

When they arrived, the coachman twisted to speak to the duke. "I'll be going a longer ways, Your Grace. I can hear that demonstration down by Whitehall even from here, and it's best to give it wide berth."

Once in the carriage, pique got the better of her. "I don't even know why you came. You did not have a wife to worry about. One might say this evening was none of your business."

"I agree. My cousins did not. Chase was inclined to blame you, which meant he blamed me."

"The man needs to collect himself. How could you be to blame?"

"His last accusation implied that if I had pleasured you better, you would not need to seek entertainments such as could be had in such houses."

"He is not to be borne. My only regret is that I may have brought his anger down on Minerva."

"Fear not. By the time they arrive home, he will be apologizing to her. He enjoyed indulging in being the outraged husband with me. He would never dare be one with her."

That relieved her more than she wanted to admit to herself.

"Are you so bored in this town that you must seek diversions such as this?" he asked.

"It was an opportunity to spend time with my sister heiresses doing something besides drinking tea. It also allowed me to find out things that otherwise I might not. Did you know that Minerva has excellent instincts when gaming? And that Rosamund has more depth than might initially appear?"

"I know about Rosamund. The gaming is new information. What else did you learn?"

She toyed with her reticule. "A bit about you. That you did not want to inherit. That you thought the title should not be yours."

The mood in the carriage changed. The silence became awkward and full of an intensity that cloaked them both.

"That is true," he said. "I have accommodated myself, but I have responsibilities I did not want and do not enjoy. It does not help that my family has a bad habit of leaving very little money to the heir, and land does not produce the income it once did."

She understood too well what he meant. The last duke's fortune had been a private one, probably accumulated after he also inherited lands and little money. Nor did he leave most of that to his heir in turn. Instead, it went to others, including her.

The duke was another member of the family who had probably hoped she was dead.

There was nothing to say in turn. They retreated into silence until the carriage neared the museum. This neighborhood was not silent or peaceful tonight. There were steps on the pavement, and loud voices and laughter. It did not sound like another demonstration, but like drunken young men making their way back from Convent Garden's pleasure spots. It would be the hour for that.

"Chase was right," he said, interrupting her distraction. "If I had pursued you more consistently, and pleasured you more thoroughly, you would never have been at that house tonight. And I would not now be sitting here battling the impulse to reach for you."

The mood changed again, suddenly and dangerously. Her breath shortened while she waited for him to lose that battle. She began hoping he would. Memories filled her, too real to deny, of being in his arms and how his kisses and touches aroused her.

The carriage stopped. They sat there, looking at each other. A group of revelers passed on the street, jostling and joking. Most of the buildings were dark. Bridget would be asleep. One word from either of them, one gesture, and they might go above stairs to her chambers. It would not be wise, but right now, with him so close and their desire meeting in the small space they shared, she almost didn't care.

To her disappointment, he opened the door. She felt a total coward when he handed her down. He walked her across the street to the bookshop.

She reached for the door latch and felt him close behind her.

His arm came around her waist. He moved closer behind her and pressed his lips to her nape.

She fell into his embrace, grateful one of them had chosen to be reckless. He pulled her closer, until she felt his body against hers and his embrace encompassing her possessively.

He stepped back into a shadow and began to turn her around and into his arms.

A sharp crack broke the night's silence.

"Damnation."

Chapter Thirteen

Pandemonium grew around him. Bootsteps pounded, growing muted as the night absorbed them. He looked to where Iris stood, shocked, staring at him. The coachman's lamp swung, casting yellow light on the scene. Something dark streaked Iris's hand.

"Go inside. Now," he told her. "Quickly."

The coachman unhooked the lamp and hurried over with it. He held it close to Nicholas. "You've been hit, Your Grace! There's blood, and your coat—"

He looked at his shoulder. Obvious damage to his coat indicated he had not been unscathed. People began coming from the buildings, asking each other if they had heard the noise.

Iris still stood there.

The door behind her opened and Bridget appeared, red hair flowing and King Arthur in her arms.

"Get her inside," he told her.

"But you have been—" Iris held up her hand that showed the blood.

"Better me than you. Now, go." He pushed her inside the door. Bridget closed it.

"Need to be finding you a surgeon," the coachman said. "If there's a ball in you—"

He moved his shoulder. It hurt, but he assumed a pistol ball inside it would hurt more. "I don't think I was more than grazed. Just get me home and we will see what is what once there."

An hour later, his valet, Johnson, prepared a bandage. The small man's face, normally lacking any expression, displayed marked concern. "Too many young bloods toting pistols in Town, if you ask me. Up to no good even when sober, and dangerous when foxed. The gods were watching over you tonight, Your Grace."

More to the point, they had been watching over Iris. He pictured those moments in his mind again. If she had been at the door alone, without him blocking the view of her— If he had not begun to move her around— The thief in the garden might have been a coincidence, but he doubted this was. Nor did he believe it had been an accident, and the result of a drunken young man discharging his pistol into the air in an inebriated display of exuberance.

"We must clean and dress it several times a day, sir. Won't want it to get corrupted. Not more than a bad scratch, of course, but the lead did hit you as it went by."

He gazed down at the bandage, so similar to one he had seen before. He knew all too well that a shoulder wound could lead to death.

Three days later, Iris stepped out of a hansom cab at a small house near Piccadilly. She gazed at her destination, planning what she would say.

A woman took her card, then led her to a small sitting room at the front of the house. It was not empty. Another visitor had come calling this afternoon.

He looked at her, and audibly sighed. She marched over and stared at his shoulder, now covered by his coats.

"Shouldn't you be resting at home?" she asked.

"I was barely wounded. It hardly calls for bedrest."

They had not spoken since it happened. She had attended to her duties in the library wondering how he fared. Eventually, yesterday, she had sent up a message asking as much. The response had been kind and reassuring but ended with a query of his own.

Have you been in any way threatened since that night?

The very notion had startled her. The duke thought it had not been an errant pistol shot caused by some young man in his cups and out of a night. He thought it had been deliberate. And aimed at her. She did not agree.

"What are you doing here?" he asked.

"I have come to call on Mr. Benton."

"Obviously. How did you learn his name? Did you ask Sanders too?"

She strolled around the chamber. Books filled every wall. More were stacked in corners, high towers of erudition. Mr. Benton most certainly was a bookman. "Is that how you learned of him. I surmised his name."

"Surmised it, did you? How?"

"I was in conversation with someone, his name came up, and I surmised he might be the bookseller who divided your grandfather's library. Since the inventory showed his name as the source of some of the best books, it just made sense."

She perched on a small chair. He sat on the sofa. She assumed that would be that.

Only it wasn't.

"With whom were you conversing?"

She sought a way to dodge the question. None appeared. "Your aunt Agnes."

He covered his eyes with his hand. She thought she heard a groan. "You didn't."

"I simply called on her and we had a chat. I thought that as an elder member of that generation, she might know something."

"You showed up at her house, presented your card, and she received you? I'm finding that hard to believe."

"If it had been me alone, she might not have. However, since I had a companion, she couldn't resist. Minerva came with me."

"Oh, dear god." He covered his eyes again.

"You were right. Chase's anger disappeared very quickly once he had her safe. He did indeed apologize for acting irrational."

He opened his mouth to say something, but just then the door to the chamber opened and a man walked in. Her heart sank when she saw him. Reed thin and of middling height, with thinning blond hair and thick spectacles, this man was far too young to have divided that library all those years ago.

From the duke's expression, she could tell he was concluding the same thing.

"Your Grace. Miss Barrington. How can I be of service?"

"Mr. Sanders, my solicitor, examined family records and learned a Mr. Benton was brought in to divide my grandfather's library," the duke said. "I have some questions about that."

"Ah. That was my father. He passed some time ago. The late duke favored him as a book trader."

The current duke began making movements to leave. Iris stood to go as well.

"I remember some of it," Mr. Benton said. "I was an apprentice to him at the time. Learning the trade at his knee, so to speak. I was only a lad, but I assisted him."

Iris sat again. "I have been wondering . . . How did he make sure the division was fair?"

"Cleverly, if I do say so. After much debating, he hit on

a solution. He made six lists of equal value. That alone took months. The library was a shambles while he did that, the tables full of lists and whatnot. When he had each list equal in value and rarities, he left it to the brothers to choose their lists."

Iris imagined how that would work. No brother could pack his share with the more valuable holdings. Whatever was chosen, no matter who chose first, there would be gains and losses for each of them.

"Quite brilliant," she said.

"This included the libraries in the other houses?" the duke asked.

"Oh, yes. It was quite a holiday, visiting them. A glorious summer for a lad."

"Is there any chance you missed something? A rarity tucked away in a cabinet, for example?" the duke asked.

"Being of small stature, I was charged with crawling into the cabinets. All were searched. Nothing was missed. My father was not the sort to be negligent in such an important task."

That wasn't true. The boy had missed the *Poliphili*. "There was a Psalter. Illuminated with full-page miniature paintings. Do you remember it? A lad would hardly forget it," she said.

His lids lowered as he retreated into thought. She pictured him sorting through memories.

"I would indeed have remembered it. Nothing like that was seen by me. Some manuscripts, of course, but nothing so grand as you describe."

"Thank you," the duke said. "We will take our leave now."

Iris resisted this quick departure. Surely if she had more time with Mr. Benton, she could encourage him to remember more. Perhaps that Psalter had been held out of the division of the library. Maybe the solicitor had taken it.

The duke all but pushed her out of the sitting room and

to the door. She faced him on the steps. "I was not ready to go. How dare you decide when I will end a visit I made without you. That man knows something and—"

"And we are done here." He took her arm and guided her to her hansom cab. "He knows nothing of value to you. Accept that. We must look elsewhere. If indeed that Psalter was among the libraries' holdings, then it will be in one of my uncle's houses. I dare say it will be a fruitless search from the sounds of things, but we will do it if you demand it of me."

Nicholas watched the cab roll away with a very vexed Iris inside. He gestured for his carriage to come up.

"Your Grace."

He turned to find Mr. Benton standing behind him.

"Your Grace, I did not want to say anything in front of the lady. However—her name. I am familiar with it."

"Her grandfather was a bookseller at the same time as your father."

"Yes." He hesitated. "There was a scandal. My father impressed the seriousness of it upon me. It cast the entire trade in a bad light."

"Well, that was another time, and another Barrington."

"Indeed. I just thought that you should know. That Psalter she mentioned—it was at the heart of the scandal. If I had seen it during the division, I certainly would have remembered it."

"Of course. Unfortunately, since you didn't, the claim that Barrington did not return it to my grandfather when the buyer declined the purchase may be true."

Benton's face fell. He appeared aggrieved, and a little frightened. He cleared his throat. "I'm afraid you have it backwards, Your Grace. Your grandfather was not the seller in that affair. He was the potential buyer. It was he who

Barrington claimed had neither purchased nor returned the manuscript."

"I see. Thank you for that information." He entered his carriage. It was such a damned ducal thing to say. Calm. Unemotional. In reality what he wanted to say was *Hell and damnation, man, are you saying that this woman is seeking proof that my grandfather was a thief?*

Iris had just donned an apron and gloves when the door to her chambers slammed open. She looked up from her box of newly purchased books to find the duke towering at the threshold, glaring at her. He was so obviously angry, so full of lightning and storms, that she took a step back before stopping herself. She forced a smile, then returned to the box, lifting one of the books out for examination.

"How nice to see you twice in one day, Your Grace. To what does our humble bookshop owe the honor."

"Do not play the innocent with me. As for your devious smiles, I am now immune to them. I know what you are about, and I will not have it."

"What are you talking about?" She made a display of continuing with the book, because she guessed what had caused this dark mood in him.

"Benton spoke further with me before I left. He provided the details of that scandal." He advanced on her. "You allowed me to think my grandfather was selling the Psalter, not buying it."

"Buyer, seller, it makes no difference. Lies were told and a man was ruined."

"It makes a big difference, and you know it. To restore your ancestor's name, you want to dishonor mine."

Enough of this. She set down the book and faced him squarely. "These are the facts. Your ancestor expressed interest in a rarity that my ancestor could obtain for him. As is commonplace, he did so, and handed it to your ancestor to examine and appraise. When it was time to either buy or return it, your ancestor did neither. The seller then accused my ancestor of being a thief."

"And now you accuse mine of that."

"It could have been an oversight. The Psalter could have been misplaced."

"You don't believe that, though. I can see it in your eyes."

"No, I don't. Because the only thing my grandfather ever said about all of this, the absolute only thing, was that it was *deliberate*."

He strode around her little sitting room, fury pouring off him. "There is some explanation that does not dishonor either of them, then."

"I don't think so."

He stopped in his tracks and stared at her. "Why not?"

"Because your uncle, the last duke, knew the truth of it. I am sure of this."

"Nonsense."

"Why else communicate with me, when I had no introduction or reference? I wasn't sure until I came here and learned about the legacy, but that proves it."

He walked right up to her. Still tight with anger, but thoughtful now. "You continue to think it was reparations?"

"What else?"

Whether it was her logic or their proximity, she did not know, but she saw his anger unwinding. A tiny smile quirked at one side of his mouth. "It has occurred to me that he did it to throw us together. It is the kind of notion that he would have found amusing."

"That is a charming thought, but I fear not the true reason. As I understand it, he changed that will before he and I met, but after I wrote to him. It was not my person that inspired his generosity, but my name."

A long moment passed, with them just looking at each

other, so close now that with the smallest move, they would be touching. Behind him the open door gaped and sounds from the bookshop below floated to them.

"I trust there have been no more thieves or errant pistol shots," he said.

"None. And your shoulder?"

"Healing splendidly. Already good enough."

Good enough for what? She did not have to ask. It was in his eyes and expression and in the air.

"Are we enemies now, each fighting for a family name?" she asked.

"Perhaps."

"We should probably decide."

He leaned down and placed a kiss on her lips. "Yes. Soon."

Chapter Fourteen

"Philip will be elated if he hears this story. Beside himself with joy." Kevin gave voice to everyone's thoughts while he called for two cards at the vingt-et-un table. Nicholas watched his cousin win yet again.

"It is certainly one hell of a story," Chase said. "Let us make sure Philip does not hear it, or anyone for that matter. It would be wonderful if Miss Barrington accepted the legacy in the spirit in which she believes it was given and left it at that."

"Would you?" Nicholas asked. "The name is remembered. She has suffered cuts because of it. I have been warned off making use of her services due to that history. She seeks to clear her name as well as her grandfather's."

"Have you decided what to do?" Chase asked.

"In the least, I will allow her to see if that Psalter is among the ducal possessions and ask the uncles to allow her to search their holdings as well. Benton may have made a mistake."

"Except you know he didn't," Kevin inserted from his other side, while accepting another deal.

Nicholas watched those cards drop. "I don't know why you bother with those inventions of yours. You could make a fortune gambling." He leaned over. "There is a trick to it, isn't there? Are you memorizing the played cards at the table?"

"I don't do that. Minerva does, though."

Chase's head jutted in front of Nicholas in order to join the conversation. "You are sure?"

"I have watched her for hours. Her play is very intense because she is concentrating on the cards so much."

Chase looked at Nicholas. Then at Kevin. He returned upright in his own chair. "I have always wondered how she does it. It is a hell of a thing to have a wife who wins more than you do." He pulled out his pocket watch. "Time to go. Finish up, Kevin. You too, Nicholas. Duty calls."

Nicholas threw in his cards. "Where are we going?"

"You have a command performance. We are charged with making sure you show up on stage."

"I don't like the sounds of this."

"Nor should you. It is one of those moments when just accepting fate is probably the wisest action, however."

As they left the gaming hall, Nicholas could not ignore that one cousin led him and one followed, as if prepared to grab him if he attempted to bolt.

"See here, I insist on knowing where you think you are taking me."

Neither replied.

In the portico, he dug in his heels. "Where? Tell me now or I will refuse to accompany you."

Kevin smiled. "It is a very special evening party. Rosamund requested I make sure you attend."

"As did Minerva," Chase said.

"They ask and you just agree? Mere days ago, you were both ready to scold them for inappropriate behavior and today you make a pact with them to deliver me to this party? I'm not in the mood for this and must decline."

His cousins looked at each other. "Miss Barrington will

be there," Kevin said. "Does that help you change your mind?"

"I trust this party is not at a male brothel?"

"Hardly."

He supposed he could attend for a brief while, just to make sure all was still well with her. That pistol shot was not far from his mind, since the reminder still pulled on his shoulder.

"I will indulge your wives for a few minutes." He settled into his coach, and they joined him. "Where are we going?"

Chase waited until the equipage started rolling. "Aunt Agnes's house."

Nicholas stood outside his aunt's house. Light glowed within and sounds of conversation drifted out.

"God help me," he muttered.

Kevin and Chase flanked him and appeared no more eager to enter than he was.

"There are very rude names for men who do whatever their wives want," Nicholas said.

"Rosamund made the request at an awkward moment when I was inclined to agree to anything," Kevin said.

"In other words, she pleasured you, then went in for the kill."

Kevin shrugged.

Nicholas glanced over at Chase. "You too, I assume."

"Well, it *is* Aunt Agnes. They must have assumed they were unlikely to succeed otherwise."

Nicholas shook his head. "Such deviousness. I shall have to reconsider my opinion of both of them. Nor have I missed that both of you have been well paid for this visit, but I have had no such bribes visited on me."

"I suppose we should just get it over with," Kevin said.

"Indeed." Swallowing the bile that threatened to build,

Nicholas led the way into his aunt's house. As soon as he was presented in her drawing room, he knew he was doomed. Not only Aunt Agnes hosted, but also Aunt Dolores. The party included all of his cousins except Philip. Agnes must have big plans for something if she had omitted him, thus also omitting an excuse for Nicholas to turn on his heel and leave.

A few other persons dotted the drawing room, so it was not only family. He hoped that meant that everything would remain civil.

To his right, Felicity and a red-haired woman shared unkind judgments about the headdresses seen at a recent ball. To his left, a man asked Douglas for his opinions about the demonstrations plaguing the city, and his wife, Claudine, immediately began answering for him.

"Hollinburgh," Aunt Agnes greeted loudly. She turned to Dolores. "See, sister, I said he would come."

He looked to the window where the three heiresses sat in a row, chatting. They rose and curtsied in greeting, with his aunts watching approvingly.

What were they even doing here? Had all these women become friends with his aunts suddenly? He could not think of a worse development.

"Hollinburgh." A feminine voice entered his ear. He turned to see Felicity now next to him, dressed in one of her expensive French evening dresses. Walter sidled over to join them, smiling his own greeting.

"Such fun," Felicity said breathlessly. "The aunts almost never entertain but when I learned you would be here, I could not be kept away."

"It is good to see you both. I'm also pleased that you have been accepting of the heiresses. While you have kept your counsel regarding Rosamund of late, you rarely have kind words for Minerva."

Felicity glanced toward the three women with a bare

acknowledgment. "I confess I don't understand why they are here. Oh, the two wives, of course, but this last one—" She raised her eyebrows quizzically.

"It appears Aunt Agnes has taken to her," Walter said. "Odd."

Frighteningly odd.

Just then, Iris leaned toward Agnes and said something that Agnes found amusing. When both women looked over at him, Nicholas realized he was the joke.

It was time to find out what was going on here. He broke away from Felicity and Walter and attended on his aunts.

"How good of you to invite Miss Barrington," he said to Agnes.

Dolores appeared to turn thoughtful at the mention of Iris. Agnes just beamed with delight. "She called on me. I was astonished, but there she was. Of course, I had to receive her, out of curiosity if nothing else. And she brought Minerva with her! Minerva has never called. I was so in shock. To my surprise it was a very pleasant visit. Miss Barrington was all curiosity about the family, and full of compliments regarding the ones she had met." She lowered her voice. "She is in trade, of course, just like the other two, but one can tell that she has associated with the best society on the Continent."

Agnes chattered on about the delightful visit. Nicholas pictured Iris and Minerva drawing out information that Iris sought regarding the division of the library and who knew what else. Like two big cats stalking a gazelle, the two heiresses had brought Agnes down, and she never realized they were hunting her.

"Since it all went so well, and since Minerva commented on how lovely my drawing room is and how it is a pity I never entertain here, I decided to host a small gathering." Agnes gestured to the gathering with a flourish of her hand.

So even this party was Minerva's idea. Or Iris's. Or both. Nicholas began feeling like a gazelle himself.

"I trust since there are nonfamily members present that there will be no fisticuffs," he said.

Agnes's laughter peeled. Dolores still looked thoughtful. Agnes noticed her sister's distraction. "What is wrong with you, sister?"

Dolores shrugged. "It is nothing, I'm sure. It is just that her name, Barrington, keeps tickling at me. Ever since she arrived in Town. It never did before, but now—"

Hell. "It is a common name."

"Yes, but . . ." Her brow puckered. "When Lady Kelmsly told me about that old scandal involving the grandfather of Miss Barrington, I just assumed that was it. That I must have heard something about that at some point in time. Yet it still tickles." She held out her hands and smiled, as if she gave up trying to scratch the irritation.

He did not much like evidence that Lady Kelmsly and who knew which other old matrons were gossiping about Iris, but there was no way to stop it.

He excused himself and moved over to the heiresses. He exchanged a few pleasantries for onlookers' sake, then leaned low over Minerva. "What are you doing? Don't try to look innocent. There is a plot afoot and I sense that in whatever game you are playing, I am a mere pawn."

"So suspicious, Hollinburgh," Minerva said. "Is it so hard to believe there has been a rapprochement with your aunts?"

"Impossible to believe. Just remember that when Miss Barrington's scheme is completed and she goes back to Paris or Vienna, you will still be here attending on Agnes and Dolores."

Iris sat right beside Minerva, so she heard every word. As did Rosamund, who sat on Iris's other side. He addressed his next words to Iris. "Minerva is one thing. Plotting and subterfuge are part of her profession. But I can't believe you are subjecting Rosamund to this."

"I insisted on being here," Rosamund interrupted. "Arm in arm, we can face anything, even the aunts."

"If you three want to engage, that is your affair. Pray explain why I must be here?"

"So all these other guests will speak well of the party," Iris said. "If a duke attends—"

Hell.

"Oh, Hollinburgh." Aunt Agnes's voice beckoned.

Unless he wanted to cut his own aunt at her own party, he had no choice but to go back to her. The elderly Countess of Carrington now perched on her right. He greeted them all, then waited for his aunt to irritate him.

"It is so nice to see you, Hollinburgh," the countess said. "Miss Barrington said you would probably attend, but I thought her too optimistic, especially since you missed my garden party last week."

"I regret that I had duties that could not be avoided that day. Miss Barrington guessed I would be here, you say? Do you have many conversations with her?"

"Only a few, but I so enjoy them. She is a sweet girl. She has wonderful tales of Vienna. She so enjoys stories of the old days, and I fear that I enjoy telling them more than I should. Eighty years will do that, I suppose."

Stories of the old days. Lady Carrington was old enough for the old days to be quite old indeed.

"It is generous of you to allow Agnes to host a select house party at Melton Park," Lady Carrington continued. She smiled coyly. "It will be so good to see that abode come to life again. Your uncle rarely entertained and never invited society there."

He felt the trap snap shut on his leg. "I'm delighted you are happy with the notion. The estate is beautiful this time of year."

"Oh, yes. I remember it well. I can't wait. Why, I declined two balls in order to stay the entire four days."

Four days? His mind began a ruthless calculation of the costs of this house party. "That is wonderful. Now, I must take my leave of you ladies. I have a few words I must share with my cousins over there." He glanced over his shoulder to where Chase chatted with Kevin.

Agnes smiled up at him. Dolores did too. Lady Carrington's eyes glittered with impish delight.

Upon seeing him approach, Kevin tried to broaden their circle to include others, but Nicholas was having none of it. He glared at the newcomers until they retreated.

"It is a conspiracy," he said. "And the two of you are part of it."

"It is only a house party," Chase said.

"Whose idea was this? Tell me now. No prevaricating."

Kevin shifted his weight. "Hard to say. Not ours."

"Aunt Agnes's, I assume," Chase said.

"Aunt Agnes has wanted to make free use of Melton Park for years. Uncle refused her, and so have I. Yet, somehow, I now find myself unable to stop her. Worse, you lured me here, led me to the edge of the precipice, and watched while the women shoved me over. Someone devised this ignoble strategy, and I want to know which one of them did it." He spared a moment to glare back at the three heiresses.

Chase cleared his throat. "I will explain if you promise to get that look off your face. The guests are far too curious about our conversation now, due to your demeanor."

Nicholas collected his anger and swallowed most of it. He forced a smile and turned it to some onlookers, as if to say, "nothing of interest here, so go back to your punch."

"As best I can determine, it was a matter of negotiation," Chase said. "Miss Barrington wanted something from Aunt Agnes, and Minerva agreed to smooth the way to their finding common ground."

"Minerva detests Agnes."

"Well, yes, but she very much likes Miss Barrington, and she also smells a mystery afoot, so—" Chase shrugged.

"What does—did—Miss Barrington want of Agnes that was so important that my closest family members led me to the gallows?"

"You do exaggerate," Kevin said. "I'm not really sure what she wanted or wants. The story I heard was that, in the course of conversation, Agnes mentioned how she longs to host at Melton Park this Season and the ladies—Minerva and Miss Barrington—promised to see if you could be persuaded. As for what was given in return, I have no idea. Do you, Chase?"

Chase shook his head.

"You are both useless. What is the good of having you married to the two of them if you can't even obtain vital information that would help me? A fine investigator you are, Chase."

"I tried," Kevin objected. "Only . . . the conversation veered in other directions."

"Did it now?"

"Distracting ones."

Nicholas eyed the two of them. Both had succumbed to feminine wiles. Again. He could imagine just how distracting those conversations had been. "Useless," he muttered again, then turned on his heel.

"Here he comes," Rosamund murmured, then sipped at her glass.

Iris could see the duke out of the corner of her eye. He did not look nearly as angry as after his last conversation with Agnes, but he did not look happy either. His sharp gaze speared her as he approached.

"Perhaps you two should leave so he can have his say," she suggested.

"I don't think you should have to suffer it alone," Minerva said. "I am hardly innocent."

"As he pointed out upon arrival, you will pay dearly in the years ahead. There is no reason to start your sentence today."

Rosamund rose and helped Minerva to stand. "Minerva could use some air now, I think."

"Keep him in here," Minerva advised. "He will never make a scene in a chamber with thirty people present."

Iris suspected it would be more fruitful to allow that scene, wherever it occurred. She took Minerva's advice, however, and remained in her seat.

The duke threw himself into the one next to her. "What did Agnes give you in return for the mass betrayal you organized today?"

"Betrayal? That sounds like a Shakespearean play."

"Forgive me if I feel as if I was put on stage without a script. What did you get from Agnes?"

"I hardly—"

"What. Did. You. Get?"

"Only a bit of information and an invitation to a garden party."

He peered past her toward where Agnes now chatted with Lady Eubry.

"A garden party filled with ancient female members of the ton?"

She decided to check the contents of her reticule.

"Ones who could regale you with stories about better times?"

She worked the knot on her reticule's strings.

"Other than Benton's name, what else did you learn?"

"Not nearly enough."

"How sad. And at such a cost too. Minerva may never forgive you."

"Minerva did not gainsay my plan at all. If anything, she encouraged it."

"She would."

"I did learn that, when alive, your grandfather kept the better part of his library at Melton Park. Not here in London. So at least during this house party, we will be able to do a search there. I'm not inclined to accept Mr. Benton's assessment of its contents. He was only a lad, and it was long ago."

Silence beside her. She turned to see him contemplating her.

"Miss Barrington, what makes you think you will be invited to this house party? I have some say in the guest list, even if my aunt will try to pretend she owns the estate."

Oh, dear. "As it happens, I have already received my invitation."

Storm clouds. Lightning. "The invitations have already gone out?"

"You didn't know? I must say, your aunt is very bold."

"Fine talk coming from you. As you will soon learn, your new friend Lady Agnes Radnor is overbearingly bold."

His body remained relaxed, but a tempest brewed in his eyes. She tried a nice smile to calm him. "It might be a very enjoyable party. We had to search that library eventually anyway. Just to make sure the Psalter isn't there."

He stood. "Since it is my aunt's party, I may even have an hour or so to do that. I must insist on being present when you search. Now that I know why you seek that manuscript, I intend to keep a close watch on you." He looked down at her. She gazed up innocently. In the half minute that followed, the one storm cleared from his expression, and a different sort of fury took its place.

"I resent the insinuation that I would do something to prove a falsehood. I promise you that while I am under your roof, I can be trusted," she said.

"If only I could say the same. In fact, the notion of this party and having you under that roof is growing in appeal by the minute." With that, he plunged into the party milling around them.

Chapter Fifteen

"It was good of you to ride down with me," Nicholas said. Kevin stood beside him at the library's front window, facing the drive. Two large wagons and three carriages were pulling up. He had been forced to transport most of Whiteford House's servants here to accommodate the party's needs.

This was why dukes needed money, he thought. This and these houses that rambled on for miles, with roofs that required constant maintenance and elaborate gardens in need of tending. And their stables and their own wardrobes and their wives' demands. And the tenants' needs, of course—far less frivolous and a constant concern.

This rather small house party would cost him dearly. Aunt Agnes, as expected, had felt free to not only use the property but his purse. Already a stack of bills had arrived, with more coming.

"I was glad to. It spared me being part of the family caravan, following these servants," Kevin said. "You know that Chase will demand frequent stops and a sluggish pace. It is a wonder he allowed Minerva to come at all, and he is sure to treat all of those coaches like he is a field marshal and they are troop transports."

That caravan, set to arrive later in the day, included not only the carriages bringing the wives but also Miss Barrington. Others had joined in, including the carriages transporting the cousins, and those bringing the rest of the guests. There were far too many of those, in his opinion. This select house party would number close to forty people. Two of his uncles would join for dinners but stay in Uncle Quentin's nearby manor house.

He and Kevin had arrived hours ago. His only activity thus far had been to demand a tour by the housekeeper regarding the allocation of chambers. He had barely listened to the woman, except when she showed him the one that Iris Barrington would use. Since she was neither family nor titled, and not even officially an heiress yet, she would be tucked into a smaller chamber at the back of the house. All Nicholas had cared about was its positioning for discretion. Its door stood behind the staircase, and it was a mere one flight above the ducal apartment. He had paced out the distance in his mind too many times already and began to do so again.

He walked to the reception hall with Kevin in tow and watched the servants pour in and hurry above and below stairs. There were too many of them to use the servant entrance without jamming the stairs, so rare permission had been granted for them to jam this entrance instead. Outside the door, his cook from Whiteford House was pointing a wagon overflowing with provisions around the house to the kitchen entrance.

"You will have to teach me how you gamble, Kevin. My accounts will never recover otherwise."

Kevin gestured to the strange collection of primitive artifacts that decorated the walls of the hall and the stairwell. "Why not just sell some of this? Or something else? Uncle collected more than any man needed. You may as well clean the properties up a bit and make some blunt in the process."

"It is probably time to do that. I hesitated because it felt unseemly to just tear down the home he knew. But time has passed and so has that sentiment. There are a few very rare items that I will probably bring back to Town and see about selling."

Kevin peered out the open door to where the last wagon was rolling away. "How long until the hordes descend? I brought my papers with me and am inclined to go up and—"

"Indulge yourself for a few hours. You won't be missed until dinner."

Kevin nodded and started up the stairs. He paused. "She ordered a new wardrobe, just for this party."

"Who did? Rosamund?"

"Miss Barrington."

"I'd think there was hardly time for that."

"Rosamund knows some newer modistes who were willing to work their seamstresses around the clock for the chance to have their creations among such company. One was willing to do it for free, but Miss Barrington insisted on paying."

He wondered where she got the money. Perhaps she had decided to live on her expectations after all. Or maybe Uncle Felix's books had brought enough commission to pay for a few dresses.

No sooner had Kevin disappeared up the stairs than the London butler approached. Powell had come down days earlier, to oversee the preparations. "Your Grace, a word if you would be good enough to indulge me."

Butlers wanting a word just prior to a party was never good news. Nicholas waited for it.

"The ladies, sir. They are insisting on a most impractical dinner the last night."

Aunt Agnes and Aunt Dolores had come down two days

ago in order to complete their plans. Nicholas had managed not to see them since his arrival. "Go on."

"They want it to be at the lake, sir. With Chinese lanterns hanging from the trees and—" The aggrieved man suppressed a sigh. "And fireworks after the meal, such as they have at Vauxhall Gardens. I have explained that to transport all the tables and chairs, the china and silver, the linens, candles . . . It makes no sense, Your Grace. And what if it rains after all of that? Even with the extra staff from Town and those hired from the village—"

"Hired from the village?" A throb began behind his right temple. "How many?"

"Four girls and two young men. The ladies demanded more, to ensure the guests were well served, but I convinced them that six would more than suffice. I have explained that it is much more difficult to do a dinner *en plein air* than a luncheon. Luncheons can be placed in baskets and served on blankets in a most charming and informal manner. As for fireworks, we don't have any, nor do I know where to obtain them in time, short of sending a man back to Town to see if they can be bought."

"Tell them that I forbid the dinner at the lake. Also, that there will be no fireworks after any dinner."

The butler licked his lips. "Your Grace, I don't suppose you—"

The hell he would. He had intended to spend the next few hours in his study with some papers that needed attention, but he pictured Agnes descending on him with demands and complaints. "Courage, man. I am off to ride the estate, so it falls on you to deliver my decision."

Iris contemplated fomenting a revolution. The coach moved at a ridiculously slow pace despite the very decent road. Across from her, even Minerva was losing patience.

Outside, one could see Chase ride by every few minutes, always slowing to peer inside at his wife as if to reassure himself that he had not made a terrible mistake in allowing her to come.

"I doubt we will arrive before nightfall at this pace," Minerva said. "If we stop again in the village ahead, I may scream."

"He is only trying to ensure your comfort," Rosamund said. "Women in your condition usually welcome frequent stops, as do the older ladies in the carriages following us."

"I am well aware of a pregnant woman's need for frequent visits to the necessary, but not every half hour," Minerva said. "I am not nearly so far along to require that, or this pace that will take three times the normal to arrive at our destination. If we do not move along, we will spend yet another night at an inn. Iris, perhaps you could have a word with Chase and—"

"I'm sure that you can be more persuasive than I ever could be," Iris said.

Rosamund swallowed a giggle. Minerva sighed.

The next time Chase's horse appeared outside their window, she stretched over, opened the curtain, and beckoned him. All Iris could see was Minerva looking up and a man's leg hanging down the side of a saddle.

"My dear, I grow concerned that such a long time in this coach is not healthy for anyone. Might we perhaps increase our speed?"

"I don't want you jostled by the road."

"I know, and that is so thoughtful. Yet I am barely being jostled at all, and a tad more speed will not matter, I think. I promise to let you know if it is too much."

"I don't think—"

"Iris has threatened to interfere with the coachman if she sees any indication that I am being made uncomfortable. You know how willful she can be, and she didn't even think

I should come. Since you and she are of like minds regarding my condition, I am sure that she will remain vigilant on your behalf."

Iris gave Minerva's foot a little kick. Minerva ignored her. She smiled up at her husband instead. Chase managed to bend down enough for his head to appear beside his leg. He looked inside the coach at Iris. Suspiciously, she thought. She tried to appear disapproving and stern.

"You will alert me at once if Minerva is bumped around, Miss Barrington? If I have your word on that, I suppose we can make better speed."

"I will have the coach stopped at once if I see such a thing," Iris said.

The horse disappeared. A moment later the coach moved more quickly.

With a smile of satisfaction, Minerva settled back against the cushion. "So, what adventures are we going to plan in order to make this house party bearable?"

Iris watched the servant girl unpack her wardrobe. The trunk was full of silks and lace, feathers and fine handwork. Several new headdresses purchased at Rosamund's millinery shop completed the ensembles.

The chamber was small, charming, and perfect. Set at the rear of the house, its two long windows overlooked the garden. If she opened the window she could look down on a large terrace. The late sun showed the windows faced east.

"Will you be wanting anything else, Miss Barrington?"

The girl couldn't be more than fifteen, and visibly nervous. Her hands had shaken while she unpacked the dresses, and her fair face flushed up to her blond hairline whenever Iris addressed her. This was not one of the servants who had come down from Town, she assumed. As the guest with the least status, she would be assigned a servant of equal ignobility.

"Not at present, Kathleen."

The flush started anew. "Then I will leave you to refresh yourself. There is water waiting in the dressing room, and I'll bring more for when you prepare for dinner. I'll come then and wake you if need be, and help you to dress, unless you would prefer to call for me when it suits you."

"Your plan all sounds fine for this evening."

After Kathleen left, Iris made use of the warm water in the dressing room, then quickly changed out of her travel ensemble. She donned one of her new dresses, a deceptively simple raw silk that had a gorgeous deep rose hue. She was resettling her hair when a low knock sounded on her door. She trusted Kathleen had not returned already. The sun had not even set yet.

She opened the door to find the duke outside it.

"At long last, you have all arrived," he said.

"Are you visiting the guests to welcome them? How generous of you."

"I would never do that. It might reinforce the notion that they are my guests, when I want it understood they are guests of my aunts."

"That seems a fine line."

"A necessary one, unless I am willing to play host for four days without pause, which I am not." He entered her chamber uninvited and looked around. "It looks smaller than I remember. I can have you moved."

"It suits me, so please do not. The housekeeper has enough to do now. Also, where else would she think I belonged? I half expected to find myself brought up to the attics where the servants sleep, since I am little more than one presently."

He peered out the window. "That is hardly true." He

turned and gave her a long look, taking her in from head to toe. "That is a lovely dress. It becomes you."

She felt herself flushing worse than Kathleen.

"Were you going somewhere?" he asked. "You do not appear ready to rest."

"Did you think to find me in dishabille?" It just blurted out, sounding more flirtatious than she intended.

"There was always the chance of that."

"I have rested for hours on end in that coach. I thought to do a bit of exploring."

"Not the library, I trust. I said that I must be with you for that."

"And so you will be, it appears." She strode to the door and slipped out.

Outside her door she looked around. One other door gave off the landing back here behind the staircase. It would be difficult to see that the duke had visited her and entered her chamber, but not impossible.

"What is that door?" she asked when the duke joined her.

"It leads to a staircase that goes up to the roof. I will take you up tomorrow if the weather is fair. You can see most of the county from its heights. Right now, I will give you a tour of the public rooms."

They strolled around the staircase and down to the next level. He explained the ducal apartments were there. Down another grand staircase and they passed the drawing room and the ballroom. Down once more to the main entry level. They passed through the reception hall filled with primitive artifacts, and he guided her to the library, which filled the entire back of the building.

It was a glorious library, such as one dreams of owning. Superb cases lined all the walls. Comfortable furniture dotted the carpets. Lamps everywhere, to be lit for late reading. Two large tables occupied the back area, where the eastern exposure would provide light for serious work. A huge fireplace held pride of place on one wall.

Not all the cases were full. There was room for more books. Or rather, the departure of books had left large gaps.

"It must have at least twice as many books as the one in Town," she mentioned, strolling along those cases, noting the organization. She became so engrossed in the bindings that she almost forgot he shadowed her. Almost. His presence and proximity created a tension, like a vague pull, that demanded attention.

Outside the eastern doors, a stairway led up to the terrace she had seen from her window. It had been built over that end of the library. She gazed out beyond the garden to the rolling hills. "What is that over there? It looks as if a bridge is being built, but I see no river or stream."

"That is one of Kevin's projects. It is an aqueduct, such as the Romans had. It starts at a spring-fed lake to the north, then aims to this house. He believes he can transport water here that way."

"How ambitious. What happens once it gets here?"

"It will go into a cistern. His thinking is that he can find a way to have it move up to the chambers. He is devising a pump to do that, so water will be readily available on each level whenever it is desired." He shrugged. "I am allowing him to try. I think he is adapting pumps used in steam engines or something. He would be happy to explain it all to you. Ask him should you find yourself next to him at one of the dinners to which we will all be subjected."

She turned and craned her neck to look up the façade of the building. "It is impressive. Far more than one man needs. Perhaps it is a good thing that people will fill it for a few days."

He laughed and shook his head. "Do not say that aloud again, especially in the presence of any member of my family, I beg you. Come with me. I have something to show you."

They returned to the house, passing through the ballroom, and went up to the level of the ducal chambers. There he led her to a door. She wondered if he would be so bold as to escort her right into his apartment. It was one thing to realize the possibilities existed for intimacy during this visit, and another to try and explore them before she even had one meal.

Instead, the door opened on a large study. A rather messy one. Unlike Whiteford House, here the study appeared well used. Papers littered the top of a desk and several portfolios tottered on a table beside an armchair near the fireplace.

He went to a cabinet and took out a good-sized mahogany box. He set it atop the papers on the desk. "I think you said your father was an art seller. Did you learn much from him?"

"My interest was books, but it was hard not to learn a bit. I have turned a few paintings over the years."

"Tell me what you think of this. I found it hidden, probably by my uncle. He had a habit of doing that. Usually gold coins, but in searching for more of those, I came upon this." He opened the box.

She stepped over and looked down, which meant she moved right next to him, so close that their bodies almost touched. She indulged in the way that pull tightened between them, then fixed her gaze on what the box held.

There inside, nestled in a thick bed of ochre velvet, lay a magnificent dark blue-gray glass vase with figures in white relief around its circumference. The entire thing looked like a huge cameo of a vase, with light penetrating the material even while it remained in the velvet.

"Goodness," she breathed the word.

"It is probably very valuable, I expect."

"Since the late duke had priceless Chinese urns tottering

on pedestals, ready to be destroyed by any passing visitor, I would assume that an object he hid was much more valuable than those."

"It reminds me of that Roman urn. The Portland Vase. That one is darker and a bit larger, but the artistry is similar. At least to my eyes. Do you agree?"

She ran her fingertips over the surface. The raised white figures had been superbly crafted, and light created shadows and highlights on their iridescent forms. "I think so too."

"If it is of similar age to the Portland Vase, would you say it is more valuable than the *Poliphili*?"

"It would be much more valuable than any printed book. It is one of a kind. It is exceedingly rare. Its similarity to the Portland Vase increases its value enormously. And any person can appreciate its beauty, while it takes a trained eye to fully do so with the *Poliphili*."

He began to lift it, but she quickly placed her hand on his, to stop him. "Have you ever taken it out before?"

"Never, but I thought you might like to see it in the light."

He did not move his hand and hers remained on it. She noted its strength and form, its warmth and the feel of his skin. How masculine it looked compared to her small, smooth one. "Please don't remove it now, on my account. It is very fragile. If you dropped it, I would be horrified. Just leave it there, safe."

He hesitated further, his hand still on the vase. Whether he proved indecisive or was enjoying this brief touch of each other, she did not know.

Finally, he moved his hands and closed the box. "Do you know someone who would buy it? Do any of your collectors also favor ancient vases?"

Still stunned by the beauty of the vase, and the delicious brief contact it had afforded, it took her a moment to understand what he was requesting. "There are maybe a handful of collectors who have holdings of this caliber in this country, and I would never risk transporting it abroad. If I were you, I would start with the Duke of Devonshire. You will not need a go-between with him either."

"Duke to duke, you mean."

"Yes. Place a very high value on it and see what happens."

"How high?"

She considered the appeal of such a rarity to a man who had one of the largest fortunes in the world. "Start with two thousand."

Their conference on the vase over, they stood there, neither one of them moving. This might not be his apartment as such, although she guessed it connected to it. The privacy they shared pressed on her and invited improper musings of pleasant ways to pass the next hour.

From his expression she guessed he speculated on the same thing. Yet both knew something stood between them that would make such a diversion unwise. Soon they would have to decide if they were enemies, he had said. Not yet, however. His hesitation said that as clearly as words.

"I think I will return to the library," she said, and edged toward the doorway. "These papers suggest you have duties awaiting your attention. I promise not to remove anything, or in any way put your family at a disadvantage while I am there. I hope that you can trust my word on that."

She slipped out, lest she not leave at all when she knew she should.

Dinner wasn't nearly as horrible as Nicholas had expected. All of the relatives behaved, and their guests clearly enjoyed being at Melton Park again. Stories abounded about parties during his grandparents' days.

He couldn't avoid acting as host, although he had made

it a point to arrive at the gathering of the guests late enough
to arrive as a guest himself.

Aunt Agnes had put his uncle Quentin to his left. Quentin
had his own property not far from Melton Park, although
he rarely left it even to visit the ducal estate. He preferred a
quiet life outside of the gossip and machinations of the
ton. A tall, gray-haired man with a retiring manner, he
maintained a formal relationship with his sons, Walter and
Douglas. Quiet like the latter, he spent most of his time
during dinner observing.

Other than pleasantries, they spoke little until near the
end of the meal.

"She is a handsome woman," Uncle Quentin said. "Miss
Barrington, that is."

"She is at that."

"Not beautiful the way Felicity is. Few women are as
lovely as Felicity. That is the problem with her."

Nicholas looked down the table to where Felicity was
speaking with Lord Carrington.

"It is as if she had her portrait done by the best artist,
then became the portrait," Quentin continued between
sips of wine. "All you get is the surface beauty. Now,
Miss Barrington is forthright. Her depths are almost tangi-
ble. Her grandfather was a little like that."

Nicholas's attention sharpened on his uncle. "You met
him?"

"Never. I heard about him, however. There was this
scandal surrounding him. Since it also involved our family,
I was curious."

"I am familiar with the scandal."

Quentin didn't respond to that. Nicholas wondered if it
had been a warning. He began to turn his attention to Lady
Carrington, on his right.

"He didn't do it, of course," Quentin said, as if their conversation had never ended.

"Who didn't?"

"Barrington. Why would he? It isn't as if he could sell that manuscript if he kept it. What good would it be?"

"Perhaps he just wanted to own it."

"The man traded in such things. He would not risk being called a thief because he coveted one of those rarities. I wouldn't. Nor would you. Why would he?"

Nicholas let that question sit there. "You are saying that your father lied about returning the Psalter to Barrington. You are calling your own father a thief."

Quentin mused over that. "Perhaps there was an explanation that had little to do with the value of an old manuscript."

"Do you have a theory about that?"

"None at all. My father, like my brother, had a large personal fortune. If he wanted it, he could have just bought it."

"More likely he returned it."

"Is that why you are letting this woman search the family libraries? To prove it isn't in one of them?"

"It is. She would like to search yours, if you will allow it."

"She is welcome to do so, but it will be a waste of a day. I sold half of it, the better half, several years ago. All the volumes were examined and accounted for at the time. Neither of my sons cares enough about incunabula and other rare printings to leave such books to them. They will much prefer the funds that those books created."

"Walter certainly will."

Quentin sighed and shook his head. "You are aware of that? I suppose the whole family is. Walter lives beyond his considerable means. That takes concerted effort, since his means are handsome enough. Unfortunately, he has a wife who thinks she should live like a duchess, and she spends accordingly. Did you see how all the women took note of her dinner dress when she entered the drawing room? She lives for that. Unfortunately, my son is besotted with her. Always has been. She will be the ruin of him."

"I doubt it will get that bad. Walter isn't stupid."

He looked down the table at his sons. "Felicity is one reason why I rarely go up to Town. I dislike being with her. I sense she is always calculating the state of my health, with the hope of finding it is failing."

Nicholas didn't like Felicity much, but his uncle's criticism seemed extreme. Walter's wife was no worse than many fashionable women of the ton. Yet the look on his uncle's face made him pause. "And is it failing?"

A long sigh. A wavering smile. "A malady of the heart. It won't be long before I see your father, Nicholas. That will be nice, at least. I have missed him badly."

The turn in the conversation sobered Nicholas. He gazed hard at his uncle and saw a resignation in his eyes that indicated this news was not exaggerated. Now that he paid close attention, he also noticed a drawn quality around the eyes and mouth that might not be the result of advancing years. "Do Walter and Douglas know?"

"I told them late last year."

His uncle drank some wine, then grimaced. He faced Nicholas fully. "I told him not to do it. That it was not worth it. Frederick himself commanded him to stand down. But he was determined to force a retraction of a stupid rumor that no one would ever believe."

Nicholas experienced an odd chill. They were speaking about his father now. "What rumor?"

His uncle moved back his chair and stood. "No reason to drag that up, especially since he died to bury it. Excuse me, now. I need some air."

"Do you require assistance, Uncle?"

"I will be fine after a few minutes."

"When would it be a good day to bring Miss Barrington to see your library? We can forgo that entirely if it—"

"Come. Not tomorrow, though. I have agreed to allow my sisters to make use of my property for a luncheon beside the river. The ladies can gossip while the gentlemen fish. The day after would be best."

His uncle walked away. Nicholas watched, noticing that Quentin appeared far more frail than he recalled.

He turned his attention to Lady Carrington, who treated him to the on-dit regarding the wife of a viscount who had disappeared with her son's tutor. But most of his mind churned with curiosity about the rumor that had led to his father's death.

Iris strolled through the drawing room, chatting with guests. She had already talked with most of the ladies either before dinner or after, when the women retreated here and left the men to their port. Now all had reunited, and the evening was winding down.

In each conversation she drew the discussion toward this house, and the man who had reigned two generations ago. If she had hoped for the insinuation of bad character, or even an unkind one, she had been disappointed. Agnes had selected her party to include friends of the dukes, and all of them thought the last two the most excellent of men. None of them even raised an eyebrow to suggest other opinions that remained unspoken.

The current duke appeared to be enjoying himself, despite his prior moaning about this party. He acted more like the host than he knew, and attention moved to wherever he strolled. Ladies beamed with appreciation and gentlemen ingratiated themselves. Being guests of a duke was no small matter, even if one had a title oneself.

Eventually hers and the duke's paths crossed. He paused to pass the time. Anyone watching would assume they discussed the latest balls.

"You have been busy," he said, smiling all the while. "Have you learned of any nefarious deeds by my ancestors?"

"None at all. Of course, this party is not composed of the sort to relate such things to me."

"Maybe there are no such tales to tell."

"Every family has at least a few secrets."

"If so, I am as ignorant of our secrets as you are."

She almost believed that. The truth was that some families were very good at keeping their secrets, even from family members. She believed that the Radnors were such a tribe.

"Have you received permission from your last uncle for me to see his library?" The uncle in question, Quentin Radnor, had been difficult to draw into any conversation. A countrified gentleman, he looked like someone who preferred shooting and riding to events like this. He clearly found small talk, and any feminine talk, boring.

The duke turned just enough to be able to speak very quietly. "I spoke with him. Meet me on the terrace and I will reveal what he said."

She glanced around. The party was ending. Several of the older couples had already departed, and Agnes and Dolores now made their way to the doorway. Slipping out would not garner much attention soon. "I will be there in five minutes."

Minerva and Chase were walking out, and the duke ambled along with them. The last of the guests started to retreat in earnest with the duke gone.

Iris bided her time until the drawing room emptied. Then she made her way to the ballroom, walked through it, and stepped out onto the terrace just as the duke mounted the steps from the library below.

"We had little time to talk," he said as he came to her. "I didn't have the chance to tell you how lovely you look."

She glanced down at her ensemble. "I could not resist the color. Like celadon pottery."

"I thought I recognized it. It is good that you are indulging yourself a little."

"I can hardly go back to the Continent without a few new things." The truth was she had indulged herself more than she could yet afford. If something delayed that legacy too long, she would be in dun territory, and she always avoided that possibility. "What did your uncle Quentin say?"

"He has agreed to open his library to you. Tomorrow next. However, he said he has sold the better half and that no rarities remain of any kind."

"Is he likely to know that for certain?"

"He is not a bibliophile, if that is what you are asking. However, he has scholarly interests and is a man who would know the worth of his property."

"'Tis a pity I was not aware he sought to remove the best books from his possession. I would have liked to arrange their sale."

"You were probably busy fascinating men in Paris much like you were doing here tonight."

"Is that a scold?"

He looked down at her for a long moment. "Not at all. It was a compliment. There are not many women who could hold their own so well with such company under these circumstances."

She felt her face warming. "I have had some practice."

"I expect so."

Suddenly they seemed very much alone, as if the entire house had yawned and fallen asleep. Except them. Two torch sconces still flamed on the terrace, but she doubted any servant would come to snuff them while the duke was here.

"Did your uncle have nothing more to reveal? You made is sound like you had news from him."

He turned toward the garden, which brought him right next to her. His side brushed hers, or at least she reacted as if it had. A wonderful shiver scurried up her back.

"He knew all about the scandal and the Psalter. It happened before he was born, but he learned of it."

"How?"

"I suppose he asked about it and someone told him. He finds it a conundrum. Two men claiming two things, neither of which makes much sense. Your grandfather would not risk his entire trade by taking a manuscript that he could not sell without proving he was a thief. My grandfather would not keep a manuscript that he could easily purchase if he wanted it."

That did lay it out very neatly. "I suppose that means it really was not about the Psalter at all. It was just a way to ruin my grandfather. He did tell me it was deliberate."

"I don't think they knew each other well enough for there to be a reason for that. A few books passed between them, but there is no indication that they were friends, or enemies, or even had social dealings. One was a bookseller, and the other a duke."

Preposterous, in other words. Even those few sales may not have brought them into each other's company. It could all have been done through an intermediary, like a secretary.

"I don't suppose anyone who served your grandfather is still alive," she said.

"Unlikely." The word murmured close to her ear.

More shivers. Wonderful ones.

"Thank you for learning what you could from him. I suppose if he knew about all of that, the late duke might have too. That explains why he knew my name, and who I probably was. Perhaps someone who served him would be able to—"

His fingertips came to rest on her lips, stopping her. "There is no point in continuing to speculate, since I am hearing none of it anymore. My attention is completely on how similar the night sky is to your eyes. The flames behind us are creating tiny stars in them."

No, the fires doing that were inside her, rising from the embers that had burned ever since she first saw him. She loved what they did to her. Low and deep excitements moved and pulsed, and her shortening breaths belied how her chest swelled with aching need.

They still stood inches apart, the small space creating an exquisite ache. Only his fingertips touched her, still resting on her lips. She looked into his eyes. Then she opened her mouth and gently bit one of his fingers.

He just watched her, but she knew what it did to him. She knew she shouldn't. Mustn't. None of that mattered when he swept her into his arms and dragged her into the shadows.

Passion, immediate and forceful. It poured out like a dam had been breached by rushing water. Her mind retreated and she only felt the cascading pleasure while they kissed and clung and shared each other's hunger. His hand pressed her through the silk in caresses designed to madden her. Her exhilaration undid her, especially when his embrace lifted her so he could kiss her décolleté and his hand cupped her breast.

If they could have remained there and made a bed on the terrace pavement, or if they had been mere inches from one of their chambers, they might have continued like that and allowed the overwhelming desire to have its way. Instead, there was only the railing and a wall if they followed that path. She began urging him with her kisses and caresses to consider the latter.

A sound. Small and discreet. A door opened and shut.

They both froze. She broke out of his embrace and stepped aside.

She caught her breath, trying to make room for rational thought within the chaos muddling her mind. "A servant, perhaps."

"Most likely." He grasped the railing and gazed into the dark, then right at her. "This will not do."

"No."

"I have decided we are probably not enemies." A slow smile broke. "Actually, right now I don't give a damn if we are." That smile turned dangerous. "I could reach your door without anyone seeing me. If I do, will you open it to me?"

Yes, yes. She closed her eyes so the mere sight of him would not sway her. Her current emotions urged her to encourage him. Invite him. But a deeper sense warned that if she did so, she would pay dearly for an hour of heaven.

"I think not."

He turned his attention back to the night. "Go inside now, before I also don't give a damn that you are at least half convinced that is the right choice."

Her legs still wobbled from how dazed she had been, but she obeyed and walked away.

Chapter Sixteen

"I am so glad that I begged off the luncheon." Minerva lay back on the blanket and looked up into the tree. "This is so much better, and after last night's dinner I have talked enough to last a week."

Iris nibbled on some cheese from the basket they had brought. Rosamund had obtained it from the cook before he left to tend to the picnic being served to the other guests at Quentin Radnor's property. "I'm also glad you begged off, so we could, too, in order to keep you company. Although I don't want to be present if Chase learns that you drove one of the gigs here."

They were enjoying a lake north of the manor house. Of good size, it offered grassy shores in various places and shallows in the little nook they had chosen for their respite.

Rosamund removed her pelisse and set it aside. "It is unseasonably warm today. No threat of rain, so it should be a successful luncheon for Agnes. Did all the gentlemen go, too, to fish?"

"I saw so many rods being packed onto a wagon to say they all went," Iris said.

"I hope that means we will have fresh fish at dinner tonight," Minerva said. "Oddly enough, it sounds appealing to me." She sat up and removed her spencer, then flopped back down.

Iris watched the lake's placid surface. Other than little eddies lapping the shore nearby, it looked like blue glass. The sun shone high in the cloudless sky.

Her thoughts drifted back to the night before, and the wonderful pleasure of the duke's kisses and caresses. Stopping that had been hard. She did not regret her decision to do so, but that did not mean she had liked denying herself the fulfillment of that bliss.

He probably would be disagreeable now. Perhaps he would not take her to his uncle's house tomorrow. He might even thwart her from learning what she needed to know. If so, she would be disappointed, but probably relieved that she had not confused matters with more intimacy.

"Are any of the servants the same ones who served the last duke?" she asked her companions.

"I think some are, but not the important ones," Rosamund said. "Kevin said that the will pensioned off the servants the duke would have dealings with, like his valet and the cooks and a few others."

"Melton Park was as poorly staffed as Whiteford House when I first met Chase," Minerva said. "That is how I gained access to observe the family. I was placed as a servant at the house for a few days."

"You never told me that," Rosamund said.

Minerva turned onto her side and told them about her first days as an heiress, and how she investigated the late duke's death. "I was under suspicion, so I thought it best to try and find out what was going on with this family."

"Yet you never learned the truth about how he died," Iris said.

Minerva made a peculiar smile, then laid on her back again. "His valet lives not too far from here. I called on him. He is not nearly old enough to be pensioned. The late duke was as generous with his loyal retainer as he was with strangers like us."

More for the cousins to resent, Iris thought. The current duke may have disowned Philip, but it was as if the last one had disowned everyone. What would make a man do such a thing, and give his money to servants and three women he barely knew? Whimsy? Anger? Had there been some family argument of which even the cousins were unaware?

The sun had moved since they arrived. Minerva's blanket still lay under shade, but the one on which she and Rosamund sat now faced full sun.

Rosamund dabbed at her neck with a handkerchief. "That lake begins to look very appealing." She removed her shoes and stockings, stood, and gathered up her skirts. She walked barefoot down to the water and stepped in. "It isn't too cold, since it is fairly shallow here." She came back and began disrobing. "I'm going to swim."

"Does it get too deep out there?" Iris asked.

Rosamund shook her head. "Not until you near the northern end. Kevin has studied this lake for his aqueduct project, and he says the land is sloped beneath the water. At this end it never gets more than perhaps six feet at its worst and that is only in places. I will be safe if I stay near the shore." She removed her stays with remarkable agility. Down to her chemise, she returned to the lake and began wading in.

"It is very nice," she called back before she plunged forward. Soon all that appeared was her blond head.

Minerva sat up and watched. "I am so envious, but I dare not."

"Would you mind if I join her?" Iris asked.

"Not at all. A day like this should not be wasted, and there is no one about."

* * *

"I'm so glad that we begged off that luncheon," Chase said while he, Nicholas, and Kevin slowed their horses to a walk. "Who would think that in a house that big it would be so hard to escape Aunt Agnes and Aunt Dolores? The notion of an entire afternoon sitting on a riverbank listening to them opine on every topic under the sun was enough to inspire a deep melancholy."

The three of them dismounted and walked toward the eastern tip of the lake. Kevin, who had instigated this excuse to avoid the larger party, walked with purpose.

Nicholas followed, wondering if agreeing to accompany Kevin to the head of his aqueduct would make fishing with Uncle Quentin an hour of paradise in comparison.

"See here." Kevin pointed to where the shore had been replaced by a stone wall. "It is quite shallow in summer, but in other seasons the water pushes out as the spring fills the lake from the other end. So instead of the slow growth of the lake, such as has been happening, I am going to have a path out through this wall and into the aqueduct. We are higher here than at the house and I have calculated that the correct slow angle for the flow can be achieved without much building."

Nicholas studied what had been constructed so far. When he gave permission for this experiment, he had no idea that Kevin's plans were extensive to the point of walling in this end of the lake. At least he hadn't suspected it until that bridge-like structure spanning a dip in the hills began appearing in full view of the house's terrace.

Chase squinted at the wall. "Impressive. I trust you don't plan to make Nicholas pay for his own water once it is all done."

"Of course not." Kevin spoke distractedly while he leaned over the wall and poked at it underneath the water.

"Then how will you earn a shilling from this?" Chase asked.

"Others will want one." Kevin's head all but disappeared upside down while he examined his wall. "Rosamund thinks we can form a corporation to offer such things to other large estates. Once this is done, everyone will want good water to arrive in unlimited supply at their houses."

"If Rosamund considers it a worthwhile endeavor, I suppose it is worth the risk," Chase said.

Nicholas wondered what Kevin's investment in this project amounted to thus far. Chase was right that Rosamund would never have allowed it if the numbers did not make sense to her, so there was risk but not a terrible one, he supposed. Giving Rosamund half of Kevin's company had probably been one of the wisest decisions that Uncle Frederick had made in those peculiar bequests.

Minerva had received a share in a company, too, and from Chase's telling, it threw off a sizable income. Only the ones bequeathed to Nicholas himself had been problems. He didn't even think of them as benefits, but only as several more thorns in his side. Once more the textile mill had rebuffed attempts to examine the company's books, and the transportation corporation had just issued a call for further investment. He and Withers and Sanders had a long meeting arranged for when he returned to Town. Perhaps Chase's agents would have something to report on the mill by then.

Kevin started walking around the edge of the lake, past the curve of the wall to where the water deepened. A clearing opened where some grass grew and the shore sloped down to the water.

Chase craned his neck and looked up. "Not a cloud to be seen, and the sun is hot. I think a swim is in order." He shrugged off his coats and went to work on his cravat.

"That is a splendid idea," Kevin said. "If we wade

around this bend, the water deepens enough for proper swimming."

Nicholas joined them in stripping. Leaving their clothing to bake in the sun, they all walked into the lake.

Kevin was the first to splash. Soon they used the lake the way they had as boys, sending showers of cold droplets onto each other, and wrestling to dunk each other beneath.

Chase struck out to round the bend to deeper water. Nicholas followed and was just finding his stroke when he crashed right into Chase, who had ceased swimming and just stood there, waist deep. Nicholas cleared the water from his eyes and saw what Chase saw.

Two hundred feet away, near the shore, two heads bobbed. Another figure reclined under a tree. The heads moved and a squeal reached his ears.

The water broke beside him, and a very sodden Kevin emerged from where he had been swimming underwater. He had Chase's leg in his grip and a devilish grin on his face, but when he saw that the fun had ended, he stood and joined them in their observations.

"Rosamund said that she and Miss Barrington intended to keep Minerva company while she rested," Kevin said. "I thought she meant at the house."

"Didn't we all," Chase muttered.

"Not me," Nicholas said. "I assumed they were with the others." He assumed that because he had deliberately avoided seeing Iris this morning. After last night, the mere thought of doing so was enough to cause pleasure and pain, both the result of an almost instant arousal, such as he now had despite the cold water.

"Although Minerva is indeed resting and they are keeping her company in a fashion," he felt obligated to point out.

Chase's head slowly turned until he treated Nicholas to one of *those* looks.

"You are deciding to blame me again, and I won't have it," Nicholas said. "None of this is my doing."

Kevin hadn't spoken, but now he grinned. "What fun." He lowered his body until only his head appeared and began moving forward. Halfway to the unsuspecting women, his head dipped and he disappeared.

Chase held his hand over his eyes and examined the shore. "One gig. I wonder who drove it."

"I expect any of them could. Just as any of them could have come up with this idea."

"Except we both know who did come up with it, don't we?"

"See here. There is no reason to assume that—"

A loud cry interrupted him. Bodies flashed and water spewed. Rosamund rose from the water, barely covered by her sodden garment, then flew back and landed with a huge splash. Kevin's laugh echoed over the lake.

Iris saw it, then immediately looked to where he and Chase stood. She sank lower in the water. Minerva sat up, and her gaze also aimed at them.

"Now he's done it," Chase said.

Kevin and Rosamund were having a wonderful time, splashing and grabbing and acting like water spirits. Iris kept looking at him, then at the shore, then back again.

A gentleman should turn his back. A kind man would not leave her there, getting cold, wondering how to make a decent exit.

He didn't move.

Minerva stood. Chase waved his arm. "I'll go back and bring my horse around and take you back in the gig," he called.

Whether she agreed or not couldn't be seen, but Chase turned to retrace his path.

Kevin had other ideas. Not being one to give a damn what anyone thought, he walked out of the lake, naked,

strode to a blanket and scooped up some garments. He
returned to the lake with the bundle high over his head.
He and Rosamund started in Nicholas's direction.

"I'll bring her back on my horse," Kevin announced
once they were close. "I'll bring yours around when we
leave."

Nicholas averted his gaze when they waded by so as not
to embarrass Rosamund. Her giggles suggested she
wouldn't care much whatever he did. He suspected it might
be a while before his horse came around.

That left Miss Barrington still in the water.

The lake absorbed Rosamund's laughter and she and
Kevin frolicked their way around the finger of land that
obscured the end of the lake. Behind Iris, Minerva called
to ask if she wanted the gig sent back for her.

"I will bring her back to the house," Nicholas called back
in a tone that brooked no argument.

Minerva hesitated, then bundled up her blanket and
walked to where Chase was tying his horse to the back of
the gig. Minerva reached to the saddle, then trod back to the
tree. She set a pile of clothing on the blanket that was left.

Then they were gone.

Iris faced Nicholas across the water. Even from this distance she could read his eyes, and knew trouble was brew-
ing. He had not been pleased by the interruption last night
on the terrace, and she doubted he would be easy to reject
this afternoon.

Not that she really wanted to. It was one thing to marshal
your reasons for restraint while kissing on a terrace and another to do so while isolated at a lake, naked.

He most definitely was that. Sunlight glinted off his
torso and sculpted his body with vague shadows that revealed his muscles. Damp, dark hair tousled around his

head, making him look roguish. He and his cousins may have lived lives of privilege, but they clearly used their bodies in sport if not labor, and the duke's lean strength, gleaming so close, made her stir.

"You and your cousins seem determined to ruin our fun," she said.

"We did not expect to find you here. You are supposed to be at a luncheon, being bored by Lady Carrington."

"As are you."

Only her shoulders showed above the water, because she almost kneeled on the lake bottom in the shallows. The thin batiste of her chemise floated around her on the surface, shifting around her body, creating luxurious caresses.

"You are welcome to continue swimming," he said. "It is better out here where the lake deepens. I'll keep watch to make sure you don't drown."

If she swam out there—if they got any closer at all—her teeth clenched against the titillation rippling through her at the mere thought of what could happen. Would happen. She had barely found her voice last night. She knew she never would now.

Unwise. Wrong. Trouble. Doomed. The arguments tried to enter her mind, but memories blocked them. The potential for pleasure untold beckoned.

He remained where he was. He would not come to her, she knew. He was letting her decide. Again.

Maybe being lovers for a short while would be worth whatever sorrow it brought. Perhaps he would not forsake her when she proved the truth. Possibly they could know something sweet for at least a short time . . .

Desire swelled within her until all she knew was his gaze and beauty and the pull of how much they wanted each other.

She made no decision. It was beyond that. Her body moved in the water toward him. He let her float forward.

His expression firmed. His eyes burned. When she was halfway there, he strode forward, thrashing through the water, emerging as the water grew more shallow until he reached her. One reach, one hold, and he lifted her up into his embrace and fierce kiss.

His body warmed her, banishing the water's chill, heating her to her core. Deep kisses, invasive and possessive, unleashed a torrent of craving inside her. She encircled his neck with one arm and his shoulders with the other and joined him in dueling kisses, a battle of mutual urging and taking.

Hands splayed across her back and bottom, he raised her high, until her head towered above his own. She looked down as his teeth gently closed on her nipple through the transparent batiste. A sharp pleasure shot through her, and she exhaled deeply in wonder at the power of it. More then. She clutched his shoulders while he pleasured her to the edge of insanity. Eyes closed, reeling from the intensity of her body's reactions, she relinquished control of her senses.

He moved her until he carried her in his arms. Water splashing and dividing, he walked to the shore, laid her on the blanket, and joined her in a full embrace. He caressed and kissed her until she was moaning with impatience and need. Then he stripped away her wet chemise so they were both naked under the sun.

He had wanted her for so long that his body urged him to ravish her at once. Instead, he leashed his desire to something manageable so he could savor the desire pounding through him and luxuriate in her embrace and hold.

Her eyes proved even darker in passion, and the lights brighter. Her lips, swollen from his kisses, parted slightly in a way that maddened him. The chemise had hidden little, but naked she was beautiful, all white and dark and visibly aroused. He moved his mouth down her body, along the long line that ran from her neck, between her breasts, over her stomach, and to the dark hair below. He caressed her breast with one hand and her thighs with the other, parting them so he could kiss the softness at their top and venture another kiss between them. He flicked his tongue at the pink flesh there and her entire body responded with a long, deep, sinuous flex.

"So you plan to drive me mad first?" Her quiet voice flowed down to him.

"Yes."

She parted her legs more, in invitation.

Surprised, but not too much so, he moved so he could use his mouth and fingers to explore the edges of pleasure. She gave herself over to it, rocking from the growing abandon, her breaths shortening and her low cries rising in a crescendo of need. Almost blinded by the fury of passion, he moved up over her, rose on tensed arms, and looked down while he slowly entered her.

Perfection. Unbelievable pleasure. Her velvet hold took him in and their sighs of relief met in the space between them. He stayed there, not moving, absorbing the stunning sense of completion while he turned his shoulders and dipped his head to arouse her breasts. Her hips flexed, asking for more, but he still did not start. Her fingers gripped at him and her cries grew louder and insistent as her arousal climbed even higher. When she tottered on the brink, he withdrew almost entirely, then thrust deeply. She gasped sharply and bent her knees, opening more. *Yes,* she exhaled with each thrust. *Yes.* Permission granted, he did not hold back but thrust harder while passion's storm broke in him. He heard her own cries of completion right before lightning crashed through his mind and soul and a vibrant pleasure drenched his essence.

* * *

They did not speak afterward. She was thankful for that. She did not want to ruin the peace of being in his arms.

He held her protectively, which she found touching. After a while, when their passion had cooled, he reached over, thrust his garments off the blanket and drew its edge over her, as if he guessed that the lowering sun meant she would be getting cold.

They stayed entwined in silence for what seemed a long time. Finally, he spoke. "I suppose we have to go back."

She resented the obligation. She glanced over at their piles of garments. While they lay here naked, they could be any two people, but once they donned those clothes and returned to the house, they would also don their respective roles. He the duke and she the bookseller heiress. He the man of duty to country and family, she the upstart who had intruded on his world.

He the man sworn to protect the title and its legacy, she the woman determined to prove some of it was a lie.

He reached for those garments and they began. He helped her with her stays and her dress's tapes. Being dressed by him felt almost as intimate as being undressed would have.

He lifted her onto the saddle of his horse, then swung up behind her. Arms surrounding her, he took the reins.

"I expect the luncheon party will have returned by now," she said. "We should not arrive like this."

"When we are close, we will walk. I'll say I was out riding and found you wandering lost on the property."

"So you will be the chivalrous knight and I will be the stupid woman."

"We can't say you found me wandering lost. It is my home."

She had to laugh. She leaned back against him and felt

him press a kiss on her head, then her neck. "Will we still go to your uncle Quentin's tomorrow?"

"If you want."

"Minerva said your late uncle's valet lives nearby. I would like to call on him, too, as long as we are near him."

"Chase has already learned what little can be had from him."

"I would still like to speak to him."

He laughed quietly. "I suddenly understand why Chase and Kevin keep getting distracted by their wives. I am inclined to allow you to do whatever you want right now, even if my better judgment says not to."

"Then it is decided. I will visit the valet."

"*We* will visit him."

"Your uncle will want you to fish with him for a spell."

"My dear Miss Barrington, know this. I will accompany you when you visit this valet."

So much for distracting him beyond reason.

Chapter Seventeen

Dinner that night was sheer torture. Nicholas sat there, trying not to devour Iris with his gaze, avoiding having their eyes meet down the table. Instead, he conversed with Lady Kelmsly about something, nodding and smiling while his mind relived that hour, and counted the minutes until he could repeat the performance.

"Hollinburgh." His aunt Dolores's low voice penetrated the din around the table to call for his attention. He gave it to her.

"I thought you should know that tomorrow night at dinner we will have two additional guests. Miss Paget and her mother are coming over from Stevening, where they are visiting her ill cousin."

He managed to contain his annoyance and say something appropriate. When he had finally seen the guest list, he had been relieved that no appropriate young ladies had been invited. Agnes would know that at a party several generations removed from that of debutantes, to have one or two present would create expectations and gossip. It appeared that Dolores refused to be deterred, and she had arranged for her preferred young lady to appear. Mrs. Paget must have scoured her whole family tree to find a relative who resided within two hours of Melton Park.

He did not want to dance attendance on this girl. He was not in the mood for demure and appropriate. He fully intended to spend what time he could on worldly and ravishing instead. He had no intention of marrying Miss Paget or anyone like her, and duty to the title be damned.

The party retired after an interminable time playing cards in the drawing room. He subtly managed to walk a few paces with Iris as the guests moved to the stairs.

"May I visit later?"

"Only if you promise not to tire me so much that I am not fit for our outing tomorrow," she murmured while she sent a smile in the direction of one of the elderly guests.

"Sooner rather than later then."

"Unless you want to find me asleep."

"I could wake you, slowly."

The glance she shot him was so sinful that he almost tripped. "Perhaps I will make it a point to be asleep then."

He moved away lest he turn into the worst ass then and there. He bid the guests good night and urged them up the stairs.

Iris straightened and rose up over him. She shifted and squirmed until he filled her completely. The way he made her quiver down there had her swaying in a blissful pleasure.

"Come here." He eased her down over him and took her breast in his mouth. The new sensations at her breast shivered down to join those below, intensifying them so she came alive there, and very conscious of how he stretched her and felt inside her. She felt herself becoming frantic in her pleasure and anxious for the resounding end she had known in the afternoon.

His mouth still busy, his hand slid between them and he touched and pressed at the nub that screamed with sensitivity. She lost control in mere moments, and he sent her over the edge to where pleasure split apart and flowed through her blood.

She collapsed on him, spent. A caress on her back. A kiss on her cheek. Then he grasped her hips and began moving in her. She gasped at how quickly her own arousal returned and at the heights it renewed. Only this time it centered on where they joined, and the quivers became demanding aches and astonishing echoes of orgasm, like soundless calls to experience it again.

She did. Thoroughly and totally with more power than she had known before. And still he thrust, holding her to a ravishment that left her breathless.

She lay atop him while her senses righted and she collected herself. Their embrace made them one, as did their minds in the aftermath.

"What an excellent idea my aunt had with this house party," he said.

"Thank you."

He lifted her shoulders and looked in her eyes. "Are you saying you encouraged her so we could be together like this?"

"Not for that reason, although the possibilities did not escape me."

"I confess the notion did not vex me nearly as much as it would have normally once I also realized the possibilities. Of course, you could have just stayed after your time in the library, and we could have taken our pleasure without the trouble of all these guests."

"Is that why you asked me to do the appraisal? Because you saw possibilities there too?"

He quirked half a smile. "It entered my mind."

She rolled off him and nestled against his side with his arm around her. Such sweetness she experienced like that. Comforting and peaceful and protected. She understood the way sating desire created bonds, but this was different. She dared not contemplate how or why. The poignancy frightened her a little.

She angled her head so she could look up at his profile. A bittersweet sensation stabbed at her heart.

"Does this mean you have decided we are not enemies?" she asked.

"I never saw you as an enemy. A source of vexation, yes. Baggage full of trouble. Reckless and far too desirable. But not an enemy." He turned on his side so they faced each other. "However—"

She waited for it. He would not be Hollinburgh if he did not try.

"Suppose you are right about all of this, and we find the Psalter. What then? Time has passed, as have the men involved. How do you think to rectify the damage done? Will you take out an advertisement in the *Times* announcing it?"

He said the last as a joke, but she did not laugh. "I will inform anyone who disparages my name or my grandfather of the truth. And refer them to you, for confirmation."

Not laughing now. Not even smiling. "If it is true as you say, what could the reason be? I can't think of one."

"Nor I. Yet your uncle believed me. Hence the legacy."

"If he saw it as compensation, isn't that enough?"

Was it? Could it be? She had embarked on this little crusade full of righteousness. The inheritance blunted her outrage a lot. As, she suspected, it was intended to.

"I do not want this to be tainted with the past," he said quietly, before he kissed her cheek. "Let us be done with this."

She heard an offer in his soft words. One of more intimacy, and no barriers. Her heart twisted with yearning. She kissed him, because there was nothing to say.

"You should probably go now," she said a short while

later. "We must leave early tomorrow, since Miss Paget will be arriving in the afternoon, and you should be here."

She heard a sigh beside her. "You heard about that, did you?"

"Your aunt Dolores made sure that I did. I think she is suspicious of us."

"If either aunt is, it would be Dolores who saw it." He sat up and reached for his banyan.

She did not expect him to disavow any interest in Miss Paget, so she was not disappointed. He had to marry such a woman.

He turned again to embrace her and give a parting kiss. She smiled into their locked lips. "Did you think to get me at a weak moment and convince me to stop my little quest?"

"Hell. It works the other way, I'm told. Women convince men of all sorts of things in such moments." With that he strode to the door. "We will leave at nine, if you can be ready by then. I'll meet you in the reception hall."

She laughed to herself. She would never betray other women by revealing the truth. Men lose power in the act of love. Women gain it.

"We are arriving soon, Your Grace." The coachman's muffled voice interrupted a furious kiss.

Nicholas released Iris with regret and helped her right her garments. He opened the carriage curtains so the passing air could cool them both down.

"I probably look a fright." She tucked tendrils of hair back into place, then pinned on her hat. "You are very naughty. I should have guessed your intentions when I saw the coach. It is hardly needed for a journey this short."

"I would have gone mad riding in an open carriage. Forgive me for being so ruled by desire."

"I don't mind." She leaned forward and kissed him on

the lips, tempting him to order the coach on a detour of at least half an hour.

She looked out the window at the river they drove along. In the distance the manor house loomed. "It is a handsome property," she said.

"He received it because he likes to hunt and fish, and it has good forests and the river. My grandfather was judicious in his bequests."

"Shouldn't the last duke have received this property?"

"Not all families entail property. Ours has only entailed the major ones. Each duke is free to bequeath the other lands to whomever they choose. Or even sell it, not that any of my ancestors would do that. For some reason, my grandfather decided to give each son some property. It is probably why my uncle Frederick turned to industry to secure his own fortune. The lands left did not produce sufficient income for his needs and preferences."

"Did he also give property to others?"

"All of what he had received came to me. He merely gave the money away, and most of the industrial partnerships." He smiled ruefully. "You might say he gave away the future to others and left me with the past."

Her brow puckered. "I wonder why."

"One can go mad trying to explain my uncle's whims. He was a most unusual man with some odd ideas. Here we are. Let us see what is in this library."

No sooner had they stepped down from the carriage than a servant approached and asked for a word with Nicholas. He stepped aside with the young man.

"Your Grace, I regret to say that the master is ill and will not be able to join you. He told us to tell you to do what you want regarding the library."

"How ill?"

"A physician came this morning and stayed a long while. I don't know what was said."

"I will escort Miss Barrington to the library, then go and see him."

"He asked that you not do that, Your Grace."

"I will see him."

He returned to Iris. "Come now. I will settle you in the library. Then I need to attend to my uncle."

She did not ask any questions, for which he was grateful. The footman brought them to the library and Nicholas left Iris there, telling the footman to aid her in any way she required. Then he went up to his uncle's apartment.

The butler hovered near the door, looking worried. Inside the bedchamber Nicholas found Quentin's valet trying to make a sick room fresher. Even with the windows open the scent of vomit lingered. His uncle lay on the bed, drawn and spent.

Nicholas leaned close over the bed. "Is it the malady we spoke about, Uncle?"

His uncle shook his head. "I ate something bad, I'm told. That was the physician's conclusion from the effects on me."

"Something at the luncheon? No one at the house has been sick."

His uncle closed his eyes. "Maybe it was the lemon tarts. They tasted off. I ended up putting them in the bin for the pigs."

"Before the luncheon was served?"

"After. I saw them before. I favor them. The cook said they were for you since they are your favorites and that there was not enough lemon to make them for the whole party. I came back early and when I returned, they were still in the kitchen, so I took one. I shouldn't have. Too much sun and I was already feeling poorly, but I indulged to my regret." He sighed deeply. "I think I'll sleep now."

Nicholas waited a few moments while his uncle dozed off. It reminded him too much of standing beside a different bed years ago, watching a man weakened before his time, grasping for strength that alluded him. Quentin's generation of Radnors did not have a lot of luck in living long lives.

When he left the apartment, he cornered the butler. "Has word been sent to his sons?"

"He instructed us not to do that, Your Grace."

"I now instruct you to send a rider to them at once. They are less than an hour away and should see him. Tell the messenger to also tell the cook to learn discreetly from the servants if any of the guests were ill last night."

"Yes, Your Grace."

Nicholas then went down to the kitchen. Quentin's cook stood at the hearth, stirring a big cauldron. Upon seeing Nicholas enter, he jumped back and quickly wiped his hands on his apron. "Your Grace!"

"Tell me about those lemon tarts."

"Weren't mine, I swear. Your cook, the one from London, brought them already made. Only six of them there were, on a nice little plate. That one there." He gestured to a small china plate on the worktable. "He said they were for you alone, since there weren't enough lemons in the orangery to make enough for the rest of the guests. Just for you and the lady who favors Viennese sweets. A special recipe, he said."

"Yet they were still here after the luncheon, according to my uncle."

"They were to go back after, when it was learned you were not coming, nor the lady. By the time we all returned to pack up what came from Melton Park, they were gone. Into the pig bin."

So those tarts had been made in his own home, and probably early in the day. They had sat in the kitchen there, and here, for who knew how long. Perhaps they had merely been tainted with some spoiled ingredient. Or perhaps someone had interfered with them.

For him and the lady. That would be Iris. He pictured her devouring those Viennese pastries out on his terrace in London. If she had tasted these tarts, she might well have become very ill. Or worse.

Would the strong flavor of lemon mask the worse one of poison, should someone look to make trouble? He wanted to tell himself that he was seeing more in this than was logical, but his instincts kept calling a warning.

He turned to go find Iris. "Send someone to the yard where the animals are kept. See what has become of the pigs."

"Nothing," Iris announced when she saw Nicholas enter the library. "He told the truth. He has sold the best of it."

Nicholas looked around the library in a distracted, indifferent manner. Iris removed her cotton gloves and went to him. "How does your uncle fare?"

"Not well, but it appears he will mend. I have sent word to Walter and Douglas."

"He did not?"

He shook his head. When he looked at her again his distraction had cleared. "Did you check the cabinets?"

"I had that footman you left with me crawl into the lower ones. Most are empty. There are no secret treasures here."

"I think if there were, Uncle Quentin would have long ago found it."

"If he had, would he have sold it, along with the other rarities, do you think?"

"Possibly. Only he did not find what you seek. He would have said so if he had. He is an honest man."

"Of course he is." Only she didn't really know that. Nicholas could assume as much, being a loyal nephew, just as he assumed his grandfather had done nothing ignoble about the Psalter all those years ago. Her own view of human nature was not so generous, especially where this family was concerned.

For now she would have to accept what her own search had revealed, however. Quentin Radnor did not have the Psalter, and most likely never had.

"Are you ready?" Nicholas asked. "We can still call on Uncle Frederick's valet."

She had worried that the illness above would put an end to that plan, so she was delighted to accompany him back out to the coach. On the way, the butler asked for a word and spoke lowly in his ear.

"I think when we meet him, you should allow me to speak with him alone," she said once they were seated in the coach.

"I disagree."

"He will never reveal anything if you are there."

"He will probably reveal more if any questions come from me."

"Because of the authority of your title? Because the duke requires an answer?"

No reply to that, but his expression said, *Exactly.*

"You can be very charming in your assumptions," she said. "He will never tell us what I need to know if you are present, precisely because of who you are."

"If a duke tells a servant to speak, the servant tends to speak."

"He is no longer a servant, and he was never your servant. He was your uncle's servant. Your uncle made very sure that he would not speak to you, or anyone. Why else give such a young man that pension?"

"Because my uncle was by nature a very generous man."

"Not to his family. Those pensions paid off the servants for their silence. The money also ensured they would not be available to be asked lots of questions.

"Such cynicism does not become you."

"I know servants far better than you do, Your Grace. I must ask that you allow me a few minutes with him, alone."

He scowled at her. She smiled at him. The scowl faded. He looked to the heavens. "A few minutes. No more. I will also take a few minutes alone with him. Fair is fair."

"Do you promise to tell me what you learn, no matter what it is?" she asked.

"Do you promise the same?"

It was not a promise she thought it wise to give. His gaze turned a little smug.

"On another topic, tell me, Iris. Do you favor lemon tarts?"

An odd question. "They are among my favorites."

"Mine too. We seem to have this is common, along with so much else."

Their locked gazes spoke of the "so much else," with warmth.

"Did you ever mention how much you enjoy lemon tarts, in the company of anyone at the house?"

An even odder question. "I believe I may have. The first afternoon. We were on the terrace and strawberry tarts were served. I mentioned how good they were, but how I prefer lemon."

"Who was there?"

"Why do you ask?"

"Indulge me. Who was with you when you mentioned that?"

She pictured that terrace in her mind. "Most of the ladies, and also your uncle Felix and uncle Quentin. Both had just arrived. The refreshments were really for them, but of course all the ladies wanted some too. Your cook from Town had taken command of the kitchen, and the treats were extremely good."

He appeared to ponder that.

"Again, why do you ask?" she prodded.

"I'm not sure. However, it might be a good idea not to eat anything prepared especially for you during the rest of the house party. I have reason to think that Quentin was accidentally poisoned with lemon tarts intended for us."

Chapter Eighteen

It took a good hour to arrive at their destination. Nothing was said about the time, but Iris approached the valet's cottage aware of the sun moving in the sky. They would have to make quick work of this in order to return in time for the duke to be present when Miss Paget arrived.

He seemed oblivious to that appointment, however. Perhaps he intended not to be present for that greeting. If he did not favor this girl, he might wait to see her at dinner, thus making clear his lack of interest.

She knew better than to hope for that. None of that, of Miss Paget or the girl who replaced her, involved her. The marriages and alliances among the aristocracy existed in another world, one that had a gate that never opened for such as she. Oh, this inheritance might allow her to visit for parties or dinners, even for calls and gossip, and certainly for pleasure and even love, but their marriages had rules and requirements that did not include her.

Nicholas had written to the valet yesterday, saying he would call, so Mr. Edkins was waiting for them at the door of his handsome half-timbered cottage when they approached. He was a man of perhaps fifty-five, with closely cropped brown hair and spectacles. He affected the dress of a country squire and wore high boots and a quite decent frockcoat of rustic tweed. He ushered them into a nicely appointed sitting room and invited them to sit. He himself remained standing, a habit, perhaps, from his servant years.

Nicholas introduced her. Did she only imagine that Mr. Edkins's gaze sharpened on her for a second? His expression otherwise remained in the bland demeanor that servants learn to use.

"Perhaps you knew of my grandfather?" she said before the duke could command the discussion. "He was a bookseller and had dealings with your master's father."

"I don't recall ever meeting him."

She gave the duke a sharp look, then shot a glance to the window. He almost sighed, but he drew himself up. "Edkins, I am going to take a brief turn in that fine garden you have out there. Miss Barrington would like to speak with you in private about a matter that concerns her, if you would be so good as to indulge her."

"There is a lake no more than seventy yards beyond the door, Your Grace. It is very pleasant there, with good fishing."

"No time to fish, I'm afraid, but I will stroll down to it."

Once the duke was gone, Iris addressed Mr. Edkins. "I hope you can help me. I think you recognized my name, you see. I beg you to tell me if you did."

Still bland. Still reserved. Not so deferential now, however. "The name may have rung a bell, so to speak."

"Do you recall why?"

He paused and his brow puckered in thought. "Did you write to my lord per chance?"

"I did. The winter before he passed away."

"I do recall his receiving that letter."

"Why would it be notable? He must have received hundreds of letters. Please, I know you are bound to discretion, but this is very important to me. He left me a very large bequest, you see, and no one can understand why."

The news of this bequest did not surprise him, or at least

he showed no such emotion. "How fortunate for you. I'm afraid I don't understand why either."

"Yet you remember his receiving my letter."

"Yes. He appeared surprised by it. I assume that was because it came from the Continent, and you were unknown to him."

"Is that what he said?"

"He said nothing at all. He received the mail while dressing, he opened it, read it, and set it aside with the rest of the mail so I could shave him. I could see he was surprised when he read it, however. That is all."

She heard the finality in his tone. "I have one more question, please. Did you ever see an illuminated manuscript in his possession? Or anywhere in the house? It would have been a book of Psalms, with paintings. Vellum, not paper. Small, perhaps a quarter folio in size."

He turned that bland face on her. "I never saw that, I'm sure. I would have remembered it."

Her heart sank. She did not know whether to believe him or not. He might never tell her if he had seen it. Why should he?

She stood. "I thank you for your time. I believe the duke wants a word with you now."

She left the house. Nicholas waited outside. "He remembers my letter, but nothing else of use," she said.

He barely nodded, then swept past her.

"You are wasting your time, and we should return to the house," she said to his back.

He ignored her.

Edkins was all deference. Even the manner in which he stood in his own home assumed a servile pose. Nicholas made himself comfortable.

"I have need of some information, Edkins. My cousin Chase suggested you might have it."

"I trust he is well."

"Yes. He and his wife anticipate the birth of their first child."

"Such happy news. Please convey my felicitations."

"I will do so. Now, about Miss Barrington. I think you recognized her name."

"As I told the lady, I did."

"Did you also recognize her? Was she the woman who visited my uncle the day he died?"

Edkins's expression broke. His gaze turned wary. "As I said last year, I did not l see that lady. Only her hat, from a distance."

"Did my uncle indicate to you in any way who that lady might be?"

"He did not."

"Did Miss Barrington visit on another day, either in Town or here in the country?"

"If so, I did not see her."

"Why did you remember her letter? That is odd."

Edkins licked his lips. "The letter upset him. At least it appeared that way to me. He said nothing to me, but of course I had come to know him well. He was restless all day, in a dark mood. I can't account for any of it, but I think that letter was the reason."

"Is that all you know? You must tell me if there is more. I understand your loyalty to him, but this is not a minor matter that I ask about."

"I truly know nothing else, Your Grace."

Nicholas hesitated before going on. The questions crowding his tongue were ones he never thought to ask anyone, least of all a servant. He wasn't even sure that he wanted to know the answers.

"I now must ask you about something more personal to

me, Edkins. The duel my father fought. I have been told it was a matter of family honor, and that my uncle commanded him to stand down. Do you know what that duel was about?"

Edkins's face fell. He looked away. "It was a sad time, Your Grace. I had never seen the duke like that. Even his wife's early death did not affect him so. Nothing after did either. Even when his own father died, he did not take it so hard. But, of course, that was different in many ways."

"How so?"

"They were not close. His Grace and his father. He loved your father, however. He mourned him deeply."

The emotions in the chamber were such that neither of them spoke for a few moments.

"It has always weighed on me that I lost him and didn't even know why," Nicholas confided.

Edkins looked at him with genuine sympathy. No longer duke and servant in that moment, but just two men. "When the duke got word that the wound had killed him, he grew very angry. Furious. He said—I will never forget it because he yelled it more than spoke it—*What a shocking and terrible waste. I told him it didn't matter to me. That I could live it down.*"

"Are you saying that the matter of family honor had to do with my uncle?"

"I don't know, Your Grace. I only know what I heard."

Whatever barrier separated them, it had been breached in the last few minutes. Nicholas decided to see if perhaps he might learn more for Iris.

"My uncle had a habit of hiding things," he said. "Valuable things. I found most of the gold, I think. And the Roman vase. And at least one very valuable book. If you were to advise me to search for more such things, where would it be?"

"He did like to hide things. Those false bottom drawers

and trunks. Did you find the hiding place behind the panel at Melton Park?"

"I did. By accident. We went to hang one of the paintings there, and the nail found no wall beneath the panel."

"I suppose you might look in the attic at Melton Park. It is full of his passing fancies."

"Do you know of anything in particular I should look for? Something of particular value to him?"

Edkins hesitated. His lips folded in on themselves. "When his father lay dying, he was called to the bedside. He was there for some time. When he returned, he carried an ebony box. He was much distracted by the meeting and left that box on the settee in his dressing room for days. A week at least. Then one day it was gone."

"What was in it?"

"I don't know. He never showed it to me. He never even spoke of it. It was heavy, however, but then an ebony box would be. He carried it in two arms when he returned with it."

"I suppose I should look for an ebony box. Something handed over that late in life would be of importance."

"I expect so, Your Grace."

Nicholas stood. "I thank you for agreeing to meet with me, and for answering my questions as best you could. I know that it was difficult. I hope that I have not made you feel that you betrayed any trust he had in you."

"Of course not, Your Grace. And please give my best regards to Miss Barrington."

Nicholas took his leave. He found Iris pacing beside the coach.

"What did he tell you?" she demanded as soon as she saw him.

"Nothing that touches on your search. Most of what I learned had to do with my family."

She stomped her foot. "I refuse to believe that a servant

who knew your uncle so well, who probably knew your grandfather, is so ignorant."

"He may not be, but there are things he will never reveal. He finally told me about a box that my uncle received from his father at the deathbed. An ebony box. I have never seen it, so I expect it is somewhere in one of the houses."

"What was in it?"

"He didn't know, but it remained in the dressing room a week, unopened."

"An entire week?"

"So he said."

"Oh, tosh. He opened it." She turned on her heel and aimed back to the house.

"Iris, you mustn't accuse the man of prying into my uncle's affairs."

"Of course, he pried. What else do servants have to occupy their time?"

Then she was gone, through the door, not even bothering to wait to be received.

Iris sped through the doorway. She found a shocked Mr. Edkins still in the sitting room.

"What was in that box?" she demanded.

"Miss Barrington, you astonish me. I have no idea—"

"It sat in the dressing room a week. You walked past it dozens of times. You had to be curious."

"I would never—"

"Of course, you would. I would. I daresay the duke would. Especially with the duke about to inherit and become duke himself. Something handed over from a deathbed would be enough to drive any person insane with curiosity." She advanced on him. "What was in it?"

He paced away. He fidgeted, his fingers intertwining. "I must insist that—"

"No one will ever know that you peeked. It may be something of significance to the title. His Grace probably would have received it in turn, if the last duke had died in the normal way."

He paused upon her mentioning the title. He looked back at her, over his shoulder. "It has entered my mind that he should have it. Find it. Considering the circumstances of how my master came by it. The timing. His reaction."

"So you did look inside."

He glanced out the window to where the duke waited. "I could not bring myself to admit to him that I had betrayed my master's trust like that."

"You did it because you were concerned, I'm sure."

He nodded. "It was not much of interest, in the end. A few letters that I dared not read. The signet ring."

Her heart sank. "That is all?"

"Not entirely." He faced her. "There was also a book inside. A very old book. I think it may have been the one you were asking about."

"Was he aware you had seen it?"

"I don't believe so, but perhaps he was. He was clever that way. It was the next day that the box disappeared, too, so he may have wondered at least if I had pried a bit."

She went over to him. "Mr. Edkins, I thank you for confiding this in me. I am more grateful than you can know."

He looked out at the duke again. "I expect you will tell him now. He will know."

She gazed out too. The duke leaned against the coach door, his arms folded, his gaze downcast and his brow puckered.

"I probably will. However, whatever was said during this visit, I suspect information about my book will be the least of it for him."

Chapter Nineteen

Nicholas tried to be gracious. He forced his attention on young Hermione Paget even though most of his mind turned over what he had learned today about his father and uncle. She in turn smiled sweetly and pretended that her dinner dress did not cost half the income of Melton Park's harvest.

He wasn't sure that demure was the right word for her this evening. Her entire manner appeared more mature. Even on occasion, bold. She had entered the drawing room alongside her mother and waited, center stage, for him to approach her. The women in the chamber had all but fallen silent at the perfect image of fashionable young beauty that she presented.

Even now her dress was the subject of discussion among the older ladies, much to Felicity's annoyance. Felicity had worn one of her new Parisian garments, and a battle of sorts was unfolding. Felicity had joined his conversation with Miss Paget and quickly turned the topic to Paris and its shops. The two ladies were engaged in a competition regarding which shops were best and which of the best they had patronized. Miss Paget seemed likely to win the prize.

He smiled and smiled and tried to appear interested while he assessed Miss Paget. She knew her own worth, that was certain. He got the impression that if he were slightly less tall or slightly less handsome, she would decide he would not do.

He hated the name Hermione. All those vowels and syllables. Nor did he much care for the little huff she had given when he finally greeted her, out on the terrace, an hour after she arrived. He and Iris had spent too long on their outing, and then he needed to dress, so the delay could not be avoided unless he had chosen to wait for her arrival all day, which she probably assumed he would do.

Duty, duty. Thirty thousand a year. It was a hell of a chant to resort to in order to remain civil.

He managed to keep his gaze off Iris. Barely. As if to emphasize that she was not a Miss Paget, she had resorted to her blue silk tonight, the dress she had brought to London from her travels. On the rare occasions when their gazes met, he saw impatience in her. On the way back he had mentioned how Mr. Edkins had recommended a thorough search of the attics, and she wanted to be doing that, not listening to Aunt Agnes opine about how the army should be called into Town to shoot all the ungrateful demonstrators.

With Felicity and Miss Paget suitably engaged with each other, he excused himself and eased away. Just then, Iris did as well. She ambled to the terrace doors and, fanning herself, slipped out. He could see others out there, so he felt little concern about joining her. He was merely a host chatting with a guest.

"I hope we go down to dinner soon," she said when he sidled nearby her at the terrace balustrade.

"You are hungry, I assume. We were out a long time."

"I am impatient for the meal to begin so it can end. I intend to claim a headache and retire soon after, and then go find the attic entrance."

"Would it not make more sense to wait until I can bring

you there? It is full to the rafters, and you can hardly move furniture and chests on your own."

"I doubt you will be available for a good while. Mrs. Paget has wheedled an invitation for the two of them to stay tonight, so you will be engaged tomorrow morning, too."

"Bold of the mother."

She slid a sidelong glance at him. "She hopes you are so bedazzled that you will propose if given enough time. She really is a very beautiful young woman, and, although her fortune was only mentioned in the lowest of voices, I heard it is stunning. Is it?"

"Larger than most."

"Larger than most of the girls hoping to marry dukes? That is stunning indeed."

He hated talking about this. He didn't like Iris's arch commentary on his marital situation and how it implied that none of it mattered to her. Which it didn't, of course. Her blithe acceptance of that struck him as too cool by far, and even a little cruel.

He closed his eyes. He was being an ass again. What did he expect? That she would weep here on the terrace because he was destined for a Miss Paget?

He scrutinized her profile in the torchlight spilling over the terrace. Eyes bright and smile knowing in true experienced sophistication. Yet he also saw something else, beneath the stars. Fortitude?

"I intend to speed their departure tomorrow morning, now that I know they will still be here. I will announce I have appointments starting at ten o'clock. Instead, you and I will search the attics," he said.

"I will rise early and have a breakfast brought to my chamber."

"No. Eat in the morning room, from the food put out for the guests."

"You don't still believe that those tarts were poisoned, do you?"

She had scoffed at the notion, but he had been the one to visit that sick room. "I am merely being cautious."

"If you insist. I expect others will be about early since they will be traveling tomorrow too."

Fewer guests now dotted the terrace. He ventured a step closer. "Do you still intend to beg off after dinner? I can find an excuse to do so as well."

She giggled softly. "I think that would be too obvious, don't you?"

"I'll risk it if you will."

She turned those eyes on him. "If you can manage it, the door will not remain locked."

He was about to steal a quick kiss when the French doors opened, and Miss Paget and her mother emerged to take some air. They strolled over to the other end of the balustrade, never once looking in his direction.

"You should go now," Iris said. "Your absence has been noted."

He didn't give a damn. He wanted to grab her and kiss her hard, right in front of the two women making it a point not to look their way.

"Go," she commanded again in a whisper.

Duty. Duty. Damnation. He turned on his heel and returned to the drawing room.

"I think they are calling for us to go down."

The young voice sounded right in her ear. Iris turned to see Miss Paget by her side. Her mother still examined the gardens from the other end of the terrace.

"It will be a few minutes still, though," she added.

Iris wondered if the girl felt the need to alert her to the way things were done among the nobility. *I have dined with princes and kings, child*. She glanced at the dress beneath that fair face and blond hair. The pearls looked to be real ones, not typical dressmaker embellishments. The embroidery was no doubt the finest silk. The fabric of the dress announced its high cost and each tuck on the sleeve probably cost ten pounds.

She was beautiful. Truly beautiful, not just fashionably so. Iris wondered what it was like to peer into a looking glass all of one's life and see such perfection gazing back.

She did not want to talk to this girl. It had taken all her composure to play her role this evening. All her strength not to watch the duke with Miss Paget, and picture them together in the years ahead. Quite a picture they made, with him so handsome and Miss Paget so exquisitely lovely. Nicholas would have to be made of stone not to be astonished by her. With little trouble he could probably love her, if that was what he wanted.

She wished she had not come to this house party. She had not expected to have to watch the two of them together, to sit on a bench against the wall while her lover danced attendance on an ethereal beauty who was in every way appropriate.

Even now, standing beside this girl, Iris felt common and ordinary and clumsy. She was not so much jealous as envious. If she looked like Miss Paget, if she had this girl's birth and pedigree, and wealth and family, she and Nicholas might . . . She dared not even finish the thought, but its abrupt intrusion into her head made her heart ache.

"You have made good friends in Hollinburgh and his family, it appears," the perfect beauty said.

"They have been kind to me."

"His Grace seems to enjoy your company."

"That is probably because I am not very English, so I am a novelty."

"It appears you are more a friend than a novelty."

"As I said, the family has been kind to me, and included me in a few parties like this one."

"I have not seen you at any others. No balls, for example."

"I have not been invited to any."

"Perhaps next Season, once your inheritance comes in."

"Perhaps, if I am still in England then."

"That's right. I had forgotten. You are Italian."

"My mother was Italian, as was my grandmother. My grandfather was English."

They did not face each other while they spoke, but rather watched the darkness of the garden. They might have been overhearing each other's thoughts, rather than having a conversation.

"It is good for dukes to have friends," the girl said. "My mother has explained to me that they all do. It is commonplace. My father has had good friends too."

"Everyone can use friends."

"I am only saying that I understand all of this and will not mind if you are his friend."

"How good of you. And how practical."

"It is the only way to be in these matters."

Iris suddenly felt bad for this girl. She couldn't be more than seventeen, if that. What a sad view of life to have at such a young age. "Actually, it is not the only way to be. One could expect more out of a lifelong alliance. Love, for a start. A great passion, if you are lucky. You can have any life you want, unlike most women. You do not have to agree to this practical plan that your mother has written."

As if she knew she was being discussed, that mother looked down the terrace at them.

"But I must marry a duke," Miss Paget said. "This one is young and very handsome, and most of the others are old."

No hesitation sounded in her voice. She had clearly agreed that the plan made excellent sense.

"Well, if you have to submit to a man for dynastic purposes, it might as well be a handsome one," Iris said.

Miss Paget visibly stiffened. She looked at Iris, aghast. "It is not proper to speak of such things."

"Such things are the essence of marriage, Miss Paget. You forget that at your peril. Now, I fear that we are holding up the procession to the dining room. Let us join the others."

"Uncle Quentin has shown good signs of recovery," Chase said. He sat beside Nicholas while the gentlemen enjoyed their port after dinner.

"So I assume because his sons returned here. He appeared at death's door when I saw him."

"Bad tarts, they said."

"Bad enough to kill a young pig and sicken two others."

Chase leaned closer at that. "I was wondering what in lemon tarts could go bad and almost kill on one bite."

"Nothing intended to be in them, I suspect."

"You should have come to me at once if you thought uncle had been deliberately harmed."

"What could you have done? The tarts were gone to the pigs, and the physician credited uncle's age to the sickness's severity. I learned all that you could." He told Chase about the cook making those tarts and keeping them separate for Nicholas and Iris. "I don't think he really made them for me, but for her. She has charmed him because she enjoys his more creative endeavors, and always sends word to him of her appreciation. He was showing off for her sake. Saying they were for me only ensured no one would think twice about there being so few and reserved for the duke."

Chase glanced around the assembly of male guests. "Who? Why?"

"One of us, I assume, if Miss Barrington was the intended victim."

"Only it might have been you too."

"Then someone who doesn't care what happens to me."

Chase's gaze came to rest down the table, where Uncle Felix was laughing loudly with Lord Carrington. "Perhaps Felix, in a fit of pique over Miss Barrington's legacy impoverishing his son, and your own actions regarding Philip, decided to—"

"It is a neat theory, but somehow I don't think he has it in him."

"Well, they all leave tomorrow, so hopefully there will be no more such mischief. Until then, the two of you should eat and drink only things prepared for the entire party."

Nicholas had to smile at his cousin. "I have already warned her about that."

"Good. Now tomorrow, after the guests have departed, I need to talk to you about the investigation into that textile business. Jeremy arrived here late this afternoon on his way back to Town. He believes he has discovered what is going on there."

Mrs. Paget and her daughter retired soon after the gentlemen rejoined the ladies. Thank God for that. Nicholas was all chatted out and only wanted the evening to end. Then come morning, he could pack the girl and her mother off to wherever they were going.

The party drifted out of the drawing room at a good hour but not quickly enough for him. Finally, only Uncle Felix remained, well into his cups. He beamed a big smile at Nicholas and gestured to the chair near him. "Sit and talk. Normally the last night at parties like this go on well into the night, but these old ladies don't have much stamina."

"Nor do I, I'm afraid, Uncle. It has been a long day."

Felix's brow furrowed. "Damned thing, to call on Quentin and find him like that. It must have been a shock."

"Did you go with Walter and Douglas to see him?"

"What? Me? No, no. I'm of an age when attending on deathbeds brings on melancholy. Quentin and I were not close even as boys. I always did better with your father, and Chase's. Sad to lose them both." He swallowed a good amount of the spirits in his glass.

Nicholas almost took advantage of that to slip away, but he hesitated. "Do you know what that was about? My father's duel?"

"Family honor."

"So he said himself." A memory invaded his mind, of begging for an explanation from a man delirious from fever brought on by a corrupted wound. "You know more, I think."

Felix looked at him over the brim of his glass, which again had traveled to his mouth. He set the glass down. "I know very little. Something was said in his presence. A scurrilous lie about the family that he could not let stand. He challenged the rogue and they met, and—you know the rest. When your father grew ill from the wound, the other man fled to distant shores. America, I think. He knew a noose waited if he didn't. You can't go killing a duke's son in a duel, even if it was unintended. Almost an accident, really. Your father shot wide, as did the other fellow, but the other was such a bad shot that his ball actually hit—well, you know all of that. Hell of a thing."

Felix's memories seemed to absorb him. His head lulled down and his filmy gaze aimed at the floor.

"Was the lie about grandfather? Did he call him a thief?"

Felix's head rose. He peered at Nicholas, surprised. "About my father? Hell, no. At least from the little I learned. It was about my brother Frederick."

Nicholas finally left Felix to his whiskey, half relieved

but mostly perplexed. He mounted the stairs but did not enter his apartment. Rather, he went back to the stairs leading to the roof, and finally stepped out onto the walkway that ran behind the parapet.

He walked around to the spot from which Uncle Frederick had fallen, then moved on until he was well away from it. He stopped and looked up into the night sky. He understood why his uncle had favored this place at night, high up under the stars. On a clear night like this one, it was like being under a blanket of tiny lights. One never saw skies like this in London, not even in the parks. Standing here, looking up, it was as if one had a taste of eternity.

The confusion dimmed and the relief had its way. He had wondered—no, he had come close to concluding—that the matter of family honor had to do with that Psalter. It weighed on him, the idea that his father had died because a rumor—or worse—regarding that sorry episode with Barrington had reared its head years later. If it had been that, and Iris proved his grandfather had lied and had indeed kept possession of that manuscript, it would mean that a good man had died in vain.

No, not in vain. The truth would not have mattered. It didn't work that way. Honor was honor. If a man called you a scoundrel and in fact you were a scoundrel, you still could not let it stand.

Even so, her search, her determination, had touched on those memories regarding his father. And he had wondered.

Now Felix had laid that to rest, if he could be believed. Not a matter of honor regarding grandfather, but Uncle Frederick. He tried to imagine what anyone could have said to cast aspersions on Frederick's honor.

He never remarried. Never fathered a child. Possibly someone had suggested he preferred boys. Only Frederick would not have cared about such a stupid rumor. Besides he was a frequent patron of the best brothels in London, and everyone knew it.

He couldn't think of any insult that Frederick would have taken seriously. Of course, it was not Frederick who had challenged a man to a duel, but his brother. Nicholas's father.

Iris had the girl prepare her for bed, then sent her away. Once alone, she made a few adjustments. She removed the undressing gown and let the nightdress drop to the floor before replacing it with another far less demure. She moved the lamp to the side of her chamber so it cast a more distant light. She released her hair from the white cap into which it had been stuffed after brushing. Then she lay down on her bed.

He said he would come tonight. If he did not—well, then Miss Paget had impressed him more than he admitted.

She laughed at herself, but the chuckle stuck in her throat. Even so, he would come. He was a man. He was a duke. She was a "friend." Even if he intended to propose to that girl in the morning, he would not deny himself tonight.

It was a cynical thought, and unworthy of her. Nicholas had done nothing to deserve her assumption that he merely dallied while he courted others. Except he had no choice but to treat this, to treat *her,* as just that. A dalliance.

Her memories drifted back to her first foray into selling books. A few good ones remained in the house after her father died, the final remnants of her grandfather's trade. When her mother passed away and the house quaked empty and the larder even emptier, she had turned to those books and the other flotsam of a man's ruined career. She had found the names of old colleagues and collectors among his papers.

She had taken one rare book to a bookseller in Florence.

He had a shop in the shadows of Santa Maria Novella. Perhaps he took pity on her, because he paid her well for the book, then sat her down and gave her advice. Do not use the name Barrington, he had said. Buy a decent dress. Do not be too proud to flirt a little, because men are happy to be fools for a pretty woman. Make friends for whom you can serve as a middleman, which will spare the high cost of inventory.

She had taken his advice, mostly. She had reworked her mother's best dress. She laid plans to go to Milan with the books that were left. She forced herself to put grief aside and find her own soul again. The only advice that she had not followed had to do with changing her name. Her father had done that, so he would be accepted in the world of art dealing. When she had her cards printed, however, she used the name Barrington.

Perhaps perverse pride led her to do that. Mostly it was an inner anger that their family had been ruined over a lie. To use another name meant accepting that lie had instead been the truth. It meant acquiescing to an injustice.

The rest of the advice had proven valuable. Nor did she believe her name had hindered her much. Time had passed. Few remembered that story imported from Britain. Of the few who did, some were curious enough to see her when otherwise they might not have.

Melton Park fell asleep the way only old homes do. Sounds more felt than heard ceased. A hush blew on the breeze.

Suddenly he was there, near the door to her bedchamber, still dressed in his garments from dinner. He released the tie of his cravat while he walked toward her. He shed his coats when he reached the foot of her bed.

She sat up and watched him undress. Enough light came from the lamp for her to see his expression. He appeared haunted. Distracted.

"You were discreet?" she asked.

"No one saw me. I came down from the roof."

"Were you thinking about your uncle? Did it make you sad?"

"Because he fell from that roof? No. Nor is it a sad place because of that. You can't be sad long under that sky. It breeds thought, not sorrow."

Not sad, perhaps, but still in his thoughts. Wherever his mind had traveled up there, it had not yet returned to earth. Nor did she believe that sorrow did not touch him in some way.

She unbuttoned her undressing gown and shrugged it off. She crawled on the bed to him and knelt to help him finish with his garments. When he was naked, she stepped off the bed and embraced him. She allowed one deep, long kiss, then moved her mouth down his neck and shoulder, his chest and torso.

Lower then, lowering to her knees until she could take him in her hands and caress him. His breath caught when she ventured a kiss on the tip of his cock. She kissed more fully while she stroked him. A moan reached her ears. She ventured further.

It took some time for his regular breathing to return. He held her against his body while he recovered. She had astonished him. He had not realized she was *that* worldly.

As his mind found its bearings, he considered what had happened. There had been little expertise in her boldness. Not that it mattered to him in the slightest. She almost had him begging with the first kiss. Still, he did not think this was commonplace with her.

"Thank you."

She turned in his arms and kissed him, then nestled into

the nook beneath his arm. "Your thoughts did not seem with me. I thought to claim them for myself."

"You succeeded."

"That probably means I did it right."

Not at all commonplace, it seemed. "You damned near killed me."

"Oh, good."

He slid his arm away and rose up on his elbow to look down at her. The waves of her dark hair spread on the pillow and spilled over her shoulders. Even with her lids half closed he could see the bright flashes in her dark eyes. "You, however, have been ill served."

Her gaze slid over to him. "Only if you intend to leave now."

"Heaven forbid. I am a gentleman." He brushed her hair away so nothing hid her body. Her breasts still showed signs of arousal. "In the necessary interlude, I'll tell you about tomorrow's plans while I admire your beauty."

He reached out and gently touched one breast. The nipple immediately tightened. She closed her eyes a moment and smiled slowly. "Plans? Other than saying good-bye to Miss Paget, what plans are there?"

He would rather not talk about that girl, but he supposed they should. "Our parting will be brief. I was not favorably impressed. She knows her worth rather too well."

"When a girl is worth thirty thousand a year, of course she knows her value. When she is also beautiful, her expectations are high."

"Who told you what she is worth?"

"At least two of the ladies. Her mother has never recovered from marrying the second son of an earl and has groomed Hermione from birth to marry the highest title possible. She has been attending on your aunt Dolores for years in anticipation of this Season."

"That was clairvoyant of her, since I only became duke recently, and by accident."

"You were not the duke her mother had her sights on."

"Uncle Frederick? I think I'm insulted to be treated as a mere substitute. Nor did my uncle show any interest in remarrying after his wife died. He found London's brothels preferable, and less complicated."

"Perhaps that first marriage had been a love match and he never ceased mourning her."

"I don't know. He could be odd in his decisions, as you well know. More likely he knew he had plenty of potential heirs if he neglected that duty. My father prepared to take his place with the lords if it came to it. Educated himself."

"Did you as well?"

"Hardly. Even after my father passed, I ignored the looming duty. My uncle was in his fifties then, so there was plenty of time, I thought."

Her curious gaze penetrated his eyes. "Do you dislike being a duke? You said you have accommodated it, but do you dislike having to do so?"

Did he? He was growing accustomed to it. The weight had become more bearable, and he found himself thinking like the duke he was supposed to be. He had crammed the last year full of his own education so he might acquit himself at least acceptably. "Only a fool would dislike it. Few men have more status and power. There are times when I still find that complicated. Also, how it came to be is never too far from my mind."

She reached out and caressed his face. He kissed her hand, then her shoulder. "In this light, your Italian half is very apparent."

"More than half. My grandfather married a woman from Milan. My father married a Florentine."

"Yet your English is perfect."

"That was my grandfather's doing. He insisted we speak

it at home, and he corrected any mistakes in pronunciation or accent. He told my father that we needed to speak it well, so if we returned here, we would not be marked as foreigners as soon as we spoke. However, in most ways my family was very Italian. I was even known by the surname Borelli as I grew up."

"Not Barrington?"

"My father adopted his mother's maiden name when he came of age. It was an informal change. Everyone knew about the Barrington name on those lanes. Memories are long there."

"Was it because of the scandal?"

"It was not only the scandal. He sold pictures, and he told me it was easier to sell Italian pictures to foreigners if they thought they were buying from an Italian. Also, during the war years, it was safer to be Borelli."

"Were those years hard on your family?"

"It was full of changes and confusing at times, but we did not suffer much. We all survived. Then, after it was over, the agues kept coming. That was much more dangerous. There was no quinine yet to help with the fevers like there is now. A few more years and perhaps my parents would still be alive."

"I am sorry you suffered that loss." He pictured her, almost a girl still, seeing all that she knew slip away.

"You did as well."

"I had a family. My uncles and my cousins. I did not face it alone."

"The neighborhood was there for me."

But she had indeed faced it alone. Small wonder that she clung to the memories of all of them, including the grandfather she had revered. "Why did you start to use the name Barrington again?"

"It is my legal name."

She fell silent. He occupied himself with lightly caressing

her breasts, grazing his fingertips across the tips, teasing at them until her breasts filled and swelled in response.

"You spoke of plans," she asked breathlessly. Her body flexed beautifully into her arousal.

"I have a meeting with one of Chase's agents after all the guests are gone. Before that, however, we are going to attack the attics."

"Haven't you already searched them?"

"Not thoroughly. When you see what is there you will understand. There are generations of accumulation. I barely got through the closest deposits when it appeared I had finished with my uncle's things. However, I think we need to look into all of it."

She squirmed a little as he continued the slow caresses and flicks. "That could take a week."

"If we worked alone. However, we will bring an army." He lowered his head and darted his tongue at one nipple while he rolled his palm over the other.

She bit back a moan. "Army?"

"Chase and Kevin will stay to help," he said between licks and nips. "We will marshal the servants. We will empty those chambers if necessary."

He used his mouth and hand more aggressively. Her breathing shortened and her hips rocked. She reached for him, but he caught her hands. He gathered them over her head and continued, enjoying her growing abandon.

"Is the interlude not over yet, Your Grace?" she whispered with a ragged breath.

"I believe it is, but I am enjoying this. I am totally aware of every reaction you have. Every swallowed cry. Every shiver of sensation. You are even more beautiful in your passion, and I am enthralled." He caressed down her body. "I want to see your complete need. Your peak of desire." He touched her inner thigh, then stroked at the damp, soft flesh of her vulva. Her back arched and her breasts rose and a low moan emerged. He caressed more deliberately, and a melody of frantic cries poured from her. They rose along with her increasing madness until, with a scream, she crashed into her completion.

He released her hands and knelt between her legs. He lifted her hips and drove into her, holding her legs to his hips, watching still as he brought her with him once more until his own finish blinded him.

Chapter Twenty

The army arrived. Nicholas served as field marshal, with Chase and Kevin as his generals. "We are going to methodically search these attic chambers," he announced to the troops.

Eight footmen faced him. They and the gentlemen were down to their shirtsleeves, their coats stacked in one of the servant bedchambers that flanked the corridor leading to the attic storage that occupied one end of the roof. Iris and Minerva sat on an old sofa at the other end of the corridor. Rosamund stood, journal and pencil in hand.

"We will remove every item of furniture and deposit it in one of the servant chambers after one of the three of us does a thorough search of it," Nicholas continued. "You are to bring me anything you find that appears to be of value. If I decide it is, you will bring it to Miss Barrington to judge further. In particular, we are hoping to find a medium-sized black box. If you see such a thing, alert me at once."

Orders issued, they began. The attic chamber was so stuffed with the flotsam of past Hollinburghs that only two of them could enter.

"So this is where those animals went," Chase said when

they opened the door. "At least you relieved the house of these."

Nicholas almost groaned when he saw the taxidermy facing them. These used to be displayed on the primary landing here, growling and striding in frozen gestures. They were among uncle's most eccentric decorating choices. He gestured for the footman to haul it all out.

Chase commandeered three other footmen to make more room. Then they began removing furniture to create an aisle down the center.

Nicholas watched a large, heavy desk hauled out. The servants set it in the corridor and he went to work on it. He had examined it eight months ago and found some gold coins tucked deep into one of the drawers. Now he checked every other inch and began feeling for false bottoms.

"Use this." Kevin handed him a long measure. "Outside then inside. You will know at once if there is a space below what appears to be the bottom."

"I knew you would prove useful."

"It was Rosamund's idea."

Halfway down the corridor, Rosamund was jotting something in her journal.

A servant squeezed past Chase and carried over a small statue. "Looks like gold, Your Grace."

Not gold, but gilt. Still, the statuette appeared to be a quality item. "Bring it to Miss Barrington."

And so it went. Once they had their aisle, things progressed more quickly. An array of objects surrounded Iris's feet while she and Minerva wrapped others in old linens. Those must be the valuable items, Nicholas assumed. They looked like two servants themselves, all covered in aprons and caps to protect their garments from the dust growing thick in the air. He ordered more windows opened and returned to his labors.

His attention remained on the attic, but his deeper thoughts dwelled on last night and this morning. Seeing Miss Paget off had been a trial, especially after the deep intimacy with Iris. His polite farewell had been met with knowing smiles from the girl, her mother, and his aunt Dolores. All three probably knew too well the financial situation with this estate, and fully expected him to avail himself of the girl's beauty and fortune. Only a fool would think twice.

Not only was he thinking twice, but he had also cursed silently all the way back into the house. Such a marriage might be tolerable if Iris agreed to continue as they were. She said she was never a mistress, but they could be lovers. Only he knew, he just *knew*, she would not agree at all.

Nor did he really want her to. Such arrangements were common and accepted at large. But even if society knew, even if Iris was openly acknowledged as his paramour, even if she was received when she attended dinner parties on his arm and no one even whispered when he danced with her at balls, it would still be—unseemly. An odd word, but there it was. Insulting to her, and a living lie by him.

He scoured each cabinet three times over, half hoping he would find a huge hoard of those damned gold coins, so thirty thousand a year would not taunt him.

"Your Grace." The young voice spoke loudly from within the attic.

Nicholas left his current position and walked down the aisle. A young footman stood in front of a table. On top of it was a black box. Nicholas's heart rose to his throat on seeing it. It was small enough for a man to carry, but large enough to hold quite a lot.

He opened it with a hard thrust and peered inside. Time froze for a moment. Then he laughed. Dolls. The box was full of old dolls. He glanced to the wood. Not ebony. The box had been painted black and was of low quality.

He returned to the corridor and his search. He tried to ignore what his reaction had been on first seeing that box. Both horror and elation had crashed through him, the first for the implications for his family, and the second for what it meant for hers.

The strange part had been which emotion had been stronger.

"This is quite a haul," Minerva said while she wrapped an ivory goddess in an old towel.

"Dukes don't stint on their decorations."

"How much do you think it is all worth?"

Iris had been keeping a running tally to the extent she could, but so much had been dragged out of that big attic that she had lost count. "I'll know better when I see Rosamund's inventory. I'd say with little effort it would all go for maybe ten thousand."

"No black box, though."

Iris glanced to Minerva. She was showing more now, and Chase had only agreed to her joining them if she sat back here, away from the worst of the dust, and if two windows in flanking chambers were open to allow a cross breeze. Even so, Iris thought Minerva should retreat soon and rest.

"No black box." Her spirits had been high when they began. Partly that was some of the euphoria left over from her night with Nicholas. Even watching him take his leave from Miss Paget had not dimmed that too much, although spying on him from a high window had said more about her feelings than she wanted to admit.

The passing hours had been matched by growing disappointment. They were far into that attic now. She thought it unlikely that the last duke, upon receiving that box from his father, had dug his way all the way back, through furniture and chests and old carpets, to hide it.

Minerva shifted on the sofa. She set her bundle down and stretched her back.

"You are growing uncomfortable," Iris said. "You should go below and rest."

"It is not my condition, but these cushions. Dukes may not stint, but one of them did with this seat. There is not nearly enough down beneath me."

Iris did not say that her cushion was just fine, and that Minerva did not want to admit defeat. "It appears they are almost finished. Four hours of hard work for all of them. Too long for you to be tortured by an uncomfortable cushion."

It did appear that they were finishing. Chase walked toward them. "We are done. Come with me, darling. You are no longer needed here."

Minerva took his hand and rose, with some difficulty. She bent and kissed Iris. "I can see from your expression that this did not end as you had hoped. Come and see me if you want. I think Chase and Nicholas will be sequestered in the morning room dealing with other matters after this."

Rosamund handed her journal to Nicholas. "It seems to me that the good furniture from storage might remain in the servants' chambers, and their old furniture placed out of sight instead. If you agree, you might simply give them all an hour or so to decide where to place what."

She and Kevin followed Chase and Minerva to the stairs. The servants filed by. Finally, Nicholas came over to Iris.

She stood and shook out her apron. A cloud of dust rose. She pointed to the wrapped bundles. "There are many good items here. There is no reason to put them back. You should have them removed to a chamber below where they can be brought to Town and put in one of the good auctions. I'm sure that they will fetch—"

"Iris."

She turned her attention from the bundles to Nicholas.

"You did what you could. I thank you. I suppose I need to accept that all the searching may not result in what I seek. Mr. Edkins must have made a mistake."

"Iris, I'm sorry."

"Are you? Family honor is very important to your sort. Your own father died protecting it. Perhaps your uncle burned that book, if it was evidence that his father had done something ignoble. Why not? It wasn't as if he cared about its importance or value. Maybe—"

He pulled her into his arms and smoothed his palm over her cheek. "Hush now. You are disappointed and I understand that. I was more than half hoping we would find it, and you would have your proof. I will continue looking for you until there is nowhere left to search."

She rested her forehead against his chest and struggled to contain her desolation. Her heart apologized to her grandfather for failing.

"Come," he said. "It is dusty and dirty up here."

She touched his offered hand but withdrew her own. "I will come down soon. I want to accommodate myself to this first."

"I will seek you out after I am done with Chase." He kissed her and left.

Tears flowed as soon as his steps faded on the stairs. The servants would return soon to clean and dust and make their chambers livable again. She would be an intrusion.

She sank back onto the sofa and allowed herself to wallow in disappointment. She shifted, because the sofa no longer felt as comfortable as before. She realized she was sitting where Minerva had sat for all those hours. More curious than sad now, she eyed the cushions.

She stood and looked at the whole of it. All the cushions appeared the same. She pressed where she had sat during the search and it felt like typical upholstery, all plump with down. She pressed where she had just sat, and it felt very different.

She placed both hands on the cushion and put her weight into it. Instead of giving way, the cushion hit something hard. The furniture makers had sold a duke a seriously flawed item.

Curious, she felt all around the cushion. To her surprise, the fabric at the back was loose. She pulled it up at one corner and it fell back, as if it had never been tacked down. She pulled harder and it folded away.

She stared at what she had uncovered.

There, nestled into the down of the cushion, covered with a thin layer of white fluff, she saw a black box.

She pushed away the down that covered it and lifted it out. It was smaller than she had expected, no more than a foot square and at most six inches high. She set it on the other cushion. With trembling hands, she opened it. Her breath caught.

Inside was an old book bound in ancient leather. Not daring to hope, she lifted the front of it and paged through. A manuscript. A Psalter. She stopped when she saw the illumination of David as king, seated like Christ in Majesty.

She lifted it out to examine it better and saw that a folded paper rested beneath it. Her heart beat hard. Perhaps it was the correspondence from her grandfather, arranging the sale to the duke.

She flipped it open but immediately folded it again. Correspondence to be sure, but not what she sought. She had glimpsed a feminine hand. Disappointed, she dropped it back in the box. She had no desire to intrude on the personal letters of the Radnor family.

Turning her attention back to the Psalter, she noticed the letter again out of the corner of her eye. She could see the recipient's address, since the letter had landed with that side up. Her heart began beating so hard that her head ached. *Reginald Barrington . . . Firenze . . .*

Her grandfather's name.

Her hand trembled when she lifted the letter again. This time she read it.

For the first time in her life, she thought she was going to faint.

"I told Jeremy to stop here since it was on his way back to London. It will save time," Chase said. "His wife, Elise, contributed to what you will be told but she is above, resting."

Nicholas examined the young man sitting across the table of the morning room. The remains of a meal were being cleared by two footmen. Chase and Minerva flanked Jeremy, and all faced the duke, their client.

He knew enough about Chase's profession to remember that this young man had started in Minerva's employment long before she and Chase formed an alliance of both marriage and business. He was a tall fellow, with chiseled features and longish hair. He currently wore the garments of a worker, but Nicholas had seen him before dressed like a gentleman. One of Jeremy's talents was the ability to appear a part of any company he kept.

Minerva pushed a vellum document across the table. "I asked Sanders for the partnership agreement regarding that mill, in case we need to refer to it."

Nicholas fingered the edge of the vellum. "I assume the news is not good, if you are all here."

"No, it isn't," Chase said. "I fear it may be worse than you expect. Tell him what you learned, Jeremy."

"I arrived in Manchester and found work at the mill easily," Jeremy said. "I've experience in the machines, so between that and Mr. Withers's letter, the mill supervisor was glad to hire me. A few pints after hours with the other lads, and I began learning the secrets."

"Atkinson is stealing?"

"He is, but not the way you might think. Not simply

embezzling from the till, in the typical way. He is using the machines at night, for a totally separate business. Different workers, different customers, different everything."

"Except not everything can be separate," Minerva said. "The building and its costs are not, nor the machines and their upkeep, nor the warehouse—"

"This is why he resisted giving a full accounting of one business. It would lead to questions regarding the excess costs," Nicholas said. "Atkinson is far more clever than I thought."

Jeremy glanced to Chase, then cleared his throat. "The real problem is that other business. It isn't wool weaving. It is cotton."

Nicholas reached for that vellum, opened the large document, and quickly read it to ensure his memory was correct.

"This mill is much like the business uncle left to Minerva," Chase said. "Uncle had conditions that he insisted be included before he gave over any money. In our case, it was the lowest wage that was to be paid. In yours—"

"It was the requirement that they only produce wool, from native-raised sheep. Uncle could be odd at times."

"It wasn't that he wanted to encourage sheep raising so much, as I heard it," Jeremy said. "It was that he specifically did not want to weave cotton."

"Of course." Nicholas had known his uncle well enough to know why. "He always spoke scathingly about the mills importing all that cotton from America. Cotton picked by slaves in their southern states. We have outlawed slavery here. Our navy stops slave ships on the high seas, but our mills buy all that cotton that makes slavery pay across the ocean. I don't suppose Atkinson is getting his cotton from India or somewhere else?"

Jeremy shook his head. "I've seen the raw cotton brought

in. Seen where it is stored and where the yarn is spun. I broke into the warehouse so I could see the markings on the bins, to be sure."

"You cannot break into a property owned by a man for whom you are doing a service," Minerva said. "You showed initiative, as you so often do."

"And I thank you for that," Nicholas said. "I now know how to deal with Atkinson, and this particular partnership."

The table had been cleared and coffee served. A plate of cakes stood in the center. They looked like the kind of delicacies that Iris would enjoy. Perhaps he would carry them up to her. He pushed back his chair and stood, to go look for her.

No one else moved.

"There is more," Chase said.

Nicholas sat again. "More initiative?"

"Yes, and you should hear it." Chase nodded to Jeremy.

"I knew our office was taking a look at the last duke's business associates. Partners and such. With respect to his accident," Jeremy said. "So I got the lads to talking about Atkinson. Elise did the same with the women. He has managers who do most of the watching and such. He visits at times but not often. I only saw him once while I was there. He himself lives away from the mill now. And he does a lot of traveling."

"To where?"

"Not Paris or anything. Not America. No need to go there when the cotton ships here. Mostly, as far as I could tell, he visits London. Not family visits. His missus doesn't go with him. Just him. I had a long night with one of the manager's coachmen over a bottle, and he knew about this from Atkinson's coachman." Jeremy reached into his worn vest and withdrew a piece of paper. "Best I could learn, those are the approximate dates when he was in Town."

Nicholas studied the short list. There were a few dates last year, then a stretch very recently. One at the top caught his attention, however. "What is this here, with the initial date but a star beside it?"

"Not London. They visited the country that spell. This county, as best I could learn."

Nicholas eyed the dates. If Jeremy was correct, Atkinson had been in the county on the day uncle Frederick had died.

"This will need looking into," he said to Chase.

"We are already learning what we can about his time here. His coachman can be bought, I'm sure," Minerva said. "However, I think you are missing that which concerns us far more than that." She reached over and tapped the last line on the paper. "He has been in London recently, but did not call on you, did not request any of your time. His presence in the city was unknown to you."

"Your persistent questions about the mill were a danger to him and his wealth," Chase said. "I have not read that partnership agreement. It only arrived by messenger this morning. However, Uncle could be ruthless in his business dealings, and Sanders is a very good solicitor. My guess is the penalties for not adhering to uncle's conditions in the management of the mill were not ones that Atkinson would want to face."

The implications sunk in. "I have read it, several times. He would be ruined."

"Hence our concern." Minerva tapped the list again.

"Every time Miss Barrington was in danger, you were with her," Chase said. "Perhaps someone was trying to harm you, not her."

What to do? *What to do?*

Iris paced in the library while that question repeated in

her head. A stupid question. An unnecessary one. There was only one thing to do, even if it broke her heart.

For the third time in the last hour, she strode from the library and made her way to the morning room. The doors remained shut. This meeting was taking a long time.

She approached the footman manning the door. "Please tell the duke that I would appreciate his company in the library as soon as he is finished in there."

Back in the library, she tried to distract herself by perusing the Psalter. She tried to appreciate its superior execution, but this manuscript, so sought for so long, now seemed to mock her. Even King David's expression looked like an unkind sneer. *Not what you thought. Not what you expected. Too bad.*

She closed her eyes and dug deeply into her heart for courage. Too much interfered with her finding it. Love urged her to find another path. Cowardice tempted her to pretend she remained ignorant. If she hid the box, or burned it, who would ever know?

She would know. She would lead the man she loved into living a lie. She experienced real pain at that thought. To have waited so long to love, to have assumed she never would, and to have it come to this—

"I brought you a treat."

His voice startled her. His arm reached around her from behind the sofa and set a plate with pastries on the little table beside its arm. "The chef outdid himself. I don't think he realized you would not be at the luncheon with us. I trust you dined with Rosamund."

Her eyes blurred with tears. How thoughtful of him to carry that plate to her, through the entire house, as if he were a servant. How like him to notice the pastries at all during that meeting and think she might enjoy them.

"I was not hungry." She stood and came around the sofa

to embrace him. She savored how he held her, making it last while she concentrated on every touch and warmth, every inch. Then she disengaged and took his hand and led him to a table near one of the windows. "I found something after you all were gone. It was in the cushion of the sofa on which we were sitting. Look here."

He went still while he looked down at it. Then he set his fingertips lightly on the top. "Zeus," he murmured. "Is it—"

"Yes." She opened the box to reveal the Psalter. Nothing else lay within.

He lifted the manuscript and turned a few pages. "It is impressive."

She spoke to fill the heavy silence while he examined the Psalter. "Perhaps the sofa was even in his dressing room and was the one on which his valet saw the box all those years ago. In any event, here it is."

"Yes, here it is." He placed the Psalter back in the box. "You were right. A grave injustice was done. My grandfather stole this and ruined your family in doing so."

"He might have forgotten about it. He was a duke, and busy with many things. The sale of one book would hardly signify."

"I am a duke, and I would not have forgotten it."

"Not now, but in ten years, when your life is full of duties and the fate of the realm, when all that being a duke entails rests fully on your shoulders and time has layered responsibilities on you, you probably might forget such as this."

A vague smile slowly formed. A knowing one. "You are being kind. However, it is what it is, and I won't pretend otherwise." He closed the box and handed it to her. "Take it. Do what you want with it. Sell it. It is small recompense for the way it was used against your family."

She did not accept the box. "Perhaps it would be better

to return it to the man it belongs to. It was not stolen from my grandfather as such. He was just a go-between."

"Yes. Of course."

"I think you should include a letter. It can merely report what is true—that in clearing out the attic this was found. You have learned that it belongs to him, and you are returning it with apologies for its long absence."

"I doubt that will clear your grandfather's name. Or yours."

"Yours is a small world, and mine is even smaller. With time, the accidental misplacement will become known to those who matter."

He drew her into his arms and rested his forehead against hers so their gazes became close and intense. "You are very generous."

"I find it doesn't matter nearly as much as I thought it would." Nor did it right then, holding each other and watching each other's souls. The Psalter and the long search, the mission and their family names disappeared during those few minutes, and it was only them together.

"What now?" The question came quietly, right before he kissed her.

"Now I return to London and my little bookshop and my auctions. And you do duke things."

A shadow entered his eyes, since they both knew what some of those things were.

"Rosamund and Kevin are starting out soon. I have asked if I can go with them," she added.

"I would prefer if you stayed here at least until tomorrow."

"I don't think that would be wise. County gossip spreads fast." She mustered a big smile, then held him close. "Now kiss me properly, so I have something to think about on the journey back."

His kiss was hardly proper. It was hot and impatient and reckless. It was the kind of kiss that could leave a woman weak and pliant and swooning from need. She offered no defense and grew euphoric from the passion.

When it was done, she offered one small kiss on his lips before she walked away.

Chapter Twenty-one

Iris was avoiding him. Nicholas could not deny that any longer. His invitations were declined. His letters received sweet, nice responses that deflected his impatience. Finally, he tracked her to a house auction, but she did not sit with him.

He guessed it was because of Miss Paget. Thanks to Aunt Dolores, gossip was spreading. His aunt had the temerity to write and imply that he should declare himself soon lest the girl's reputation suffer.

"I have done nothing to deserve this," he complained to Kevin while they rode in Hyde Park, far from where they might be seen by any ladies lying in wait. "I didn't even invite her to that dinner, let alone to stay the night under my roof. It was all the aunts. I haven't even called on the girl, which is almost rude, yet there are all these whispers creating something out of whole cloth."

"I'm told you danced with her at a ball two nights ago."

"One time. I danced with three other girls too. One time each." That had only left three more mothers plotting, unfortunately. "It isn't fair. No one wanted their daughter to marry me two years ago."

"You have to marry someone now. It may as well be her. You won't do better financially."

How like Kevin to just come out and say that, as if it was all that mattered.

"Don't look at me like that. You do need the money. It was why uncle married. And grandfather, I assume. The Radnors have a bad habit of leaving heirs too much property and not enough blunt."

Damned if that weren't the truth.

"What do you have against Miss Paget? She is lovely as well as wealthy."

"Don't forget accomplished. At that ball Aunt Dolores and Mrs. Paget cornered me—I am not using a metaphor since they actually backed me into a corner so I could not escape—and extolled her many achievements in singing, playing the pianoforte, equestrian skills, writing poetry, and many other impressive virtues."

"Sounds perfect. You should propose at once." Kevin moved his horse so he could look Nicholas in the eye. "Is the problem not who she is, but who she is not?"

Nicholas surveyed the view behind Kevin's head.

"I thought you had ended that," Kevin said. "Word has it the two of you haven't seen each other since returning from Melton Park."

"Word has that, does it?"

"So it is said."

If Rosamund had told him that, it meant the other heiresses were still seeing Iris. She had not just disappeared. "Miss Barrington has no more need of our friendship. She has found that which she was seeking." Not him, clearly.

"If that matters to you, I am sorry to hear it."

Hell, yes, it mattered. Much more than it should. She haunted him.

"Have you decided what to do about Atkinson and that mill?"

"I have sent Jeremy back with a big purse to bribe information out of the man's servants, regarding his visits here and to Sussex. As for the mill, I am meeting with Sanders in an hour to discuss strategy."

Kevin angled a bit. His expression changed. "If you have an appointment, I advise that you do not turn around."

"Why not?"

"Just don't. You say Miss Paget is an excellent horse-woman? Does she know of your habit of riding in the morning here in the park?"

Did she? He might have mentioned that at some point. If not, Aunt Dolores might have.

"I ask because two women are riding at a canter in our direction. That is why I warned you not to turn around. Once you see her you will never escape unless you want to cut her. Once you are snared you will not make any appointments today."

Damnation. "I suddenly feel the need to exercise my horse at a full gallop. I leave it to you to say something polite when they overtake you."

"I am happy to be of service."

Nicholas moved his horse hard and gave it its head.

"Are you feeling well?" Bridget asked the question after laying some linens on Iris's bed.

"I am fine. Why do you ask?"

"Because you sit in that chair a lot, staring at a fireplace with no fire."

"I am thinking."

"And because King Arthur is on your lap, and you don't seem to mind, or even notice."

Iris blinked and looked down at the large orange mane on her lap. The cat was asleep and sprawled so its back legs hung down on one side.

She had not even noticed him hop up.

How stupid of her to suffer such melancholy. How

womanish to succumb to this heartache. It wasn't as if the liaison with the duke truly meant anything. It was just one of several such affairs that she had enjoyed in her life. There would probably be others. There was no future in such tendres with men of his station. One enjoyed the moment, then looked to the future when it ended.

"I have been thinking that I will return to the Continent soon." She gave the cat a long stroke over his fur.

"So soon?"

"Not right away. I'll still do the partnership of this shop. I fancy having a home to come to here."

"You are always welcome here, even if you don't buy into the shop."

Iris looked up, into Bridget's concerned expression. "I am fine. Truly."

"Don't look it. Don't act it. You cared for him, didn't you? Did he throw you over? Such men aren't particular with other people's feelings, I expect."

"I did care for him. Far more than I expected. Much more than was wise. He did not throw me over, however. Nor was he cruel with my feelings. It was time for it to end, that is all."

"Why?"

Because she had learned a secret that changed everything. And explained everything. "It just was."

"If you say so. I've some fish for dinner. I'll call up when it is ready."

As if he understood Bridget's words, Kind Arthur was instantly awake and alert. He hopped off Iris's lap and padded out after his mistress.

Iris rose and walked to her little desk and the books stacked there. She tried to occupy herself with preparing them for sale. Her gaze kept drifting to a simple, practical book on the back corner of the desk. A letter was hidden in it. An old letter.

It had not really been time to end things with the duke, but it had been necessary.

Nicholas considered all that Sanders had explained. The solicitor had, in his calm, capable manner, listed the various ways Nicholas could confront Atkinson about the breach of contract regarding the mill. Being a very good solicitor, he had not made it any prettier than it would be. The time and costs of going to court had loomed large in the little lecture.

"If he were merely making use of equipment and facilities to conduct a completely separate business, that would be one thing, as I said," Sanders concluded. "One need only sue that business for costs owed. However, it appears Mr. Atkinson was not clever enough to do it that way. Instead, he has taken the business in which you are a partner down this path, only hidden the activity, and profits, from you. That was why he could never supply a complete accounting. Taking legal action will be a very lengthy endeavor."

Nicholas had visions of years of endless legal complications, during which time Atkinson would withhold any income distributions in retaliation.

"I will, of course, do whatever you choose," Sanders said. Sanders knew the condition of the estate's finances better than anyone. Nicholas had heard cautions in the advice, even though Sanders would never say look away and pretend ignorance.

"What I choose to do is hang the man," Nicholas said. "I have another idea, however."

"Do you now."

"Rather than sue him, I will let him sue me, if he wants."

Sanders cocked his head. "Indeed?"

"I am a full partner. Where is it written that Atkinson controls the mill and I remain in the background? I will send a new manager and simply replace his with my own.

He will be barred from the premises. I will also send book-keepers to conduct a full accounting. Let Atkinson complain to the courts, if he dares."

Sanders smiled slowly. "Bold, but possibly effective. May I suggest that if you intend this insurrection that you do it all at once, on one day, and send some strong arms to ensure it unfolds peacefully?"

"I'm sure Chase will know some men who can serve that purpose."

"No doubt. I know a man who would be excellent with the accounts, if you need him."

"Then I will plot the campaign and set it in place. Now, on another matter. What have you learned about Miss Barrington?" He half hoped Sanders would reveal something of what she was doing these days, now that she no longer came to his home to conduct appraisals and searches.

Sanders slid some papers aside on his desk and lifted one. "Interesting that you ask. I have just had a communication from my man in Florence. I don't think I am speaking out of turn to say that the matter should be settled soon. As she had told me, her father adopted another name, which complicated matters."

"Borelli."

He got a sharp glance from Sanders. "As a result, she was known in her neighborhood by that name, and only reverted to Barrington upon taking up her trade after his death. However, I now have received confirmation that Iris Borelli and Iris Barrington are one and the same. We can then assure ourselves that the woman now claiming the legacy is that same Iris Barrington, once a small matter is settled."

"What matter is that?"

"The physician who tended to her mother, and to her, says that the Iris Borelli, born Barrington, that he knew had a small birthmark on the back of her left shoulder. Once she agrees to be examined, that mark, if present, will prove this woman in London is the same woman who lived in Florence."

"Is this birthmark vaguely in the shape of a heart?"

Sanders looked at him. "Yes."

"Examine if you choose, but she does have such a birthmark."

Being not only a very good solicitor, but an extremely discreet one, Sanders merely nodded. "I see. Well, then we have found our third heiress."

Chapter Twenty-two

The letter came by messenger. Iris recognized the seal.
She set down the books she was reshelving and ignored
Bridget's curiosity. She walked back to the kitchen and
opened it.

> *Please call at Whiteford House this afternoon to*
> *discuss a matter of extreme importance.*
> *Hollinburgh*

He knew. That was the first thought to jump into her
head. The terse one sentence. The reference to extreme importance. The command. The signature. He knew.

She debated whether to comply. She had not seen him
since she walked away at Melton Park. Her emotions from
that day still had not settled. She should just let the day pass
without obeying this summons. That was what a smart
woman would do.

Only she did not feel very smart anymore. She felt weak,
and confused, and her heart yearned to see him again, even
if they had a row. Knowing she should not, she dressed herself for such a call, and hired a hansom cab to bring her to
Park Lane at three.

The butler manned the door this day. He escorted her to

the library, where the duke was waiting. The butler closed the doors when he retreated.

Nicholas just looked at her, long enough that she began to worry about womanish things, such as if he no longer found her attractive or whether her face appeared ruddy and unpleasant. He appeared wonderful, as always. Tall and handsome and so very perfect. She imagined his portrait being painted with him dressed just like this, in his dark coats and crisp cravat and fashionably cropped hair, standing beside the fireplace with one arm crooked and resting on its mantelpiece.

He turned and faced her squarely. "I was beginning to think you were not coming."

"It is only three o'clock."

"You tend to be early or punctual."

"I did not want to appear eager."

"And were you? Eager?"

She sat on a wooden chair. "I was curious. So here I am, although a request instead of a command would have been more polite."

"Would you have come at a request?"

Probably not. "What is this matter of extreme importance?"

He took a seat as close to her as possible, at the end of a sofa. "Your legacy. Sanders will be informing you in a day or so, but it is settled. I am letting you know first, before I inform the family. You can begin planning what to do with it."

"That is good to know."

"You do not appear very happy about it."

"That legacy has receded in my thoughts. It has become something that might happen at some point but perhaps not. I never allowed myself to believe in it or count on it." Even now, with this news, she could not summon much excitement. Perhaps that was because most of her emotions involved the man barely an arm span away.

His mere presence stimulated her. She had to build mental walls against memories. She struggled to silence the whisper in her heart. *Who will know? Who will care? It is a small deception.*

"I also wanted to let you know that the Psalter is on its way back to the family it belongs to. I sent along a letter, containing a weak excuse regarding its misplacement all these years. I mentioned that a bookseller named Barrington was ill served by my grandfather's carelessness. Perhaps, as you said, word will spread to those who matter."

Her throat burned from tears that wanted to flow. Finally, at long last. She pictured her grandfather calling her to his side so he could show her a florid, engraved frontispiece.

"Thank you. That was very generous of you. I am grateful."

"I did not do it for your gratitude."

"Then why? You could have sent it without explanation, without laying its disappearance at your grandfather's door."

He just looked at her. Such warmth in his eyes. She could no longer block the memories because his gaze held them all.

"I did it because it was the honorable thing to do."

She had no reply because looking in his eyes left her without a voice, and without defenses.

To her surprise, and disappointment, he stood and strolled away. "I have something else to talk about. A business proposition."

She had to smile, although a corner of her heart yearned for it to be the scandalous sort that she never accepted. Or hadn't in the past.

"I want you to sell the *Poliphili*. That is assuming that you will be continuing your trade at least for a short while, despite that legacy coming through."

It was perhaps the only thing that could divert her attention from the erotic speculations snaking into her mind. "You do? You are sure you want to sell it?"

"I am sure. I also want you to serve as the go-between on that Roman vase. I will give you letters of introduction to Devonshire and any others you want. I would prefer it be you, rather than a solicitor or factor."

Those letters would open the doors to the best collectors in Britain. Her elation for her trade crashed into a numbing disappointment. He was ensuring her future, even beyond the legacy. He was giving her a parting gift.

What did she expect? She was the one who had walked away. She was the one who had not responded to his two letters. She had ended it, and he had accepted that, but he was still a duke. A gentleman.

"I should probably do a sketch of the vase and take detailed notes regarding its measurements."

He walked to the table at the north window. Her gloves and apron still waited there, and her notebooks. "Since it appears you will not be finishing the appraisal, we can make use of your implements." He picked up the notebook, pencil, and measure. "I knew it was done when you did not return to complete your examination of this library. I checked every morning. Your absence said everything I needed to know."

She rose and walked over to him. "What did you need to know?"

"Whether my sense that you walked away for good that day was accurate." His expression hardened. "Whether all of this"—he gestured to the table and gloves—"was just a means to an end. Having achieved your goal, you no longer required any of it."

Her heart tore in half. He was not talking about the appraisals, but about him.

"That is not true. I did not take on the appraisals, or anything else, merely as a means to an end."

He glanced at her, and his expression softened slightly. "That is good to know. Now, the vase is above, safely hidden in my chambers. Come with me, and you can do your examination."

She accompanied him up the stairs, to the level with the ducal apartment.

"The northern light is in the dressing room. I will bring the vase to you there." He opened a door and gestured her inside the chamber.

The dressing room had more space than the entire house she owned in Florence. Big enough to hold four big upholstered blue chairs set in a circle, it also contained another one set in a corner near a window. Beside that chair she noticed a stack of books, along with another stack of ledgers. Newspapers had been strewn on a nearby table.

The northern window looked down on the famously large garden's wilderness area. Someone had moved a small table against it and set a chair facing the window.

He entered, bearing the box that contained the vase. He set it on the table, along with her measure and notebook. She reached for the notebook, but his splayed fingers got there first, pressing down so she could not lift it. His body warmed her shoulder and back.

"It was badly done, Iris. What we shared deserved better."

Her breath caught. She closed her eyes. His body, so close to hers, his voice, near her ear. His hand, so handsome and firm—

"Yes," she said. "Badly done."

"Was it the gossip about that girl and me? It is all so much nonsense put about by her mother and my aunt."

She shook her head. "Actually, Miss Paget gave me permission to continue being your lover. She thinks she is very sophisticated about such things, although I doubt she has any idea of what she speaks."

"How understanding of her."

"That is one word for it." She steeled herself and turned to face him. "I don't belong here. I don't belong with you. I am probably going to return to the Continent. Legacy or not, I will continue as a bookseller. It is what I do. I enjoy it. England is not my home, especially for that." It sounded logical, she hoped. It certainly sounded much better than the real reason.

"It could be. After you sell that book, it will be, if you choose."

"Is that the reason for the introduction to Devonshire and others? To bind my interests to England?"

"It is merely a friend helping another friend. I also think that you will get a higher price for that book than anyone else will, so self-interest plays a part." He stepped closer, if that were possible. Dangerously close. She could slip away. She should. Only every part of her, heart, soul, and body, did not want to and refused to allow it.

He lifted her chin with one crooked finger. "Are you determined about this break with me?"

Somehow, she managed to nod.

He caressed her lips with his thumb. "You are sure?"

This time she could not nod.

"A gentleman does not demand explanations or anything else, but retreats with grace in such situations," he said. "Today I am feeling more like a rogue than a gentleman and am inclined to plead my case."

She saw the kiss coming. She could have stopped it. *No one will know. No one will care. It is a small deception.*

It might well be the last time, but at least it would be one more time. He did not care that he had seduced her to something she claimed she did not want. He did not think twice as he guided her to his bedchamber and undressed her, then joined her on the bed.

Light flowed in through the windows, and he was glad for it. He wanted to see her while he pleasured her, while he used his body to praise the Iris he knew, all of her. He luxuriated in the pleasure and the poignant emotions flowing between them, touching her body and soul as he never had before but should have from the beginning. He shed all his armor and the result astonished him.

He made sure he gave her the best pleasure, slowly, bringing her along until madness claimed her. He kissed all of her, every inch, branding her with his mouth just as she branded his mind with the memory. It might be the last time, but he wanted it to be the best one too.

Afterward, while they lay entwined in the late afternoon breeze, silent in their contentment, he kissed her temple and tasted the saltiness of a tear.

"What is it?" A stab of guilt intruded on his peace. "I made you unhappy."

"No." She wiped her eyes with her hand. "I am being womanish, that is all. Sometimes our tears are of happiness, not unhappiness."

That relieved him. "Do you have a ball gown?"

"I have something that can serve as one. Why do you ask?"

"There is a ball in two days. I would like you to come. The hostess will invite you if I require it."

A broad smile broke. "It is good to be a duke."

"At times it is." He gathered her closer to his body. "I would like to dance with you."

She stilled. He waited.

"Is that wise? To be seen dancing with me in public like that? To require I be invited is bad enough, but if you then attend on me and dance with me, it will be noted."

"I don't care."

"Perhaps you should." She turned in his arms so they faced each other. "You are not thinking clearly at the moment. It is sweet, but—"

"I am thinking with utter clarity."

Her brow puckered. "Then we are not unified in our thinking. If you do this, it will be assumed that our liaison is ongoing, and more than it ever was. I told you I would not be a mistress."

"I am not asking you to be known as my mistress." He kissed her little frown. "I am wondering if you would consider being my wife."

A normal woman would swoon with happiness at a proposal from a duke. Not Iris Barrington. She disengaged from his embrace and rose up on one arm to stare down at him. "You are mad."

"I am a man in love, Iris. It is only right to call it what it is, and to do what that should mean."

"You can't. You know it. My legacy is a fortune to me, but not one to you. I know the financial problems with the estate. Minerva told me. You need Miss Paget or someone like her."

"I will manage. It is improving. You will not be a poor duchess."

She scooted to the edge of the bed and reached for her garments. "I am honored by the offer, but one of us must think straight. You cannot do this."

He stretched for her and grabbed her arm. He cajoled her back onto the bed. "I can do whatever I want. I have shocked you with this. Just consider it for a few days."

Her eyes glistened. More tears. Not ones of happiness. "I can't. I just can't."

He did not argue. He did not express disappointment, let alone the confusion she created in his heart. He held her until she composed herself, then helped her to dress.

* * *

"I will not attend, but Rosamund will be there, so you won't be alone." Minerva spoke while her maid displayed two gowns in Minerva's dressing room. "Rosamund and I favor the gray one. The silk makes it look like silver and under the candles it takes on a hue much like champagne. It should fit you well enough, and my maid can alter it quickly."

The silver-gray ball gown was lovely, and simple in its design. Rosamund held up a headdress. "I brought this from the shop. I thought it would enhance the ensemble." Tiny pearlized beads decorated the headdress, and three discreet white plumes rose from its right side.

Upon hearing that Hollinburgh had cajoled her into attending a ball, her two heiress sisters had taken matters in hand. After one glance, Minerva had decreed that the dress that might make do would not do at all and offered her the use of any gown in her own wardrobe.

"I have told him this is unwise," Iris said. "He would not hear me."

"Why unwise?" Rosamund asked. "You will not even arrive with him, but with Kevin and me. It is only unwise if he attends on you so much that it is seen as a declaration and even that would not be unusual."

"He will not do that," Iris said. "I will not allow it. Such a declaration will be seen as something I do not accept. It would also be insulting to Miss Paget."

Minerva made an indelicate noise with her lips. "Miss Paget's mother may act as if they are almost engaged, but nothing has transpired to lend credence to that gossip. He has been most careful, and most correct. Exceedingly so. It would do Mrs. Paget good to see that he does not accept her brand just yet."

Rosamund, being much more practical than Minerva,

raised her eyebrows just enough to indicate she thought that brand would emblazon Hollinburgh sooner or later.

"No matter how discreet he is, it will not fool the aunts," Minerva added. "It is not Mrs. Paget's reaction that will signify, nor that of society, but theirs. Aunt Dolores tastes victory in pushing her favorite forward and will not take well evidence that Nicholas is distracted by you."

"There will only be one dance," Iris said. "Surely that can be excused as politeness."

"They are not ignorant," Rosamund said. "Agnes was fussing the other day about the amount of time he has spent with you, and regrets inviting you to that house party. She fears you have turned his head. And now the legacy has come through, which hardly endears you to either one of them."

Turned his head. Had that been the reason for that impulsive marriage proposal? Perhaps it had merely been the result of their lovemaking, yet it had moved her to tears. Perhaps he, too, had been touched in special ways and given voice to that.

Love. That was the word he had used, as if giving no thought to it. He had shocked her with both that word and the proposal itself. How tempting that moment had been. In her confusion she had even half convinced herself that she could deceive him forever, and that, if found out, he would not hold it against her.

Impossible, of course. One could not live in such intimacy long before there were no secrets. He would not thank her when her biggest one came to light. It would be enough to kill everything, even love.

"I think the gray one is the best choice," she said, to force her mind to other things before she became melancholy over what she would lose soon. "I have a silk shawl in peacock colors that will go nicely with it. No jewels of sufficient quality, however. Still, I think the gown will be enough."

"I could loan you some jewelry," Minerva said.

"I don't think so. Perhaps I will purchase one fine piece with that legacy. The two of you can help me, after you come along while I buy a new wardrobe."

They turned to discussing what she would need in that wardrobe, and which modistes to visit. Iris enjoyed the planning. She would return to the Continent in style, at least.

Chapter Twenty-three

Nicholas tried to join Kevin's party the night of the ball. Kevin resolutely refused to allow him to accompany them in his carriage. "It is too late to inform Miss Barrington of the change, and she will not appreciate your addition without warning."

"If we all enter together, there is nothing to be said about it," Nicholas argued.

"Let me make this as clear as possible. I have been commanded to allow no such thing by Rosamund, who suspected you would attempt this. You will have to make your own way."

Make his own way he did. He entered the ball alone, not long after Kevin's party did. His gaze lit on Iris at once.

She appeared ravishing in a silver gown that glistened almost as much as her eyes. He saw her laughing with Rosamund, just as a man approached them both. He saw the introduction being made, and the man leading Iris to the dancing.

She danced very well. Of course, she did. Those years on the Continent had taught her much, and a ball such as this hardly presented a challenge. She chatted during the dance, and smiled, and enjoyed herself.

He himself danced. Once with Miss Paget, then with

several other girls to their mothers' glee. He spent some time talking with some lords about a bill being introduced in Parliament. He cornered Kevin for a spell. All the while, he kept one eye on Iris.

Other men approached her. Other men danced with her. Her inheritance now settled, she would be a catch for many of them. She did not have a fortune like Miss Paget, but she had more than enough for a younger son or a minor title. He wondered if any of them would allow her to continue as a bookseller. Probably not. Some would even lose interest once they learned she was in trade. Many more would decide she was worth the risk, since she was lovely and rich.

Finally, well into the ball, he approached her. She stood with Rosamund again, and they both welcomed him into their little circle. After a few words, he asked Iris for a dance.

One dance, she had said. One ball. One final moment, to her mind.

"You are beautiful," he said while he escorted her to their places.

"Rosamund and Minerva helped."

"I did not say you appeared beautiful tonight. I said you are beautiful. You could be in your apron and work dress and be just as lovely."

She looked at him warmly, her expression soft and revealing. The music started.

Bodies moved around them, interchanged with theirs, and separated them. He never lost sight of her. Nor she of him. They might have been alone in that dance. They might have been embracing, not doing dance steps that kept them apart. His chest filled with a heavy nostalgia. He had been careless, to allow a casual liaison to become so important.

When the dance ended, he took her hand and led her away from the dance floor, toward Rosamund.

"Thank you," he said. "It was the finest dance of my life."

"And mine," she whispered.

"Shall we take another turn?"

"If you are going to dance twice with someone, it should not be me."

"I would rather dance with no one except you. Since I am a duke, I can do whatever I want."

"No," she said. "You can't."

They had arrived at Rosamund, whose own expression was unreadable. "I think the two of you have attracted some attention," she said. "Dolores is headed this way."

"Then allow me to retreat," he said. "I'm sure she wants to congratulate Miss Barrington on her inheritance."

He walked away, trying not to think how ignoble a parting this might be, if indeed it was the final one.

"Hollinburgh."

The voice, low but feminine, sounded behind him. He turned to find Aunt Dolores bearing down on him at full stride. He had no choice but to stop and greet her.

"A word, please," she snapped.

She did not look happy. Her expression was more distraught than angry, but her dark eyes looked full of tiny daggers. Both of his aunts were forces to reckon with when vexed, but Dolores in particular took no prisoners.

She continued to advance on him, so much that he had to step back. Then again. They continued like that until his back hit one of the walls. Her mood was so obvious that bodies near them flowed away, as if to avoid the danger.

"How. Dare. You." She whispered each word emphatically, but they came out like three spits.

"I have dared very little recently, so you are exercised for nothing."

"Nothing? You bring that woman here—"

"I arrived alone in case you didn't notice."

"You have her invited then, only to dance with her in a way that creates a spectacle."

"You are the one creating a spectacle. Please compose yourself, Aunt, or remove yourself before tongues wag badly."

His scold caught her up short. She closed her eyes, and after a moment her shoulders sagged. When she looked at him again, he could see she was weeping.

"Everyone noticed how you looked at each other during that dance," she said forlornly. "Mrs. Paget certainly. Her daughter probably. They have left the ball, hopefully only for a short while, but you all but announced that woman is your mistress. She will not do, I tell you. You must break with her at once."

"By 'that woman' you mean Miss Barrington, I assume."

"Yes." She grit her teeth when she said it, as if acknowledging Iris's name pained her.

"Aunt Dolores, I must insist that you not interfere with my life so boldly, especially to the point of cornering me at a public ball and trying to upbraid me in a—"

"She knew him," she blurted. Her words seemed to shock herself, and her mouth gaped.

The woman was beside herself about something.

"Who knew whom," he asked while he took her arm and guided her farther down the wall, then turned them both so he blocked the view of her with his body.

She hesitated. "Her name has nibbled at me ever since she arrived. I couldn't understand why. It had been in the will and had no effect on me, but when she showed up it began this irritating nudging. It must have been her story, about living in Florence. Yes, that was probably it. Barrington and Florence must have raised the memory."

He just waited while she dug a lace handkerchief out of her reticule and dabbed at her eyes.

"When I saw you dancing with her, suddenly I remembered

why that had happened. Barrington and Florence." She looked up at him. "My mother knew him. Barrington."

"I expect she knew his name, since he sold grandfather books."

She shook her head, irritated, as if he were too stupid to understand her. "Not the name. She knew *him*. When she was sick and failing, I would sit with her. Agnes would avoid that duty, but then, Agnes has always been weak that way. So I would sit with her. One day she said she had a special favor to ask of me. She gave me four letters that she had written and asked me to post them for her. Myself. She gave me the money to send them postage paid. One of them was to Barrington, in Florence. I thought it odd that she would be writing to the Continent, but it did not signify much. However, now that I am remembering, I can see that address as if it were yesterday."

Most likely his grandmother had written to apologize for the business about the Psalter. "Did you send them?"

Dolores flushed. "I confess that I handed them off to the butler. A friend called and wanted to go out to the shops, so I asked the butler to see to it instead. I assume he did."

"I think you are troubled by this more than you should be. You promised to do a service for her and failed to do it yourself, but all came out the same in the end."

"It isn't that. I just have this feeling that her family and our family have bad business between them, somehow. I can't explain it. Certainly, you should not risk losing a future that will ensure the estate due to her, of all women."

"There was indeed bad business between the two families, and I will explain that at a later time, when half of society is not watching. However, that old history has been laid to rest, I promise you. It is not something to distress you. As for the rest, I remind you it is indeed my future we discuss, and I shall live it as I see fit. Now, I will escort you to your sister, and I suggest that you sit a spell until you are feeling more yourself."

He brought her to Agnes and suffered a brief conversation with his other aunt. Then he retreated to the terrace.

Dolores's revelations were insignificant and should not occupy his mind at all. Yet they did. They moved around his head, along with other things said and remembered, bumping into questions still unanswered.

It was deliberate. That was what Iris claimed her grandfather said about the lost Psalter.

The ball had been glorious, but also bittersweet. She had hoped Nicholas would come by to talk later in the night, but he had disappeared. Now she sat in the carriage with Rosamund and Kevin, talking about the event the way people do, pretending she had not been disappointed by her lover's lack of attention.

What did she expect? She was the one ending things, not him. She had promised one dance, and nothing more. It was stupid to think he would find ways to extend that dance into something else, at least for this one night.

"Here we are," Kevin said. The carriage rolled to a stop in front of the bookshop. A footman opened the door and lowered the steps.

"I will assist the lady." A man came out of the shadows and held out his hand. Iris looked at Rosamund, who shrugged in a way that said this had not been planned.

Iris had no choice but to accept the duke's hand. She stepped down. The door closed. The carriage rolled away.

"This is bold of you," she said while she opened the bookshop's door.

"I needed to see you, and this was one way to do it."

"You could have called tomorrow."

"I chose not to."

"What of my choice?"

"I require this meeting tonight. Do not worry. I do not expect more than your time."

He was talking in his ducal tone and using his ducal words. *I chose, I require, I expect.* His Grace addressed her, not her lover.

Once in the shop, he walked to the stairs and extended his arm to guide her up. Bridget's door opened a crack as they passed, then closed quickly.

She cast aside her shawl once in the sitting room and lit a lamp. She removed her headdress, then faced him. He opened the window to the garden, then crossed his arms and gave her a long look.

"When we met with Edkins, the valet, he described that box to you. An old book was inside, you reported he said. A signet ring. Also some letters."

"The old book was the Psalter, as you know."

"And the signet ring was on my uncle's finger when he died. What became of the letters?"

Her heart drummed inside her chest.

He strolled to her desk and the books resting there. "My aunt was so angry about our dance that it caused an old memory to emerge." He told her a story about Dolores being given letters to post by her dying mother that, instead, she handed off to the butler. "I asked myself, if that happened in my household, what would Powell do with those letters."

She tried to speak normally, but doubted she succeeded. "Post them, I assume."

"You do not know butlers well. It may appear they serve the household, but in truth they serve the master. If Powell was handed those letters, written by a dying woman to persons at large, he would bring them to me, so I could make sure that unseemly deathbed confessions were not being sent out into the world."

She shrugged, as if such things mattered not at all to her, but she was sickening in the worst way.

"Iris, Dolores said that one of those letters was to your grandfather. I have wondered why a duke, who could well afford an old book, would deliberately hide it and allow the bookseller to be known as a thief. It was not something that was normally in his character, as he has been described to me. Not at all."

"I wouldn't know. I did not know him. Nor did you, not really. And apparently, he did just that."

"It is the why that we don't know. Maybe he would do it in anger, if that bookseller had cuckolded him and had an affair with his young duchess."

"I don't—"

"I think the letter she wrote on her deathbed was to her long-ago lover. Final words, long after they could hurt anyone."

She tried to wave it away, with a gesture that spoke to how wrong he probably was. "That is conjecture and nothing more."

"Is it? It would explain my uncle's bequest to you. If he also read that letter and understood what had been done to your family and why, he might have wanted to make recompense for the way a man was ruined. Deliberately."

She sank into her reading chair, mostly because in that position she did not have to look at him. "Perhaps you are right. It makes a certain sense." She held her breath, praying he took her agreement as a final word of sorts.

He walked over and stood right in front of her. He lifted her chin so she had no choice but to see his face, and him hers. "You found that black box, and brought it to me, and everything changed between us, or at least you tried to change it. You walked away and avoided me afterwards. I told myself that all you ever wanted was that damned book and having found it nothing else mattered, that it was all a long game on your part. That even our passion was a means to an end. Only I didn't believe it." He touched his chest. "Here, I didn't believe it."

"Perhaps you should have. Perhaps it *was* a means to an end, with the end being pleasure along with the book."

He smiled vaguely. "Do you think me so green I can't tell the difference between mere pleasure and passion?"

She just looked at him, her chin trembling beneath his fingers and her heart breaking. *Don't. Don't. Just don't.*

"Iris, I want the letter. Give it to me now."

"There is no letter. There was only the book."

He shook his head.

"I burned it."

"No, you didn't. It was to your grandfather. It explained much and filled a big hole in what you knew about him. Out of reverence to him if nothing else, you would not burn it."

A panic broke inside her. She beseeched him with her gaze. "Do not ask this."

"I must. I only want to read it, as you have. I, too, have holes to fill. I will leave it with you."

"No. If you read it, take it with you. I do not want to see you reading it."

"If that is how you want to do it, I will take it away with me."

She rose. On shaking legs, she went to her desk. She pulled the letter out of a book in the middle of the stack. She handed it to him.

"Take it. Read it, then burn it. Go now. And please do not come back."

Chapter Twenty-four

He waited until he was in his apartment before he removed the letter from his pocket. Like most ladies of quality, his grandmother's hand was impeccable, florid, and totally legible. *Reginald Barrington, Via Corso, Firenze.* It bore no marks indicating it had been posted.

He moved a lamp to his dressing table and opened the page. He read it once, then again. He set it down, stunned.

No wonder Iris had not told him about this.

He read it once more.

Darling,

I write this finally, long after I should have. I pray that it finds you. I do not have long and need to touch you in some way, even at this distance. To see you one more time would be my greatest wish, but of course it is not to be.

I want you to know that he was good to his word. He took his vengeance against you, but not the child. I had a choice, didn't I? Give you up or give up my son. He has not been unkind to him. The world knows him as the duke's heir, and one day he will inherit it all. I have given him other sons. I love them all, but my first will always be special to me.

*He looks much like me, but I see some of you in him
at times.*

   *I pray that you have survived the scandal that he
made for you, and that you take pleasure and solace
in those books of yours. Remember me, and what it
was like being young and reckless, holding each
other heart to heart before the implacable tide tore
us apart.*

It explained much. Almost everything. Why a good man
would cruelly ruin another of lower station and little fortune. Why uncle Frederick had never worried about siring
an heir. If he received that black box while his own father
lay on his deathbed, he learned about this soon after his
young wife died. Perhaps he felt passing the title to a
brother who carried Hollinburgh's blood would be more
honest.

It also explained, finally, horribly so, why one of those
brothers fought a duel in the name of family honor. Was this
still being whispered about then? Everyone alive all those
years ago was probably dead now, but gossip and secrets
have a way of being inherited, much like titles and wealth.
Some old relative might have said something when in his
cups, and the fool who heard it repeated the story in the
hearing of Nicholas's father. A duel was fought. There was
no choice. Such rumors could not be allowed to stand, and
perhaps spread.

This was probably why Iris Barrington had been left that
legacy too. Not merely in expiation of a wrong done to her
grandfather. Not because of that Psalter. Uncle Frederick
had changed his will after she contacted him. A name from
the past had appeared out of nowhere. A name he knew
from this letter. Small wonder he had agreed to meet her
and had left her that money.

She was related to him.

* * *

Iris pulled on her gloves after signing the documents. Mr. Sanders sprinkled the ink so it would not smudge, then folded the vellum. It had been a long meeting, but as always, the solicitor had everything prepared and in order.

"I wish I could bring you with me, Mr. Sanders. I doubt I will find as fine an advocate abroad."

"I am always here for you, Miss Barrington, should you need my services. Do you have that list I gave you of lawyers I can recommend in Paris and Vienna? If need be, they will come to you wherever you are." He gestured to the documents. "When you establish accounts at the banks over there, they will, in turn, aid you in accessing your funds."

"It is all very complicated, but your explanations have given me confidence that I will manage."

"I am so glad that you reserved a goodly sum and invested it in the funds. Not very exciting, perhaps, but quite secure."

"One must consider the future, as you said." The income from those funds would keep her in style, if not luxury. After years of frugality, two thousand a year would be far more than she could comfortably spend. She could not resist, while Sanders showed her the calculations, to do other ones that worked out just how big Miss Paget's fortune must be to have an income of thirty thousand. Huge. Gargantuan. Nicholas would be an idiot not to propose as soon as possible.

As she took her leave of Mr. Sanders and walked through the anteroom of his chambers, her mind turned to Nicholas, as it did when it was not otherwise fully occupied. Two days and no row had occurred. After he left that night, she had expected him to return, storm into the bookshop and up the stairs, and give voice loudly to his shock and dismay. He could not blame her, but he could blame her grandfather. A new familial wedge now existed, one that had started just when the Psalter went missing.

She had thought to spare him. To take the secret away with her, never to be known by Nicholas or any of his family. She could not stay, knowing that, of course. To see him, all the while holding such a secret in her heart would be the worst deception.

Being right, doing the right thing, or trying to, did not mean one experienced any triumph. She certainly had not, before he learned the truth and certainly not now. It made her sad that what they had shared must end this way, but she expected nothing else.

She exited the building and began walking to the street where the hansom cabs waited. Halfway down the block, boots fell into step beside her. She knew who it was at once. She sensed him nearby, then felt his presence as surely as if he touched her.

"You are finished with Sanders?"

"I am, for now. He was very helpful. Every heiress should have a solicitor like him to guide her."

They walked on. "How did you know where I was?" she finally asked.

"I visited the bookshop. Miss MacCallum told me. She is worried about you. Said you have not been yourself. Pining, she said."

"I do not pine. Bridget should be more discreet."

"I am glad she is not. She also told me you are laying plans to leave. Paris, she said."

"It is time to go, I think."

"I disagree. Paris is not very pleasant in the summer. I hear it smells worse than London."

"Perhaps I will go to the mountains instead. Switzerland."

"That would be better, but I doubt there are any libraries being sold there. Here, however, there will be many. The financial situation is getting worse. There will be families looking to sell fine books to raise some blunt. Me, for example. You still have to sell the *Poliphili* for me."

She stopped walking and faced him. "You can't be serious."

"I am most serious. I could use the money."

"I will send you the names of two excellent and honest booksellers who will gladly do it for you."

"I only trust you."

She walked on, wishing he would leave but yearning for him to stay. It felt so good just having him there beside her. Feeling him there.

The hansoms came in sight. This time he stopped, touching her arm and bidding she do the same. She stared at his cravat because she dared not look in his eyes. She had been tasting loss ever since she found that box, and now it almost undid her.

"I have to leave Town for a few days. Word has come that my uncle Quentin has taken a bad turn. I should see him."

"Of course, you must."

"I want you to promise me that you will not disappear while I am gone, Iris. There is much I need to tell you. Much that we need to settle. No rows, I guarantee. Just honest conversation."

She kept looking at his cravat. She realized it was not white, but a casually tied black one. Not very ducal looking at all.

"Do you promise you will delay this trip abroad that long?" he asked.

She finally looked up at him. Warmth in his eyes, and sincerity in his expression. How handsome he appeared.

How strong and magnificent. "I will wait that long before leaving."

"Good. Good." He escorted her to the cabs and handed her into one, then paid the coachman.

She looked out the window at him as the equipage began moving. "Knowing what I did, I could not—I had to—"

"I know. No honest person could."

Chapter Twenty-five

Nicholas, Chase, and Kevin rested their horses at a staging inn while they refreshed themselves with some ale. The public room was not crowded at this time, so they took a table.

"We should arrive before nightfall," Chase said.

Nicholas and Kevin just nodded. This was not a pleasant visit to be making. The word that had come said Uncle Quentin would probably not survive the week.

"As long as we are not riding hard, I have something to report," Chase added. "About Atkinson."

Nicholas turned more alert at the name.

"I received a letter from Jeremy last evening," Chase said. "The man has left again. Scotland, the manager was told. Jeremy, however, used that purse to buy information from a footman at the house, who confided it was not Scotland at all, but London."

Kevin did not like it. "No wonder you kept looking around while we rode, Chase. Seeking out a musket's end from behind the trees?"

"Something like that. You do need to be careful, Nicholas. If Atkinson is abroad, he will be dangerous. The arrival of your new manager and his displacement is sure to have infuriated him. It was probably something similar that had him go after uncle Frederick."

"We don't know for certain that he did."

"Some of his absences line up with the attempts on your life. He was not at the mill when uncle tumbled off that roof. We are inclined to believe he is the culprit of both."

By we, he meant him and Minerva. Only they really did not have any evidence that Atkinson had been behind any of it. Actually, they didn't have any proof that there had been any of it.

"I will be careful. Now, we should ride."

Two hours later, they approached Quentin's house. No black bombazine on the door yet. They had come in time, it appeared.

They handed their horses to grooms and mounted the stairs. A footman led them to the library to wait.

"I expect that Walter and Douglas are already here," Nicholas said. "And the uncles are on their way."

"Uncle Felix and Philip are on their way in a carriage," Chase said.

"My father is not coming," Kevin said. "He did not attend Uncle Frederick's funeral, and he will not be present for this passing either. His refusal to leave the house in London only increases. I fear his eccentricity is turning to madness."

Nicholas and Chase exchanged glances. Given time, without Rosamund to manage him, Kevin might have followed a similar path. Instead, she pulled him out of his mind enough that he was almost sociable these days.

Chase strolled over to the windows. "Walter at least is here. I see Felicity out in the garden. She looks dressed for riding."

"She probably intends to take inventory of the livestock, to see what Walter will inherit," Kevin said.

"That is unkind," Nicholas said.

"But true," Kevin retorted.

The footman returned. "He is awake now, if you would like to follow me, Your Grace."

The man had addressed Nicholas, but all three of them filed after the servant.

Up in Quentin's apartment, Douglas and Walter were sitting by their father's side. They left when their cousins came in.

Quentin was awake but nothing about him suggested he would recover. His breathing came hard, and he barely acknowledged them. They all paid their respects. Then Quentin's gaze focused on Nicholas. He weakly gestured him closer.

Kevin and Chase left, and Nicholas sat in a chair beside the bed. He took his uncle's hand.

"Things I should say to you," Quentin said. "Things you should know. I tried to tell you at the dinner but couldn't bring myself to do it. I need to explain about that duel, and—"

"I know, Uncle. I know why it was fought. I learned recently. I know about Frederick. I know it all. Do not trouble yourself."

Quentin sighed heavily. "We knew. Your father and I. Frederick confided in us soon after he learned the truth from—from our father. We never spoke of it again. It didn't matter. Such things are not unheard of. Not the only title to take such a turn. Probably why our sort doesn't sport those Spanish lantern jaws." He chuckled a little, but that only made him cough.

"I'm glad that you know. He thought it would be your father, but when it was clear it would be you, he was satisfied. He knew you would be a good Hollinburgh."

Nicholas experienced almost overwhelming humility that his uncle Frederick might have believed that.

"I need you to—" Quentin coughed again but conquered it. "Look to my boys, will you? Just keep one eye on them."

"They are men now, and don't need me watching them."

"Douglas maybe. That wife of his is solid. Dull, but then so is he. Walter, however—that woman will ruin him unless he stands up to her. She has his head so turned. Always did."

"I will do what I can for him should it become necessary."

Quentin patted his hand. "That brings me more peace than you can know. With me gone, he will be the heir now. You need to marry and sire a son. I'm sorry to say that neither of my sons would make a good duke."

"I will do my duty, Uncle. Now, you should rest, and your sons need to be with you."

He left the chamber. Douglas waited outside, but Walter had disappeared. Nicholas went in search of Chase and Kevin.

"So do we stay and join the death watch?" Kevin asked.

They drank port in the dining room, in order to avoid their cousins and cousins' wives in the library. Dinner had been a quiet affair, with only the most cursory small talk breaking the silence. Felix and Philip had arrived just as the meal ended, and Nicholas had suffered that particular cousin's presence out of respect for his uncle Quentin.

"I think we can leave in the morning," Chase said. "We have paid our respects and done our duty. Don't you agree, Nicholas? You have been very quiet this evening."

"I have been thinking." Mostly he had been pondering things Quentin had said. An idea had taken root in his mind, one that he did not like but which he could not pull out no matter how hard he tried.

He looked at Chase. "You think Atkinson has come south to harm me."

"I fear it, yes."

"So he may have followed me here, from London. He could have been mere hours behind us."

"I'd rather not believe it, but he could have done just that. Which is why I need you to be careful."

"I can't be careful all the time, all day and every day. What would you have me do? Isolate myself in my home and not leave? Not attend sessions? It isn't practicable."

"We will find him before it comes to that."

"I'm not sure we will. Unless we invite him to act, so it is over."

Kevin had been daydreaming but now he set down his glass. "Bait him, you mean."

"Why not?"

"Because usually the bait gets eaten," Chase said firmly.

"Only because the bait is unaware of the danger. I think tomorrow I will ride to Melton Park. Let the man follow and try his worst. The two of you can be watching and can stop him."

Chase folded his arms. He shook his head, but Nicholas could tell he was thinking.

"It would get it over with, possibly," Kevin said.

"It would take an army to protect you if, in fact, he is trying to harm you," Chase said.

"I will be a moving target, even at a trot. If he dares anything, it will have to be a firearm. How likely is it that he is a good shot? With one of you behind me, and one flanking me cross country, we will catch him."

"I think it is a good plan," Kevin said.

"That is because you are, by nature, reckless." Chase rose and paced. He scowled at Nicholas. "Your plan is that you let him fire but miss. What if he doesn't miss?"

"Then Walter becomes the duke, just the way he always

wanted," Kevin said. "Hell, Chase, what are the chances the man can hit a rider? I'm a good shot, and it would be hard for me."

"Perhaps he won't take that shot. Maybe he will wait until you are at Melton Park and try something there," Chase said.

"Even easier to catch him at it, then," Nicholas said. "I'm not of a mind to live with this hanging over me. I intend to ride to Melton Park tomorrow. I trust you will accompany me."

Chase threw himself back into his chair. "Hell."

Nicholas moved his horse along the road. A light rain kept most other riders and carriages away and he overtook few others. Behind him by a quarter mile, Kevin followed. Somewhere behind the trees and brush flanking the road, Chase kept watch.

The assignments had been easy ones. Chase, as a former army officer, had more experience. His profession as an investigator had also honed his instincts. Nicholas was not worried, as such, but serving as bait proved more unsettling than he had expected.

He kept alert with his eyes, but his mind filled with other things. Most of them had to do with Iris. He would probably arrive back in London to find her trunks packed. Even the lure of selling the *Poliphili* and the Roman vase would not hold her if she was determined to leave.

He reviewed the arguments he intended to use. They seemed eminently logical to him, but he wondered if any of them would sway her. She had uncovered a secret that she did not want to know and removing herself and all that it implied might be the only clear path she saw. He needed to convince her that while the original impulse had been honorable, such a course of action was no longer necessary.

Of course, she may want to go for other reasons. He was not so conceited as to assume continuing their liaison appealed to her above all else. Legacy in hand, she might look forward to returning to the courts and capitals that in the past she broached as a bookseller alone. He could picture her dancing under a thousand candles in a palace ballroom, being pursued by gentlemen and better.

Or perhaps she just wanted to return to her trade. She enjoyed it. She excelled at it. Most men would be loath to give up such hard-won achievements. A woman most likely would be too.

He told himself that he had not misunderstood what existed between them, that she would not want to part if a way could be found around that. He refused to accept that he had been mistaken about the depths of their—

A crack sounded. A musket, not a pistol. His horse reared and he concentrated on bringing the animal under control. A small stand of trees stood a hundred yards off the road to the right. It occurred to him that it might have been a hunter, bagging a hare.

Another shot, this time a pistol. He turned his horse and aimed for the trees. Out of the corner of his eye he saw Kevin coming, riding hard behind him.

Another horse appeared, tearing out of the trees. Not Chase's horse. The rider aimed east. A mistake, that. Kevin turned off the road and angled toward him. Even Nicholas could tell that the two riders would intersect. Kevin had calculated just how to ride for that to happen.

Nicholas went that way, too, worried that they had not seen Chase. If Atkinson had harmed Chase, he would kill the man. He pushed his horse harder. In front of him Kevin's horse ran right into the other rider's. Kevin jumped off his saddle. Fisticuffs ensued.

The rider's hat flew off. Ginger hair reflected the gray light. A man howled in pain. Not Kevin.

Nicholas pulled up right next to them. Kevin was pounding his opponent, and Kevin knew how to box effectively. Already the culprit was a heap on the ground, trying to crawl away.

"Enough," Nicholas said.

"Not nearly," Kevin snarled. "I should have killed him the last time I thrashed him."

Nicholas moved his horse so that he blocked Kevin from continuing. "I said enough."

Kevin walked away, furious still, breathing hard. Nicholas looked down at the cowering coward. "If Chase is in the least harmed, Philip, I will see you swing."

Philip shook his head and struggled to stand. "Not harmed," he gasped. He gestured toward the trees. Chase was walking toward them. No horse. That pistol had killed the animal, not the rider, so Philip could make a good run for it. He had not expected Kevin.

"Don't move. Not one step." Nicholas dismounted and walked over to Kevin, who was still collecting himself. "You did that passing well, Kevin. The slightest mistake and he would have gotten past you."

Kevin rubbed his fist. "It was simple geometry."

"Let us bring him to Melton Park and decide what to do with him. It will be slow going. We are down a horse, I think."

Kevin glared over his shoulder at Philip. "I know who will be walking."

Chapter Twenty-six

That evening, Nicholas returned to his uncle Quentin's home. Black bombazine now festooned the door. Quentin had passed. Just as well.

He made his way up the stairs. Movements coming from the master's apartment suggested the development had been very recent. He thought he heard a man weeping.

He kept going, up another flight of stairs. He checked the doors and found the one he wanted. He let himself into Walter's apartment and followed the sounds inside to the threshold of the dressing room.

Inside, the servant assigned to Walter's wife folded garments, while Felicity herself stuffed others into a valise. Unaware of his presence, she moved quickly. Her expression combined excitement and fear.

The maid saw him and stopped what she was doing. It took Felicity longer to notice him.

"You are in a hurry to leave," he said.

"No reason to stay now. He is gone."

"It is customary to remain until the funeral."

"We can return for that." She stuffed another dress into the valise.

Nicholas gestured for the maid to leave. When they were

alone, he sat on the settee against one wall. "Philip had quite a story to tell, Felicity."

She froze, then returned to her packing. "That would be like him."

Nicholas struggled to keep his temper. "You always wanted to be a duchess. It seems you found a way to do that, once you learned that your father-in-law had an illness that would take him soon."

She faced him. Proud. Lovely. Deadly.

"Philip gave uncle Frederick that push and made those efforts regarding me. Except the poisoned tarts. Those were your doing. But you encouraged him in the rest. It was all your idea, from his telling."

"Hardly all my idea. He hated you. All of you. Once Walter became duke, he would be back in the family. He would have the means to live."

"He probably would have blackmailed you for the rest of your life."

"Regarding what? I have harmed no one."

"Since we are not dissembling, tell me something. Why now? A little patience and it may have all worked as planned."

She looked into the valise and pulled out the last dress. "Maids exist for a reason. This will be ruined if it is not folded properly." She cast it aside. "You were going to marry. Miss Paget, or someone else. Once you did, if there were an heir—Walter would have been too far removed from the title. A waste then."

A waste. He assumed she meant killing Frederick. "Did you visit him that day, at Melton Park? In the garden?"

"I came to ask for money. There are some debts. Philip had some too. Many. So I came to petition him. He refused. He had so much, and he refused." She spit the last words. "I was angry. Philip had accompanied me, to get his share.

He was angrier. He wanted to argue our case further." She shrugged. "And Hollinburgh fell. An accident."

"You were quick to cast suspicion on Kevin."

"He is too peculiar to like, and he can be very cruel with that ugly wit of his. No one would mourn him much."

And she and Philip had concocted explanations for their own absences from London, but far from Melton Park.

"It must have shocked you both to learn Hollinburgh had changed his will and that accident would not benefit either of you much." He stood. "Did Walter know about any of this?"

She laughed. "He would have prayed a fever took you before you had an heir, then felt guilty for inheriting. He was not the man for this. Or much else. At least now there is the inheritance from his father. That is something, at least."

"Not for you."

She stared at him over the gaping valise. Bits of lace and silk still spewed over its edges. "Of course, for me. I am Walter's wife."

"Yet your marriage is a disappointment to you, it seems. In many ways. That makes this easier."

She stared at him boldly, but he could see her confidence breaking. "This?"

"I am offering you the same choice I just gave Philip. He is returning to London with Kevin. He will take leave of his father here, then journey to Town at once and hop the next packet. He will never return. A difficult life awaits him, but at least he will not hang. Of course, this choice depends on your being on that packet too."

"I'm not going anywhere."

"Then he will not either because he will be needed here to lay down information against you." He advanced on her. "I will not pretend this did not happen and let you go free here, living as if you did not plot in a most heinous way.

I don't care what scandal it creates for the family. Believe that, lest you choose badly."

She tried to hold her composure, but her expression cracked. Desperation entered her eyes. "I will need money."

"Take your jewels and your dresses and whatever else is your personal property. But remove nothing from Walter's home. Certainly not his children. You are to return to London immediately. I will send servants up for your baggage. Chase will accompany you and a carriage is waiting."

"Walter—"

"You can tell him whatever you choose. Or I can explain it all after you are gone."

She sniffed and wiped her eyes. She found her composure. "Tell him nothing. He is more likely to send me money if he thinks I might return."

Chapter Twenty-seven

Iris watched while the workmen carried in the new table. She had them set it in the back kitchen. She had created a little space at one end that, with some effort, might be thought of as a dining room.

Bridget sidled up next to her. "Fine wood. Too fine for this place."

"Not too fine for you, though."

"You've been spending a lot of money these last days. Off with your fancy friends to dressmakers and such. New hats. Now this furniture in the shop. The extra sitting chair near the front of the shop was a good idea, I'll grant you that. King Arthur has his own now."

The cat in question strolled in and walked around the new table, rubbing his face against each leg. He angled back his head and eyed the new intrusion this way and that. With one fast jump, he landed on its surface and continued his examination.

"He is not to be allowed on the table," Iris said firmly. "People eat there."

"He isn't dirty or anything. He just likes perches up high."

"Bridget, I mean it. You tell that cat the table is forbidden."

Bridget shrugged. "I'll try, but he's like a man. Hard to tell him what is what if he doesn't want to hear it." She angled her head. "I hear the door. A patron has come." She breezed out of the kitchen.

Iris strode to the table and shooed the cat away. He sat on his haunches and calmly licked a paw.

"Oh, for goodness' sake. Go outside and hunt some mice." She lifted him and dropped him on the floor. He looked up at her, then jumped back up and took a relaxed sphinx pose on one corner.

"You ornery, headstrong animal."

"I hope you are not insulting that noble cat."

She turned quickly. Nicholas stood just inside the kitchen's doorway. Her heart rose to her throat. "You are back."

"I returned two days ago but had matters to settle with others before I came to find you."

"Minerva told me some of it. Rosamund added a few hints. I think you were in danger on this journey."

"Briefly. Nothing that signified."

"I'm relieved to see the proof of that." She had worried horribly. Not knowing what he was doing, why he was in danger, and where it might lead, had tortured her.

"I will tell you all about it later." He went to King Arthur and petted the cat down its back. "I think I will get one. He can live in the garden. It is probably a paradise for such as he."

"It is big enough to keep any cat happy."

He held out his hand. "I rather like the one here. I have fond memories of it. Let us go sit there, where the cool breezes can find us."

She allowed it, taking his hand and letting him lead her out. He was not going to make this easy.

"Family business is finished. One major duty is completed, although I must return to Sussex tomorrow for my uncle's funeral. But now I can turn my mind to my own business. That means you."

He still held her hand while they sat on the stone bench where they first released their passion in the tiny wilderness.

"I am sorry I discovered that secret," she said. "I knew you would not want to learn about that history. It was a shock to me too. To discover we are cousins."

"Not really cousins. Oh, on paper perhaps, if anyone ever put it to paper. Half cousins even then. But we share no blood. Anyone who knows the truth of it would know we are not cousins in any form."

She pondered that. He looked at her and laughed. "Reginald Barrington married after taking residence in Florence and your father was born to him and his wife, no? Your father was a half brother to my uncle Frederick, but on my side it ended there. My grandfather was Hollinburgh. There is no Barrington blood in me, and none from the Duchess of Hollinburgh in you."

"I think you are right, but it is quite complicated."

"I am right, but to be honest, I don't really care. Even if we were related by blood, I would never regret a minute that we have shared." He turned to her. "Nor would I allow it to end for such a reason. It is no longer so commonplace for cousins to marry, but it is still done."

Marry. She had been sure it would matter. Such marriages were not at all commonplace now. "If anyone did put it to paper—"

"No one will. You and I know. No one else. Even Aunt Dolores has no idea about Frederick. Oh, she wonders who this man was that her mother wrote to, she may even suspect an affair in her mother's past, but she did not read the letter before she handed it to the butler to post. Only my grandfather did. It proved useful, I expect. To give Frederick that letter instead of explaining it all himself."

"I wonder why he even let Frederick know."

"Men have a need to relieve themselves of guilt and

secrets when close to death, I think. He saved the letter for the same reason he saved the Psalter. So his heir would know what had happened, and why a good man acted badly toward another. So his heir could expiate the sin, perhaps."

"With a legacy."

"It is a far better reason for you to receive it than the other heiresses had. Are you enjoying your good fortune now that it is in hand?"

"I confess that not having to count my pennies has been fun."

He laughed and raised her hand to kiss it. "Iris, being a duke is not easy. I'm growing into it, and finding my way, but it is not a life to spend with a woman with whom one has little sympathy, or friendship. I am not looking for a duchess, but I would like to have a good wife to share this life, with all it entails. I asked you before to consider marrying me. I am asking you again."

Too many emotions burst in her for her to contain them well. She clutched his hand tightly. "My fortune is nothing to your station. It would not last you a year or two at most."

"I don't care about incomes and fortunes and all the rest of it. I will manage that just as past Hollinburghs have. Iris, I love you to the point of distraction. Madly. Totally. You have stirred all of me and made the future promising and important instead of a series of duties and responsibilities. I want to sit with you of an evening and explain the problems I face and hear your counsel. I want to share pleasure and passion with you, and feel you touch my heart while I do." He leaned in. "What do you want?"

"I have rarely dared to want much. To love fully. To be loved completely. I think if one has that nothing else matters."

He rested his palm against her face. "I love you completely, and I assure you nothing else matters."

She tried to smile, but her lips trembled. "And I love you fully."

"Then there is nothing else to say, is there? We are agreed and will marry forthwith." He gathered her in his arms and kissed her.

"Are we really mad enough to do this?" she asked when the long kiss ended. "Heiress I may be, but that does not make me an appropriate match for you."

"I am a duke. I can do whatever I want. Marry whomever I choose."

"Your aunt Dolores will be furious. Your aunt Agnes will be appalled."

He smiled. "I know."

Don't miss Minerva's and Rosamund's stories
in these previous Duke's Heiress romances
from Madeline Hunter . . .

HEIRESS FOR HIRE

In this stunning series debut from **New York Times**
*bestselling author Madeline Hunter, a duke's mysterious
bequest brings fortune—and passion—
to three young women . . .*

Minerva Hepplewhite has learned the hard way how to
take care of herself. When an intruder breaks into her
home, she doesn't swoon or simper. Instead she wallops
the rogue over the head and ties him up—only to realize
he is Chase Radnor, a gentleman and grandson of a lord,
and a man who makes it his business to investigate
suspicious matters. Now he's insisting that Minerva has
inherited a fortune from his uncle, a wealthy duke.
Only one thing could surprise her more: her sudden
attraction to this exasperating man . . .

Chase can't decide whether Minerva is a wronged woman
or a femme fatale. Either way, he's intrigued.
Maddeningly, with her unexpected inheritance, she has set
up a discreet detective business to rival Chase's own.
She may be the perfect person to help him uncover the
truth about his uncle's demise. But as proximity gives
way to mutual seduction, Chase realizes he craves
a much deeper alliance . . .

*Available from Kensington Publishing Corp.
wherever books are sold*

HEIRESS IN RED SILK

*A sparkling new love story from a historical romance legend, perfect for **Bridgerton** fans and readers of **Sabrina Jeffries, Eloisa James, and Grace Burrowes.***

In one life-changing windfall, Rosamund Jameson goes from struggling shopkeeper to heiress—and co-owner of a new business. Not only will her sudden fortune allow her to move her millinery shop to fashionable London, Rosamund will also be able to provide her younger sister with a proper entry into society. The only hitch for resourceful Rosamund is her arrogant, infuriatingly handsome business partner . . .

Kevin Radnor is shocked that his late uncle, the Duke of Hollinburgh, bequeathed half his company to a total stranger—worse, a beguiling beauty who can only hinder his enterprise. But Rosamund insists on an active, equal partnership, so Kevin embarks on a plan: a seduction that will lead to a marriage of convenience, giving Rosamund the social status she needs, and guaranteeing him the silent partner he desires. Yet as this charismatic gentleman sets his flirtation in motion, he begins to wonder who is seducing whom—and if he can learn to share himself body and mind, without losing his heart . . .

*Available from Kensington Publishing Corp.
wherever books are sold*

Visit our website at
KensingtonBooks.com
to sign up for our newsletters, read
more from your favorite authors, see
books by series, view reading group
guides, and more!

BOOK | | / / | CLUB
BETWEEN THE CHAPTERS

Become a Part of Our
Between the Chapters Book Club
Community and Join the Conversation

Betweenthechapters.net